NOT THE MAN I THOUGHT HE WAS

PHOEBE MACLEOD

Boldwood

First published in Great Britain in 2022 by Boldwood Books Ltd.

Cover Design by Head Design

Cover Photography: Shutterstock

A CIP catalogue record for this book is available from the British Library.

Paperback ISBN 978-1-80426-249-8

Large Print ISBN 978-1-80426-248-1

Hardback ISBN 978-1-80426-250-4

Ebook ISBN 978-1-80426-246-7

Kindle ISBN 978-1-80426-247-4

Audio CD ISBN 978-1-80426-255-9

MP3 CD ISBN 978-1-80426-254-2

Digital audio download ISBN 978-1-80426-252-8

Boldwood Books Ltd
23 Bowerdean Street
London SW6 3TN
www.boldwoodbooks.com

To Gwyneth, who would have loved the adventure.

1

MADISON

Christmas Eve

I am *never, ever* drinking again.

This is the first thought that comes to me as I start to wake up and realise that my head is pounding, my mouth feels like something crawled in there and died, and my stomach feels like something crawled in there and is very much still alive.

This leads directly to the realisation that I'm going to be sick. Hastily, I throw back the duvet and run barefoot into my bathroom, where I vomit comprehensively and disgustingly into the toilet, thankfully remembering to hold my hair out of the way. Even when it's obvious there's nothing left to come up, my stomach keeps cramping, and the strain of retching is making the pounding in my head worse. I don't think I could feel any sorrier for myself than I do right now.

Eventually, the cramping eases up to the point where I feel safe to move. I stand up tentatively, flush the toilet and move to the basin, where I splash some cool water on my face and rinse my mouth out. God, I feel dreadful. I dare to glance in the mirror, and the face staring back at me is a perfect reflection of how I feel. My eyes are bloodshot, my skin is deathly pale and clammy, and there are smudges of make-up here and there – I obviously didn't remove it before I went to bed last night. My hair is hanging limply down each side of my face, as if in sympathy with the rest of my head. At least I'm wearing one of the long T-shirts that I like to sleep in, so I wasn't so blotto that I went to bed in the very expensive evening gown I'd bought for the gala dinner last night. I quickly check and find that I am, however, still wearing the horribly uncomfortable thong that I'd decided on to make sure there couldn't be even the vaguest hint of VPL showing through the tight-fitting dress. Another quick check reveals that I'm also still wearing a bra. A small part of my brain questions why I would have had the presence of mind to take off my dress before passing out, but not change into comfortable knickers, take off my bra, or remove my make-up. The rest of my pounding head quickly dismisses it though; I feel too rough to care.

A mark on my T-shirt catches my attention. It's a little bit of sick. Yuk. I rip the T-shirt and bra off, step out of the offending thong, and open the door of the shower cubicle. Once inside, I turn the shower to cool and stand underneath, letting the jets of water massage my throbbing head. After a while I start to feel a little better and turn the shower temperature up. I wash my hair, condition it, and select an invigorating black pepper body wash for the rest of me. By the time I step out of the shower and wrap warm towels around my head and body I'm still feeling very delicate, but I allow myself to hope that the worst is over.

I'm not normally much of a drinker, which is probably part of my undoing. I enjoy a glass of wine or two, but it's been years since I've had a hangover even beginning to approach the severity of the one I have now. There had been a lot to celebrate though, and, from the way I feel now, I evidently hadn't held back.

Yesterday evening was the annual gala dinner hosted by *Voyages Luxes*, a luxury travel magazine for which I do a lot of writing. I'm a freelance journalist, specialising in travel, so I spend a lot of time reviewing hotels, experiences and so on. As well as *Voyages Luxes*, I also write for a couple of airline in-flight magazines and have a regular column in a Sunday supplement, so I'm lucky enough to make a decent living. Many people equate my job with being 'paid to go on holiday' but the reality is that it's hard graft, and I probably spend more time pitching for work, or writing up in my flat, than I do actually travelling.

The *Voyages Luxes* gala dinner is one of the highlights of my year. Their head office is in Tunbridge Wells, where I live, so it's always held in an upmarket hotel in the area. They negotiate discounted room rates for anyone who wants to stay over, but to date the venue's always been close enough that it's been cheaper for me to get a taxi home. When you've stayed in as many hotels as I have, it doesn't matter how upmarket they are: I'd still rather be at home, in my own bed.

Last night's dinner was at the Hotel Royal, a spa hotel with a golf course around ten miles from the town. It was a beautiful crisp winter's evening when the taxi dropped me off, and I was looking forward to a fun evening. It's always a black-tie event, so everyone looked very smart as I walked into the bar. There were waiters circulating with glasses of champagne and canapés on trays, and a happy buzz of conversation, punctuated by the occasional loud laugh. An enormous, tastefully decorated, Christmas tree stood in one corner, its lights twinkling. One of the things I love about the annual dinner is that my job entails working alone for the most part, so it's a great opportunity to catch up with some of the other writers and swap stories. It's also a chance to do a bit of networking and, if you win one of the awards that are given out on the night, it can be a real boost to your career.

I quickly found myself ensconced in a group of fellow writers, gossiping happily about our time on the road and this, along with a couple of glasses of champagne, had passed the time very happily until dinner was called.

The main function room was arranged in typical corporate style, with lots of numbered round tables, and seating plans displayed on easels as we walked in, so we could work out where we were sitting. I was glad to see that my friend Toby was sitting to the right of me, but felt a pang of disappointment when I saw that I had Peter Smallbone, a failed writer who somehow found his way into editing, on my left. Peter feels strongly that his lack of success as a writer is nothing to do with the fact that his columns were achingly dull (I know, I've read some of them), but all because he simply wasn't in the right place at the right time. Any writer who is even moderately successful, when cornered by Peter, is treated to the same tedious monologue about how he could have made it if fate had dealt him a different hand. For some reason he particularly hates me, and even tried to get me dropped as a writer a while ago.

Last night was no different. As soon as I sat down, remarked to Toby that he looked very smart, and poured myself a glass of water from the bottle on the table, Peter had started up in his nasal whine.

'Hello, Madison. You're looking very pretty this evening,' he began, innocuously enough.

'Thanks, Peter, you're looking good yourself,' I replied, hoping that the conversation might actually take a civil track, for once.

'It's been a good year for you, hasn't it?' he continued. 'The double-handed stuff you've been doing with Toby has gone down extremely well. Of course, I had a plan to do exactly that back when I was writing, but no editor was prepared to listen to me. I suppose—' and here he looked me up and down disdainfully '— you being so *glamorous* helps you to get editors to listen to your ideas, doesn't it? A flutter of the eyelashes here, a winning smile there. Who was going to listen to me, eh?'

I opened my mouth to contradict him and tell him that he was being unprofessional, but I could see it was pointless. He was winding himself up into his usual tirade and, without thinking, I reached for the bottle of white wine and poured myself a generous glass. I was desperate for him to finish, so I could turn the other way and talk to Toby, but Peter had snared himself his favourite captive audience and wasn't going to let go easily. I steeled myself for a long and painful dinner.

By the time the desserts were being cleared away and the waiters were coming round with coffee, I'd made quite a dent in the bottle of white wine and was feeling slightly woozy. Peter seemed to be running out of steam, so I took the opportunity to break away from him and escape to the ladies'. I remember feeling slightly unsteady in my heels as I tottered in the direction of the bathrooms, and giving myself a stern warning to slow down and drink more water when I got back to the table. Thankfully, when I got back, Peter was talking to the woman on his left, so I was able to chat to Toby.

We'd barely got beyond the usual pleasantries before the waiters started circulating and putting glasses of champagne in front of each guest. As soon as they were done, a hush had fallen over the room and *Voyages Luxes* CEO, Oliver Phillips, took to the stage. On a table behind him was a row of acrylic award plaques, jokingly referred to as tombstones, waiting to be handed out to their lucky winners.

He started, as he always does, with a twenty-minute ramble about the state of the travel industry, the success of the magazine, how customer expectations were becoming more exacting, and how he thought the travel industry should plan to respond to that in the year ahead. There was polite applause at various points, and a couple of shouts of 'hear, hear' from some of the travel company CEOs in the room, but most of us (me included) were willing him to get on with it so we could get to the awards.

You're supposed to say, in any line of work, that awards don't matter, and that you do the work because you love it. However, travel writing is a fiercely competitive industry, especially if you're freelance, so an award from a company as prestigious as *Voyages Luxes* really helps you to stand out from the crowd. In fact, had I not won the 'Best Newcomer' award at the start of my career, I doubt very much that I would have enjoyed the success I have. They're that influential.

At last Oliver wrapped up his speech and the awards ceremony got under way. As each award was handed out, the recipient walked up to receive it, accompanied by polite applause, and then made a short acceptance speech, before returning to their seat as the rest of us drank a toast to them. I wasn't expecting anything this year, so I sat back and enjoyed watching the flush of excitement from each winner, raising my glass and clapping along with everyone else.

'Madison Morgan and Toby Roberts!!' Oliver's announcement caught me completely by surprise and I turned to Toby with a blank expression.

'Most innovative content,' Toby hissed in my ear as we'd got to our feet and started to make our way to the front of the room.

I have no idea what I said. I garbled some thanks I think, and Toby said some words about how much he'd enjoyed working with me, and then we fled back to the table, clutching the tombstone awkwardly between us. I remember Peter looking absolutely apoplectic, and I think we had a bit of a row. I remember deciding that I wasn't going to let his jealousy bring me down, draining my glass of champagne and heading to the bar to buy a bottle so Toby and I could celebrate properly.

After that, unsurprisingly, it all got a bit hazy.

I apply some moisturiser to my face, before padding out of the bathroom and back into my bedroom, and that's when I spot an unfamiliar lump under the duvet. With mounting horror, I realise what it is.

There's someone else in my bed.

Oh no. Please tell me I didn't proposition someone last night. I know I was drunk, but surely not drunk enough to break the golden rule? From the moment I picked up the keys to my flat, I've had a rule that no man stays the night. I'm not anti-men at all; I like men a lot and have had my fair share of boyfriends over the years. It's just that this flat is my sanctuary, a place that's just for me, and having a man stay over feels like an invasion of my space. I've stayed over with boyfriends and that's fine; I just don't want them here. And inviting someone back when I've just met them? That's not something I would ever do. What on earth could have got into me?

As I'm staring in horror at the bed, the shape under the duvet stretches, yawns loudly and sits up. A very familiar face stares at me, blinking the sleep away.

'What the bloody hell are you doing here, Toby?' I ask.

2

ELEVEN MONTHS PREVIOUSLY – JANUARY

I don't often visit the offices of my clients. Most of my work is done remotely either by email or phone, so the summons to the *Voyages Luxes* office I received a week ago is unusual. As I have no idea what the meeting is about, I wasn't sure how to dress. In the end I went for a professional look: a dark, knee-length skirt with matching jacket, a white, wide-collared shirt, black court shoes and muted lipstick. Better to be overdressed than underdressed, I reckon.

I announce myself to the receptionist and take a seat in the waiting area. It's quiet today, just me and another man. I nod a hello to him as I take a seat, and he nods back. I guess him to be around the same age as me, possibly slightly older. He's dressed in a pink floral shirt and dark blue turned-up jeans with highly polished brown brogues. Everything about him looks fastidious, from his beautifully ironed clothes to his perfectly manicured close-cut light brown hair. For some reason, my gaydar goes into high alert. I don't know what it is about him, but he's definitely giving off a gay vibe. Not flamboyant or effeminate, but the sort of guy who lives quietly with his boyfriend or husband, to whom he's absolutely devoted. His skin looks soft, like he moisturises it, and he's clean-shaven without even a hint of stubble.

I divert my attention from him and glance around the lobby. As befits a company like *Voyages Luxes* it's grand, with a high ceiling, marble floors and expensive-looking chandeliers. The chandeliers have always bothered me; they're immaculately clean, but are high enough that they'd be difficult to reach, even with a stepladder. I can't help wondering how they dust them, or stop spiders building elaborate cobwebs across them. At the back of the lobby are the security gates leading into the actual offices. I've never been any further than the lobby and the visitor meeting rooms, so I've never seen the workspace. I imagine it's much less grandiose though – probably the usual arrangement of cluttered desks, computer monitors covered in Post-it notes, and whiteboards with the hieroglyphic remains of badly rubbed out brainstorming sessions that seem to adorn most offices, if the dramas I've watched on TV are anything to go by.

'Madison!' My reverie is interrupted by Mark Stevens, the commissioning editor of *Voyages Luxes*, striding across the lobby towards me. Under one arm he's clutching a laptop and notepad, and the other is already outstretched. I get up to greet him.

'So good of you to come in, particularly at such short notice,' he says as he reaches us and shakes both our hands. 'Toby, good to see you too. Robyn asked me to apologise to you – she's running a little late. Do you two know each other, by the way?'

The man called Toby is also on his feet, and I can't help noticing that he's a good couple of inches shorter than me. I know I'm quite tall for a woman, at five feet nine inches, but he is most kindly described as 'compact'.

Our blank looks must give us away. 'Madison is one of our freelance writers – you might know her by her pen name, Lucy

Swann – and Toby is an extremely talented photographer that we use when we can afford him,' Mark continues, with a wink.

'Are you Toby Roberts? Oh, my goodness, I love your work!' I exclaim, and he smiles. Mark isn't bluffing when he says Toby is talented. Whether it's bikini-clad models in beach settings or romantic sunsets, his images are a big reason that the magazine looks so beautiful. When I'm snapping away on my iPhone, trying to capture the essence of a place, I often find myself thinking, *How would Toby Roberts frame this?* It never helps, of course. I think either you have an eye for composition, or you don't. My pictures, while serviceable, fall firmly into the second category.

'Nice to meet you, Madison,' he replies, offering his hand. I was right, his skin is soft, but his handshake is warm and surprisingly firm. 'I always enjoy reading your articles when I can. Your descriptions are so vivid I can often picture the scene without even looking at the pictures.'

'That's probably for the best,' I laugh. 'My pictures are atrocious. There's a reason why you get double-page spreads and mine are never printed bigger than passport size.'

'Much as I hate to interrupt your little love-in, can I persuade you to join me in the meeting room over there, Madison?' Mark interjects, and points towards one of the meeting rooms reserved for visitors on the other side of the lobby. The walls are clear glass with open Venetian blinds, and I can see tea, coffee and pastries have already been laid out, as they always are for visitors.

'Sure, sorry. It was nice to meet you, Toby,' I say.

'You too. I hope our paths cross again,' he replies.

Once inside the meeting room, I help myself to refreshments while Mark plugs his laptop into the projector and closes the blinds. I take a seat and turn it so I can see the screen, and then get my notepad out of my bag.

'Madison,' Mark says, as I'm taking a sip of coffee, and I notice that his voice is suddenly much more downbeat now that we're in private. A niggle of worry forms in my stomach. 'The reason I've asked you to come in is that we have a bit of a problem.'

As he speaks, he clicks a button on his laptop, and a hotel review appears on the screen. I recognise it as one of mine. My heart sinks. Did I get something wrong? Describe the wrong hotel? I always worry, particularly if I'm staying in several hotels over the course of a trip, that I'll muddle them up, but I have a system for preventing that and it's always worked so far. I always make sure that the first photo I take of any hotel or attraction shows the name. I then know that any photos between that one and the next one with a name in it are of that particular place, and this serves as my aide-memoire.

'Do you remember the Bellavista Hotel in Corfu?' Mark asks. 'You reviewed it about a year ago.'

I stare at the picture on screen, frantically trying to remember the hotel. Sometimes I struggle to remember a place I stayed in the previous week, so trying to remember one from a year ago is a tall order. Although I always do my own research before I go, each hotel generally expects journalists to attend a famil, or familiarisation session, either on arrival or soon afterwards. This is essentially a meeting where the hotel owners, the local tourist board and owners of local attractions present the area to you and the things they particularly want you to try. They would say that it's helping to get you up to speed so you can write about the place as if you were a local, but of course they carefully curate what they tell you to try to make sure you only see the good in a place. They're useful, but you also have to try to see around them to an extent, and remember which famil went with which location. If you're not very careful it can all merge into a blur very easily. I always make sure I take copious notes.

Mark gives me space to collect my thoughts. He knows what

it's like, he started out as a travel writer himself before climbing the editorial ranks. I read the opening text of the review, and a few memories start to surface.

'Vaguely,' I say eventually. 'I think it was a four-star all-inclusive boutique hotel, wasn't it? On the cusp of opening, adults only. Is that right?'

'That's the one. Tell me about the trip.'

'Fairly standard, from what I can remember,' I say, after wracking my brains some more. 'Usual famil when we got there, nice big rooms with balconies, fairly standard all-inclusive buffet, limited bar selection. Was that what I wrote?'

'And the nice big room you wrote about,' Mark continues, 'was that a standard room or one of the more expensive ones?'

'I really can't remember,' I tell him, honestly. 'But we normally get one of the more expensive rooms, because the hotel is trying to show itself at its best, so I imagine that was the case here as well. Why?'

'Well,' he replies, after a short pause. 'You must have liked it, because you strongly recommended it as a great place to stay on the island. The problem is that TripAdvisor appears to disagree with you.'

He clicks the button again and the TripAdvisor page for the hotel comes up on the screen. He scrolls through some of the reviews, giving me time to read them. Although there are a few five-star reviews, the review count against the posters is usually one and the English is poor, which indicates that they're probably posted by the hotel itself. The majority of the others are not good, and some themes quickly start to develop. The food and drink come in for particular criticism, as do the lack of sunbeds, the rudeness of the staff, and the poky rooms with tiny bathrooms. I'm horrified.

'I don't understand,' I say, after we've read and digested a few pages of reviews. 'It sounds like a totally different hotel to the one I stayed in!'

'You can see the problem though, can't you?' Mark asks. 'It undermines our credibility as a luxury travel magazine if we strongly recommend a place that subsequently turns out to be awful. It's also not good for your image, because it dents trust in you as an impartial reviewer.'

Oh shit, this is much worse than I thought. He's going to let me go. He's trying to build up to it gently but that is definitely where this is heading. I'm in big, big trouble. If he lets me go, word will quickly get out that *Voyages Luxes* has dropped me, and it won't be long before my other work dries up too. This is the worst part of being a freelance journalist; it takes years of hard graft to climb the greasy pole to the point where you can make a decent living, but only one fuck-up to send you straight back to the bottom again. It's like a game of snakes and ladders, only without any ladders. I blink back the tears that I can feel forming. I've worked so hard to get to where I am, it seems grossly unfair that a single hotel review can undo it all. I focus all my energy on maintaining my composure.

'I'm sorry,' he continues. 'You know how highly I rate you as a writer, but ever since Peter Smallbone drew this to my attention, I've been put in an impossible situation.'

Peter 'drew it to his attention', did he? I bet he was positively salivating with glee at the prospect of bringing me down. Bastard. What is his problem with me anyway?

No. No fucking way. I'm not going to take this lying down. I'm not going to let my career be wrecked by someone like Peter bloody Smallbone. My mind is whirling, desperately trying to think of a way to save this. I need *something*, and fast. If I let Mark get to the end of what he wants to say it'll be too late.

The glimmer of an idea starts to form, and I grab it. It isn't great, but it's all I've got to work with. When you're drowning, you'll grasp at anything to keep your head above water, and this is how I feel right now.

'Do you ever wonder,' I venture, 'whether the review process is fundamentally flawed? Whether we should be doing it completely differently?'

This is enough to throw him off track and buy me the precious seconds I need to try to put some flesh on the very bare bones of my idea. I've got to pitch like I've never pitched before, and without any time to prepare. Not ideal, but it's amazing how impending disaster allows your mind to focus.

'What do you mean?' he asks.

'Think about it,' I reply. 'The hotel invites reviewers to come. They know who we are and when we're arriving. They lay on the famil to guide us to all the stuff they want us to see, and they give us the best rooms. The staff are doubtless instructed to be especially nice to us. In this instance, the hotel hadn't even opened its doors to the public when I stayed; all the guests were journalists, so it was even easier for them to create a good impression. They were probably at no more than twenty per cent capacity, so it wasn't hard for them to put on a convincing show, and I bought it. I expect the others did too. Have you looked at other reviews from the time?'

Mark fiddles with his laptop and brings up a search page. Before long we've looked at a series of reviews of the same hotel from other travel magazines and blogs. We don't read them in depth, but we read the summaries and, like mine, they are universally positive. I recognise the names of most of the authors and they've all been around for a while, like me.

'What are you suggesting?' he asks.

'Why don't I go back there, but incognito this time?'

Mark sits back in his chair, tilts his head back and stares at the ceiling. I've seen him do this before when he's thinking, so I sit and wait. My heart is in my mouth; it's no exaggeration to say that my whole future hangs on his next words. After what feels like an age, he tilts his head forward again and his eyes meet mine.

'Go on,' he says.

3

JANUARY

'If I go back incognito, then I can experience the Bellavista as an ordinary holidaymaker,' I explain. 'No famil, no special treatment, and a standard room. I can find out what's really going on, and it's an opportunity for you to put the record straight. I will be up front in the review and say that I loved the hotel when I first visited, but the TripAdvisor reviews concerned me, so I decided to make a return trip to reassess. If it's still as good as I thought it was the first time, then I'll say so. We know that there are a lot of people who will write wildly critical reviews on TripAdvisor because of some inconsequential thing that nobody else would care about, and that may be the case here. However, if standards have slipped to the extent that these reviews claim, then I'll say that's what has happened.'

'So, you'd submit a negative review and expect us to publish it?' Mark asks. 'It's not really our style, is it? We're all about the idea of dream holidays. When it's cold, wet and miserable in the UK our readers want to look at pictures of beautiful hotels, beaches, safaris or whatever, and imagine themselves in those places. *Voyages Luxes* is just as much about fantasy as it is about travel. Did you know that the latest consumer data shows that 29 per cent of our subscribers have never been abroad at all? We aren't a magazine like *Which?*, where people want to know that this product is good and that product is bad. We're more like *National Geographic*, but with booking information. How does your negative review of a hotel fit into that?'

Damn. I thought I had him, but he's slipping away again. I grit my teeth and fight on.

'I know, but if I don't get the opportunity to correct this, then nobody wins. Your credibility as a magazine is dented, and my career is over,' I tell him, baldly. 'You know me, Mark. You've worked with me for years, and you're always saying how much you like my stuff. Give me the opportunity to put this right. You don't have to make a big deal of the review if it's negative. Why not review some other hotels on the island that cater to the same market, and include the Bellavista in passing? If it's as bad as TripAdvisor would lead us to believe, it could go in as "One to avoid", and I could say that it seems to have gone downhill since my first visit. If it's still good, I put it as a "Lucky dip" choice, or something like that.'

'OK, but how would this work in practice?' He's back on the hook, and I think fast to make sure I keep him there.

'It's basically a mystery shopper concept,' I explain. 'The hotel knows that a journalist is coming but, unlike our usual trips, they don't know who it is or when they're arriving. We'd need to agree what package the hotel is offering to fund in advance, of course, but I'd make the booking like a normal customer, rather than them liaising with you. They'd still want to pick and choose some experiences, I'm sure, but instead of the usual famil session, we could ask them to submit a famil pack in advance, so I have all the information without having to come face to face with them and reveal who I am. I do everything I would normally do, but under the radar. If they want, I could reveal myself and debrief the manager at the end. That way they get something out of it too.'

'I think you're forgetting something,' Mark says, after another uncomfortable pause. 'Even if you don't announce who you are, the hotel will know that someone is coming, and a young woman travelling on her own is going to stand out. They'll be on to you.'

Have you ever seen those YouTube videos of people landing large fish? This is starting to feel like that. Every time I try to reel him in, he thrashes and pulls away. I'm not done though. Mentally I grasp the fishing rod and give an almighty pull.

'You're right!' I tell him, as reckless inspiration strikes. 'So what if I didn't go alone? What's the one thing that you've always criticised in my reviews?'

'Your photos,' Mark replies without hesitating.

'So, what if I took a photographer? You'd get the writing you say you like, with decent pictures to go with it. We could pretend to be a couple and wouldn't stand out at all.'

'Too expensive,' he counters.

'I disagree. You pay photographers by the image, don't you, so there is no extra cost there as you're still buying the images at the same rate. You pay me for the submissions. The hotel covers the cost of the stay, so the only additional cost is an extra flight. I would say that the value you'd get would far outweigh the cost.'

'And which photographer would you take?' he asks.

And this is the point where my plan unravels. I wrack my brains furiously to see if I can think of someone suitable. I know a couple of photographers, but not well enough that I could ask them to come and pretend to be a couple with me. The only one I can think of who might agree is Stuart, and I'd have to spend all my time trying to stop him hitting on me. I realise that my mental fishing line has snapped, Mark is swimming away scot-free, and my shoulders slump in defeat.

'I don't know,' I say, quietly.

Mark tilts his head back again, and the silence stretches horribly between us. Now that I know it's over, I can't bear the waiting. Why can't he just deliver the killer blow and let me slink away? Suddenly he gets up and opens the door.

'Toby, would you mind joining us for a minute?' he calls.

In the seconds it takes Toby to cross the lobby, enter the room and sit down, my hope soars again. If Mark didn't think there was any merit in the idea I've just pitched, he wouldn't be bringing Toby into it, would he?

'Toby,' Mark begins, 'how would you feel about going on an incognito trip with Madison here?'

'Umm, I'm not sure what you mean,' he replies, confusion written all over his face. 'Can you tell me a bit more?'

'Madison thinks there is a problem with the way we do our hotel reviews, because the hotels know who we are and when we're coming. This has caused her, and us, to get our fingers burned. Her proposal is therefore that she undertakes an under-cover trip, where the hotels don't know she's coming, to get a more realistic flavour. However, if she goes alone then she'll stand out like a sore thumb and the hotels will be onto her in a flash. So, she's proposed taking a photographer along, which is where you come in. The idea is that you travel as a couple so you blend in, but also the quality of the pictures improves because they're being taken by – no offence here, Madison – someone who knows what they're doing.'

Before Toby has a chance to reply, there's a knock on the door and a woman, who I'm guessing must be Robyn, sticks her head into the meeting room.

'Mark,' she admonishes, 'Toby is supposed to be meeting me. I know I'm running late but that's no excuse to kidnap him!'

'Sorry, Robyn, can you let me keep him for just five minutes? I'll be as quick as I can.'

Robyn sighs, obviously knowing that argument is futile. 'Fine. I'll wait in the lobby. Five minutes though, please, Mark. I'm behind enough as it is.'

As soon as the door closes, Mark turns back to Toby.

'Well, what do you think?'

Toby considers for what feels like an age. I can see that he's not one for impulse decisions.

'When you say, "travel as a couple",' he says, eventually, 'does that mean we'd have to share a room?'

Crap. I hadn't thought about that. This plan is full of holes, I realise. This is what happens when you pitch without adequate preparation. There's really only one answer I can give though. I need to get both of them onside with this idea, and I'll have to work out the details later.

'Madison?' Mark asks.

'Yes, I think we would. I don't see any hotel being keen on giving away two rooms for free when one is the norm. Also, the whole aim of this is to blend in as much as possible. Even if the hotel agreed to two rooms and we travelled as friends, it would raise our profile. The hotel staff are going to be like sniffer dogs on full alert for anything unusual. The more ordinary we are, the better our chances of going undetected.'

'But what about the sleeping arrangements?' Mark presses.

'Look, this is a professional situation,' I counter. 'If we have to share a bed then I would expect both of us to make sure we are appropriately covered up, and I would expect us both to keep our hands to ourselves.'

'I can assure you that you have nothing to fear from me,' Toby interjects.

'So, in principle, you'd be up for a trip like this?' Mark asks him.

Toby is silent for what feels like forever, and I'm aware of my fingers pressing hard into my palms as I try my best to be patient and not pressure him. 'Yes, I think so, if it fitted in with my schedule,' he replies, at last. 'I think Madison's right about the potential benefits of an undercover review, and so it's worth a shot. If it doesn't work out then we don't have to do it again, but we won't know unless we try, will we? Listen, I'd better go. I can see Robyn fidgeting from here. Do you mind?'

'No, that's great. Thanks, Toby, I'll be in touch.' Mark gets up and holds the door open for him, and we watch Robyn rush over to him and practically drag him into another meeting room. Mark turns back to me and silence descends. I'm not completely sure, but I'm feeling more confident that I might actually have pulled this off and saved my career. He sits for a while, alternately looking at me and staring at the ceiling. Once again, I let him formulate his thoughts, and sit as still as I can, even though the waiting is agony.

'OK,' he says, eventually. 'This isn't where I expected this meeting to end up, but I'm happy. I think this is an interesting idea and certainly worth a punt. I'm not going to say "yes" right now as, although I have the ability to commission this, I want more time to consider it, and I also want to talk it through with a couple of my colleagues. I also need to see whether there's any appetite for this type of review from any of the hotel owners. It's more risky from their perspective, so I'm not sure how well it will be received.'

'That's fair enough,' I answer. 'All I would say is that this is potentially good for them too. I don't know of any hotel owners who want their guests to have a horrible time, and I'm sure the owner of the Bellavista doesn't like reading the TripAdvisor comments any more than I did. What this offers is for them to get an impartial picture of what's going on, and the opportunity to improve. If they're not interested in that, then they aren't the sort of hotel *Voyages Luxes* should be reviewing anyway.'

'Leave it with me,' Mark replies. 'I'll give you a call in a few days.' With that, he unplugs his laptop and stacks the notepad on top of it, indicating that the meeting is over. I take the cue, place my notebook back into my bag, and stand up. Mark gets up and opens the door for me.

'Thanks for coming in today, Madison. We'll speak soon.'

Once I've left the *Voyages Luxes* offices and stepped back onto the street, I exhale loudly, trying to release some of the tension of the last hour. Although it's cold, the sun is shining, and I find I'm enjoying the freshness of the air after the stuffy atmosphere of the meeting room. I make my way down to a coffee shop that I like in the Pantiles. When I get there, I order a flat white and a Danish pastry, and sit down at one of the tiny rickety tables outside to enjoy them. There's a chilly breeze but I'm warm inside my thick winter coat. As I eat and drink, I reflect on the meeting. I'm pretty pleased with how I handled it and thought on my feet, although I shudder when I think how close to disaster I was. Bloody Peter Smallbone. I know I'm not out of the woods yet, but Mark had definitely come around to the idea by the end, so I'm hopeful that it will come off. I liked Toby too, and not just because he helped to bail me out. I'm not used to travelling with anyone else and I don't know him, which is far from ideal, but he seems nice, and I have a good instinct for people, so I reckon we'll probably get on OK. What was it he had said? Oh yes, I have 'nothing to fear' from him.

Called it – he's definitely gay. I'm not saying that I'm God's gift to mankind or anything, and that no heterosexual male could possibly resist me. It's just the subtext in the way he said it, and the way he emphasised the word 'nothing'.

I'm pleased, because that will make the whole business of having to share a room much easier. I can relax, knowing that he's definitely not going to try it on, and we can get on with the work. With sexual chemistry firmly off the menu, what could possibly go wrong?

4

JANUARY – A FEW DAYS LATER

I'm at home, working on the travel advice column that I have in one of the Sunday broadsheets, when the phone rings. The caller ID shows me that it's Mark, and my heart starts thudding in my chest. This is it. Casting aside Irene from Doncaster's email asking for ideas for a big family holiday in Tuscany in summer, I take a moment to prepare myself mentally for bad news before I press the button to accept the call.

'Hi, Mark,' I say, as brightly as I can.

'Hi, Madison, how are you?' I'm trying to second-guess whether it's good or bad news by the tone of his voice, and I'm encouraged. He sounds pretty upbeat.

'I'm good, thanks. How did you get on with my proposal?' I decide to short cut the pleasantries and chit-chat that usually precede our business discussions. I need to know whether I've pulled it off.

'Well, Peter was dead set against it, saying that it was a poor use of resource and that you were just trying to use us to dig your-self out of your own mess, but I mentioned it to Oliver, the CEO, and he was very enthusiastic. He thinks it could be a unique selling point for us, so we're going to give it a trial run initially, to see how it goes. The difficulty is that the Bellavista doesn't open until April, when the tourist numbers in Corfu start to pick up, and Oliver doesn't want to wait that long to trial your idea. However, we are planning a feature for our March edition on last minute ski holidays, to try to catch the Easter holiday market. I've been in touch with three hotels in Courchevel, and they're all interested. They're going to email famil packs across to me, along with vouchers to cover the cost of the room, so I'll forward those to you when they arrive. It's a six-night trip – two nights in each hotel – and I'll need draft copy from you by the tenth of February. Do you think you can manage that?'

I do some hasty calculations in my head. It's the fourteenth of January now, so that gives me just under four weeks to do the trip and write it up. I've already got a trip to Istanbul booked next week for one of the airline magazines I write for, so the timing is really tight. A lot will depend on when the hotels can fit us in, and what Toby's schedule looks like.

'Do we have any idea of availability?' I ask.

'I checked that. They all have good availability for January at present.'

'And have you spoken to Toby?'

'No. In the end I thought it would be better if you liaised with him directly. Do you have his number?'

I admit that I don't, and he reels it off for me.

'I'll email you all the details now. Tenth of February, Madison. Don't let me down,' he says, and finishes the call.

Almost immediately, my laptop pings to announce the arrival of a new email. I click to open and read off the names and addresses of the three hotels Mark has sent me. The five-star Hotel Mirabelle is right in the centre of Courchevel, and offers direct access to the ski slopes, as well as indoor and outdoor pools, a sauna and a spa. The restaurant holds a Michelin star. We will need to include that in the review, so I check the dress code. Thankfully it's described as smart casual, but it does say that gentlemen have to wear a shirt with a collar, and jeans are not permitted. I make a note to tell Toby. I see that Superior rooms have a hot tub on the balcony, but as we're going under-cover that won't be a luxury we will be enjoying. The second hotel, La Residence, is also in the centre of Courchevel. It's only three-star, but also offers direct access to the slopes, a spa, and boasts that it has been recently renovated. I have a quick look on booking.com and it does look very modern, chic and minimalist. I like the look of it, but hope it doesn't prove to be all style and no substance. The final hotel, Les Suites de Bellevue is, as its name suggests, a set of self-catering apartments in a block, although I note that there is a restaurant and spa on site as well. Again, the pictures look promising, and the self-catering aspect will give us an opportunity to try more of the local restaurants and bars.

I dial Toby's number and, after a couple of rings, he picks up.

'Hi, Toby, it's Madison, from *Voyages Luxes*. Is now a good time to talk?'

'Hi, Madison, absolutely. How are you?'

'Fine thanks. I'm calling because Mark has just rung me with the details of a trip for the two of us. Are you still interested?'

'Yes, of course!'

I fill him in on the details. Unsurprisingly, it proves difficult to find dates that work for both of us at such short notice, but we finally manage to agree on the twenty-fourth. This isn't ideal for me, because it's the day after I get back from Istanbul, but I'll just have to find a way to make it work.

'There's just one thing you need to know,' he tells me towards the end of the call. 'I've never been skiing before.'

'But, Toby, that's brilliant news!' I exclaim. 'It adds an extra dimension to the piece. I'll book you into a ski school, and you can write about your experiences of it as a novice.'

'I thought the writing part was your job,' he replies, and I can hear the smile in his voice.

'Fine. You tell me about it and I'll write it down, OK?'

'What about equipment?' he asks. 'Do I need to get skis, poles and all that sort of stuff?'

'Skis, ski boots, poles and helmet we can rent when we get there. It saves you capital outlay and it's also something we can charge to expenses. You will need a suitable jacket, gloves and salopettes though,' I tell him.

'What on earth are salopettes?'

'They're ski trousers. Look, if it helps and you're free, I'm happy to come to the shop with you to help you get the right stuff. How about Saturday?'

There's a pause while he consults his diary.

'I've got a shoot in Maidstone on Saturday morning,' he says, 'but that should be done by midday. How about Saturday afternoon?'

'I'll pick you up at midday,' I tell him. 'That way we can grab something to eat first. What's the address?'

'Are you always this bossy?' he laughs.

'I prefer to think of it as assertive, and yes. Last thing – I need all the details from your passport to make the booking. Have you got it to hand?'

While I'm waiting for him to find his passport, my brain is already working out how to jigsaw these two trips together. I'll have to write up the Istanbul trip during any downtime I get on the ski trip, and then work flat out when I get home to finish both of them by the deadline. As long as I'm disciplined and don't get distracted, I reckon I can pull it off.

Toby gives me his passport details, directions to the studio in

Maidstone, and we end the conversation. As soon as he's off the phone, I busy myself with booking flights, transfers and the hotels. One of the joys of using a pen name is that I can remain anonymous when I travel under my real name. Lucy Swann is fairly well known in the travel industry, but nobody knows who Madison Morgan is. I book Toby into a ski school that seems reasonably accessible from all three hotels, as well as a spa session at the Mirabelle, restaurant tables at all three, and ski hire. I also book ski passes for both of us, in the hope that I will be able to get a reasonable amount of skiing in while I'm there. I need to be able to write about the slopes; they're the primary attraction for this type of holiday, after all. Although I've been to Courchevel before, it was several years ago, so I'm looking forward to re-acquainting myself with it.

The following Saturday, I find myself outside the studio just before twelve o'clock. The building is a beautiful old red-brick warehouse that's obviously been divided up into offices and work-shops. Next to the main door there are a number of buttons, each with the name of a different business next to it. The buzzer for the photo studio is just over halfway down. I check my watch and, as it's now midday, press the button. An unfamiliar voice answers, and I give my name and explain that I'm there to meet Toby.

'No worries,' the voice tells me. 'He's just putting everything away. Come on up. We're on the first floor.'

The door buzzes and I push against it. Disappointingly, the interior of the building looks nothing like the exterior. It's all drab beige partition walls and cheap brown carpet. Whoever did the conversion obviously valued low cost over aesthetics. I find the stairs and walk up to the first floor, where I eventually discover a door with the name of the studio on it. I knock and wait.

The door is opened by a man who I guess is in his fifties but is desperately trying to project a younger vibe. His long grey hair is tied back in a ponytail, and he has a little goatee beard. He's wearing a lumberjack shirt and faded jeans, with battered Converse sneakers on his feet.

'Hi,' he says with a smile, 'I'm Paul. Come on in.'

I follow him past a small kitchen area and a closed door with 'Dressing Room' written on it, into the main studio. Toby is packing up various bits of expensive-looking equipment, and he gives me a wave when he spots me.

'I won't be long,' he calls. 'Paul's a great guy, but heaven help you if you use his studio and don't put everything back exactly how you found it.'

'The place has got to look like he was never here,' Paul explains to me, smiling. 'Just because I've known him forever and he's some hotshot 'tog doesn't make him exempt from the studio rules, and he knows it.'

"Tog?' I ask.

'Sorry, short for photographer,' he explains. 'So, how do you know Toby, Madison?'

'I don't really know him at all,' I tell him. 'I just met him for the first time the other day. I know his work though. What about you?'

'I've known him since before he started out,' Paul replies. 'He pitched up here, years ago, begging me to take him on as an apprentice. I liked him, took him on, taught him all I know, and now he earns sums that I can only dream of.' Paul grins to show that he has no hard feelings about it.

'He's a good guy,' he continues. 'Of course, I would say that, being his mate, but he is. Some 'togs are real prima donnas, throwing hissy fits if the models don't understand what they want immediately, but he's always calm and explains things very clearly. As a result, the models go the extra mile for him; he really knows how to put them at ease and get the best out of them.'

'What's he been shooting today?' I ask.

'Fashion,' Paul tells me. 'The outfits were all sent down by one of the Sunday supplements – I forget which one. They arrived by courier yesterday and the editor brought the model today. The model was fine, but the editor was a demanding little bitch, like so many of them are. I was biting my tongue, I can tell you!' He chuckles again, and I decide I like him.

Just as I'm about to ask him for more details, Toby appears with a large rucksack on his back.

'Sorry for keeping you,' he says to me. 'Shall we go?'

We say our goodbyes to Paul, and I follow him out of the building. He stows his rucksack safely in the boot of his car before getting into mine.

'Where to?' he asks.

The ski shop is on a retail estate outside the town, so we decide to have lunch at the coffee shop on the same estate. As we chat over paninis and coffee, I realise that he's quite shy. I do manage to glean that he's an only child like me, that his parents still live in the house he grew up in, and that he's currently renting a room in a house-share with three other people who he hates.

'It's the mess more than anything else,' he tells me. 'The kitchen permanently looks like a war zone, and the less said about the bathroom the better. Thankfully, I'm in the process of buying my own studio in Sevenoaks, and it's got a flat attached, so, if that all goes through, I'll be able to move out soon.'

I imagine him and his boyfriend choosing curtains together, and I can't help asking the question.

'So, is there anyone special in your life right now? How do they feel about you being kidnapped for a week by a strange woman?'

He shakes his head. 'No, I'm happily single. To be honest, I've been so focused on getting my career up and running that there hasn't really been room for anything else. What about you?'

'Also single,' I tell him. 'I've had a few boyfriends over the years, but it's never been serious. I'm not sure relationships work very well with this job.'

As we finish our lunch, the conversation limps along. It's not awkward exactly, but I feel a little like I'm dragging information out of him, rather than him volunteering it. In a funny way, it's rather refreshing. I'm so used to guys who drone on about themselves without asking any questions about me that I'm pleasantly surprised by Toby's modesty. I study him as we talk. He is good-looking, with deep chocolate-coloured eyes, high cheekbones and a strong jawline. I reckon he would get plenty of interest if he were to put himself out there, but I suspect his shyness makes him hide behind his work. Shame really; he'd make someone a lovely boyfriend.

Toby and I spend a very pleasant afternoon getting him kitted out for the slopes and, by the time I drop him back at his car, any lingering reservations I have about working closely with him have evaporated. He's still courteous and very reserved, but I learn that he has quite a wicked sense of humour on the rare occasions he lets his guard down. At one point, he tells me a story about one of his flatmates having a row with his girlfriend about something he said to her parents, and he mimics his broad Geordie accent so perfectly it's as if I've met the guy. As we part, I remind him about the dress code for the Michelin-starred restaurant and we agree to meet at the airport.

Once I get home, I ring my best friend Charley. She and her husband, Ed, are expecting their first baby imminently, and I haven't spoken to her since nearly getting dropped by *Voyages Luxes*, so a chat is long overdue.

'Fat and fed up,' she tells me when I ask how she's feeling. 'Honestly, Mads, I just want the bloody thing out now. I'm eating the spiciest food I can bear, and Ed thinks Christmas has come because I keep demanding sex in the hope that it will encourage things along. I know the whole concept of growing another person inside you is incredible, but what with the vomiting in the first trimester, the kicking at all hours of the day and night, and now being uncomfortable all the time, I just want my body back. Does that make me a bad person?'

Charley and Ed's first indication that their attempts to conceive had been successful was when she woke up one morning and promptly had to dash into the bathroom to throw up. Their euphoria at the positive pregnancy test had been short-lived, as she struggled to keep anything down for weeks, and started to feel quite low about it. Things weren't helped by the fact that Ed, a divorce lawyer, had been in the thick of a hugely complex case and was working all hours. Thankfully, her parents live quite close by, so her mother had stepped up, popping round regularly with small meals for her and keeping her company in between vomiting episodes. Things did improve after a few months, but it was a grim time for her.

'You're pretty much due though, aren't you?' I ask her.

'Another week to go. They say they'll let me go up to two weeks overdue before inducing me, but I hope it doesn't come to that. I'll be climbing the walls if I have to endure another three weeks of this. Anyway, enough of me. What about you?'

I fill her in on the *Voyages Luxes* debacle, and she's suitably outraged by Peter Smallbone's attitude. When I tell her about Toby, she giggles in delight.

'Is he hot?' Her first question catches me off-guard.

'Charley, you're about to have a baby, for goodness' sake! Turn the libido down a notch.'

'I didn't mean for me, dummy. I wondered if you fancied him. It's been ages since you've had a boyfriend.'

'Two years isn't ages,' I retort. 'I told you, I'm bored of wasting my time on immature boys who can't cope with a real woman.

Anyway, he's shorter than me, and gay, so I think that kind of rules him out, don't you? He's also very shy, which I think is partly why he's single. It's not my job to sort out his sex life though, this is a professional arrangement.'

'Of course. You'd never meddle in anyone else's relationships, would you?' she laughs. She's referring to the fact that I stalked Ed, accosted him in his office lobby, and brought him back into her life after a series of mishaps meant they lost contact with each other. Given how things turned out for them, I reckon I can be justifiably proud of that particular intervention.

'Do you think he'll end up being your GBF?' she continues.

'My what?'

'Your Gay Best Friend,' she explains. 'Obviously he can't be your BFF, because that's me, but every girl should have a GBF, and he sounds like he could be perfect. Shy where you're extrovert – a yin to your yang, you know?'

'I've never heard of such a rule, and it sounds like some nineties anachronism straight out of *Friends*, or *Sex and the City*,' I tell her, frankly. 'Who's yours then?' I'm trying to work out which of her male friends it could be, but I'm drawing a blank.

'Sam Carter, obviously!' she replies, laughing.

'Sam?' I ask, incredulously. 'Sam's nothing like Toby. Toby is a painfully shy gay man, whereas Sam is a full-on, in your face, frankly terrifying lesbian!'

'Aww, she's a pussycat when you get to know her,' Charley laughs. 'You just have to see past the piercings and angry tattoos.'

'Whatever,' I reply. 'I'll keep you posted on whether Toby makes GBF status, or whatever other hideously dated label you want to pick out of the ether. In the meantime, try not to have the baby while I'm away. I want to cuddle it the moment they've wiped all the yuck off it.'

'What yuck?'

'I don't know. I was watching *One Born Every Minute* a few months ago and all the babies were covered in this white yucky stuff when they were born.'

'That's the vernix. It helps protect their skin in the womb,' she tells me. 'Anyway, much as I love you, I'm not going to promise anything. I want this thing out as soon as possible. But I will get Ed to text you the moment anything happens, OK?'

'Well, if you're going to be all selfish about it, and just pop it out whenever it suits you,' I say, jokingly, 'I guess that'll just have to do.'

* * *

A few days later, I'm sheltering from the January rain in one of the bus shelters in the long-term car park at Gatwick when my phone pings with a WhatsApp message. It's very early in the morning, and still dark, so I'm fairly certain I know what it is. Sure enough, it's Ed telling me that Charley has gone into labour.

I keep checking my phone every few minutes while I'm queueing to check in, and then in the departure lounge, but there are no further messages. Just before I board the plane, I send a message to Ed, asking for an update. He replies that the contractions are regular, but not close enough together yet to make it worthwhile leaving for the hospital. I reply, wishing them luck and sending love, and then turn my phone off in preparation for the flight.

As soon as the plane lands, I grab my phone and turn it back on, cursing the age it takes to connect to the Turkish network. There's a message from Ed, and I open it eagerly, but all it says is that they're about to leave for the hospital. I don't reply, as I know he'll ping me as soon as there are any more developments.

Istanbul is one of my favourite cities. I've been here many

times over the years, and I love the chaotic vibrancy of it. On the taxi ride from the airport to the Hilton, where I'm staying this time, the traffic is horrendous and vehicles of all shapes and sizes just seem to pile in from every direction, with no recognisable priority system. I make a note to advise against car hire in my write-up. Thankfully, taxis are cheap and plentiful, and I know the public transport system generally works well.

The Hilton is a haven of peace after the mayhem on the roads. It's not a hotel I've stayed in before, but it seems well situated and my room is a decent size, with a view out towards the Bosphorus Straits. Crucially, there's a desk that I can work at, so I quickly set up my laptop. The airline has provided a list of 'must see' attractions that have to be included in my review, but they have also left some leeway for me to use my own experience, so I set about creating an itinerary. I'm only here for two full days, so I can't afford to waste time. Night has fallen by the time I've made my plan, so I freshen up and head out in search of something to eat. I get a taxi to Taksim Square, where I enjoy a selection of excellent *meze* and a glass of Efes beer in a small restaurant. As I'm eating, my phone pings with another update from Ed. Apparently the labour is still progressing slowly, and Charley has been given an epidural to help with the pain.

Back at the hotel, I write up my notes so far. Once I feel my eyelids starting to droop, I get ready for bed and am soon fast asleep.

I check my phone as soon as I wake up in the morning, and there are a number of messages from Ed. I open them excitedly, and I'm greeted with a series of pictures of a tiny baby being cradled either by an exhausted-looking Charley, or an ecstatic-looking Ed. The final message reads:

Meet Amelia Wells, 8 lb 4 oz. Mother and baby both doing well. Ed x

I write back straight away to congratulate them both, and say that I'm looking forward to meeting her as soon as I get back from Courchevel. Ed sends back a thumbs up, along with a message to say that they're going to keep Charley and Amelia in hospital for the first night as it was such a long labour, but that they should be able to go home tomorrow.

After a fairly standard hotel breakfast, I set off for the Kabataş tram station, stopping on the way to buy and top up the card that you need to use any public transport in this city. It's a ten-minute ride to the Sultanahmet district, where many of the top tourist attractions are. I never really have time to take attractions in fully, so I usually have a quick wander round, taking photos where I'm allowed to, then buy the cheapest guidebook I can on the way out to help me fill in anything I may have missed. I also make time to stop after each one and write down my impressions in shorthand in my notebook.

It's a full-on day, but I manage to visit both the sixth-century Hagia Sophia and the Blue Mosque, named after its stunning, blue-tiled interior, in the morning. For lunch, I head into a busy café in one of the many narrow cobbled streets for Balık ekmek (an unappealing sounding but surprisingly delicious grilled fish sandwich), before tackling the Grand Bazaar, an intricate maze of small shops, stalls and restaurants. I've been here before, but I'm always blown away by the vast array of jewellery, beautifully intricate Turkish carpets and brightly coloured fabrics that assault your eyes as you wander through. There are shops selling pretty much everything you could want, and I pick up a couple of gifts for Ed, Charley and baby Amelia. I enjoy the good-natured haggling even though I know that, as a tourist, I'm never going to get a particularly good deal. A taxi driver once explained to me that most of the stallholders have three prices. The most expensive, unsurprisingly, is for tourists. Those who are obviously foreign but have enough mastery of Turkish to indicate that they're probably ex-pat residents fare slightly better, and the lowest price is reserved for Turks, who can haggle fluently in their native tongue.

Despite my comfortable trainers, my feet are starting to ache a little as I head for my final attraction of the day, Topkapı Palace. As I wander through the courtyards the sun is beginning to set so, after buying the obligatory guidebook, I head down to the Metro to catch the train back to Taksim Square. Back in the hotel I lay my spoils out on the bed and run myself a hot bath to soak the grime of the day away. Afterwards, I wrap myself in the fluffy bathrobe that is de rigueur for hotels like this everywhere and sit down at the computer to start writing up. I flick through my phone pictures, and I'm pleased to see that they've come out quite well – perhaps Toby transferred some of his talent via osmosis when we were having lunch together. I also send a message to Ed, and he replies to say that Amelia isn't feeding very well yet, but they've been told that it's nothing to worry about at this stage.

The next morning I'm up early to catch the tram down to the Eminönü Pier. One of the things I've never managed to do in my visits to Istanbul is see it from the water, and I'm determined to change that today with a trip on the public ferry. I'm planning to travel up as far as it goes, just short of the Black Sea at Anadolu Kavağı, have lunch there, and then get the ferry back in the afternoon. After the pavement pounding of the previous day this is a much more leisurely affair, and the weather is being kind, so I'm able to sit outside on the ferry and watch the scenery go by. I take pictures and make notes as we go, and I find I'm enjoying the fresh breeze. Crowds of locals pour on and off the ferry at every pier where we stop, and my eye is drawn to a small child at one point. He's obviously feeling unwell as his parents pick him up and hold him over the side. He immediately starts screaming blue murder, evidently convinced they're trying to throw him overboard, and that seems to cure his seasickness. As we're heading back past Rumeli Castle, my phone pings with a message from Ed to say that Charley and Amelia have been discharged, as Amelia seems to be feeding a bit better. I send love and tell them I can't wait to see them when I'm back.

My final morning sees me back in Eminönü for a quick visit to the spice market, before I visit a few hotels in the Sultanahmet district that the airline features in its holiday brochures. They're all expecting me, and I stick my head round a bedroom door in each, to get a flavour of the accommodation, before catching a taxi back to the airport for my flight home.

By the time I get back to my flat, it's after ten o'clock at night and I'm very aware that I have to be back at Gatwick early the next morning to meet Toby. I unpack hurriedly, shoving my dirty clothes in the laundry basket to deal with when I get back from Courchevel, dig out my ski clothes from the back of the wardrobe, and repack, before falling into bed, exhausted.

6

JANUARY

I'm up at four the next morning to drive back to the airport. Things get off to a bad start when there's no sign of Toby at the easyJet check-in area where we've agreed to meet. I try to call him, but his phone goes straight to voicemail, so I text him an angry 'Where are you?' message instead. I know he can't have checked in already, because I've got his boarding card, which I printed off just before going to bed. I can feel my stress levels rising. I'm used to travelling alone, and this sudden reliance on another person, over whom I have no control, is making me uncomfortable. By the time he arrives, slightly out of breath, I'm positively annoyed.

'Sorry I'm late,' he pants. 'I had to wait ages for a bus. It said there was one every few minutes when I booked the parking, but I must have been there for at least a quarter of an hour.'

Amateur. Everyone knows there are hardly any buses this early in the morning, as they're still running the night schedule. The bus only comes round every few minutes during peak times. I'm trying not to be cross with him, but I'm failing. If I'm being purely rational, I know there is still plenty of time to check in and get to the gate, but I feel aggrieved that he's managed to upset my routine before we've even got through security.

'Why didn't you answer your phone?' I snap, probably more fiercely than he deserves. I see the surprise flash in his eyes.

'Sorry. I always turn it off when I'm driving, and I hadn't got around to turning it back on.' He reaches into his pocket, fishes out his phone, and makes a display of turning it on.

'Well, you're here now,' I say, forcing myself to be more gentle. 'Shall we?'

As we're queueing up to drop our bags off, I feel my phone buzz in my back pocket. Worrying that something might have happened with Charley and Amelia, I fish it out, only to see that Toby has replied to my 'Where are you?' message.

'Don't look now, but I'm right behind you,' he's written. I can't help but smile. I type, 'If this were from anyone else, I'd be worried that I was being stalked by a pervert, but I don't think I'm your type, so I'll let it go,' and press send. There's a brief pause before he sends back a smiley face. My annoyance starts to fade, and I turn and smile at him. He's looking at me quizzically, as if trying to work something out.

'Sorry I was grumpy,' I say to him. 'I'm used to travelling alone, so this is unfamiliar and a little stressful.'

He smiles. 'I'll make sure I allow more time next time, if there is a next time.'

'There has to be at least one next time,' I tell him. 'You've got to experience the delights of the Bellavista in Corfu with me.'

Our conversation is cut short by the process of dropping our bags and making our way through security. I'm pleased to see that he's organised enough to have his carry-on liquids already in a see-through plastic bag; I'm always amazed by the number of people who seem to be caught out by that, or try to take more than the allowance through.

I pass through security with no issues, but Toby has to have his bag searched. When he's finally allowed to proceed, he zips it up and walks over to me.

'Would you believe that happens pretty much every time?' he says. 'You would think they'd never seen a camera, or lenses, before.'

'Have you ever been through security at Tel Aviv?' I ask him, as we set off in the direction of the gate.

'No, why?'

'This is a walk in the park compared to there. They would probably have dismantled your camera, and they would definitely have swabbed every nook and cranny. I took a simple battery-powered alarm clock through there once in my hold baggage, and they went berserk. They swabbed the poor thing so much it never worked again. Israel is an amazing country though, you should go.'

'Is there anywhere in the world you haven't been?' he asks.

'Oh yes. Quite a lot of the Middle East, for example. I wouldn't feel very safe as a woman travelling on my own there, although I'd love to go to Jordan and see Petra. I've also never been to Russia, China or Japan. I've seen quite a lot of the rest of it, though. You must travel quite a lot with your work too? All those bikini-clad girls on beautiful white sand beaches are hardly shot in Bournemouth, are they?'

'Actually, I have done a few bikini shoots in Bournemouth,' he replies. 'With photography you don't have to be in the Caribbean to make it look like the Caribbean, if you get my drift. You just need a nice sandy beach; careful lighting and Photoshop help with everything else. So I don't actually do as much travelling abroad as you might think. Also, if a magazine like *Voyages Luxes* wants stunning pictures of, say, New Zealand, they can just hire a photographer who lives out there and get the images sent across. Much cheaper than paying for me to go there.'

'I guess I never really thought about it like that,' I reply.

'What about you? Do you ever have to fake it?' he asks.

'Of course! If the guy doesn't know what he's doing, I don't want to be there all day,' I say, before bursting into laughter as the realisation of his double-entendre dawns on him and he blushes furiously.

'Sometimes, when I was just starting out, I'd research a place on the internet and then try to write about it as if I'd been there,' I tell him, more seriously. 'Nobody will fund your trips up front when you're new, so either you have to fund them yourself and hope someone will commission your article, or you have to find a way to write convincingly without actually doing the travel. For me it was a mix of both in the early days. I did fall foul of one editor, because it turned out he had actually lived for a period in the place that I'd written about and he therefore spotted all the things I'd got wrong. The funny thing was that he was so impressed that I'd managed to get so much of a feel for it just from internet research that he became one of my first regular clients. For the first couple of years, he would always demand to see receipts as proof that I had actually been to the places I was writing about, though.'

We settle into a couple of seats near the gate and a companionable silence descends. From the number of our fellow passengers kitted out in thick, brightly coloured puffa jackets I deduce that most of them are also heading for the ski slopes. It's still dark outside, but the first glimmers of dawn light are creeping over the horizon. I pull my laptop out of my bag and start reading the famil pack from the Mirabelle. Unsurprisingly, they want us to try the restaurant, which I've already booked for this evening, and the spa.

'So,' Toby asks, suddenly, 'tell me more about this place in Corfu. Why do we have to go there?'

'I beg your pardon?'

'Earlier, when we were at the bag drop, you said I had to experience the Bellavista in Corfu with you. What's that about?'

I explain to him about the mismatch between my review and TripAdvisor, glossing over the part where Mark was about to drop me, and tell him how it inspired me to come up with the idea of doing incognito visits.

'So that's what he meant about getting your fingers burned,' he comments when I've finished. He's obviously got an extraordinary memory for detail, as I don't remember anything along those lines being said while he was in the room.

I grit my teeth at the memory of that meeting and bury myself back in the famil packs. After a while the flight starts to board and there's the usual confused scrum where those who haven't paid for priority boarding try to see if they can sneak on early. An attendant spots a man with two pieces of hand baggage and descends on him like a hawk.

'I'm sorry, sir,' she tells him in a tone of voice that indicates she isn't sorry at all, 'you're only allowed one piece of hand baggage unless you've paid for priority boarding. One of those will have to go into the hold.'

He's having none of it, though, insisting that it said he could bring two when he booked. The argument that ensues is predictable; she digs her heels in and just repeats the policy while he becomes ever more enraged. The whole area round the gate has fallen silent to listen, and I find myself feeling slightly sorry for him, as this is only going to end one way. Sure enough, the attendant's immovable attitude wears him down eventually, and he hands over one of his bags. She marches off, clutching it like a prize, and he looks dejected. His jaw is still moving silently, and I'm fairly sure he's muttering obscenities under his breath.

We file onto the plane and there is the usual scramble for the overhead lockers. Thankfully, there is space in the locker above our row and we hastily cram our bags into it before sitting down. I managed to get us aisle and centre seats, and Toby very gallantly takes the middle one. The window seat next to him is currently empty, and I find myself automatically scanning the other boarding passengers, trying to work out who is going to fill it. I've lost count of the number of novels I've read where the heroine finds herself sitting next to some gorgeous man on a plane, they strike up a conversation and end up getting married. I can safely say that nothing remotely like that has ever happened to me. Sure enough, a large, middle-aged woman stops at our row and indicates that the window seat is hers. Toby and I dutifully stand up and move aside to allow her access and, after fiddling around to get a magazine out of her bag, she heaves herself into position and flops down with a groan. Unfortunately for Toby she is overflowing the seat a little, so he's forced to squash himself over towards me to make room for her.

'Look on the bright side,' I whisper in his ear. 'We're only going to Geneva. Imagine if it was long haul and you were going to be like that for eight hours or more.'

Toby smiles grimly. 'I've just remembered one of the reasons I'm glad I don't travel as much as you,' he whispers, and I can't stop a giggle escaping.

'Well, look at the two of you! What a charming couple you make. Have you been together long?' The woman has obviously mistaken us pressing our heads together and whispering as a sign of intimacy. I open my mouth to correct her, but Toby is too quick for me.

'About six months,' he tells her with a smile. 'This is our first holiday together though.'

'Aww, that's lovely. I hope you'll have a wonderful time. Where are you staying?'

'It's a surprise,' Toby replies, grasping my hand as he does so. 'All Madison here knows is that it's skiing.'

'That's so romantic,' the woman says, with a sigh. Thankfully, her attention is momentarily drawn to some activity outside the window, and I have the opportunity to pull my hand back.

'What the fuck are you doing?' I hiss in his ear.

'Getting into character!' he replies. 'It just seemed like a golden opportunity to test out how convincing we could be before it really matters.'

He grins at me conspiratorially, and my annoyance evaporates. I smile back at him.

'Are you going to be this much trouble for the next six days?' I ask, just as the woman turns back and starts looking at us again.

'I reckon you'll go the distance, you two,' she observes. 'I've got a nose for these things.'

I have to look away and hold my nose to prevent myself from snorting with laughter, but thankfully she doesn't notice, as Toby is replying to her.

'Well, it's early days,' he tells her, 'but we're hopeful.'

7

JANUARY

It's a little after two in the afternoon when the transfer minibus drops us outside the Mirabelle. Thankfully, Toby seems to have got the mischief out of his system on the plane and has reverted to his usual, slightly reserved, self.

'Golden rule number one,' I say to him. 'Don't let the porter take your bag. If they do then you have to tip them, and tips aren't reimbursable through expenses.'

He digests this information as we walk up to the main entrance of the hotel. Just as we're about to go through the door, he stops and turns to me.

'Just a thought,' he says, 'but if we're supposed to be tourists we might blend in better if we did let them take the bags. How much is the tip – ten euros?'

'That sounds about right. Five would seem stingy, wouldn't it? But across three hotels that's thirty euros of our own money. I do need to make a living, you know.'

There's a pause while he ponders the options, and I try not to be impatient.

'OK, no porters,' he replies eventually.

'I like your thinking though,' I tell him. 'That wouldn't have occurred to me.'

In the end the discussion turns out to be moot, at least as far as the Mirabelle is concerned. The receptionist informs us most apologetically that our room isn't quite ready so, once we've completed the check-in process, she takes our bags to store them. The hotel is very traditional, from what I can tell by studying the lobby. There's lots of wood panelling and soft classical mood music is emanating from hidden speakers. The lobby itself is large and contains several little seating areas, most of which are empty at this time of day. The ones that are occupied indicate that the primary target market is middle-aged and older.

'Come on,' I say to Toby. 'Let's go and sort out the ski hire, have an explore, and then I'll treat you to a glass of *vin chaud*.'

When we return a few hours later, the lobby is much busier. There is a gentle hum of chat and most of the seating areas are now occupied by couples and small groups enjoying a drink and catch up at the end of the day's skiing. Although there are some younger people like us, most of the guests are much older, and there are very few children. The same receptionist greets us, hands over our room cards, and informs us that our bags have been taken up to our room already.

'Nice touch,' I say to Toby as we make our way to the lift.

As would be expected in a five-star hotel, our room is spacious, with a superking-size double bed, a comfortable-looking sofa and armchair, and a huge flatscreen TV. There's no overhead light, but a soft glow emanates from a couple of standard lamps in the seating area, added to by the slightly brighter bedside lights. The effect is obviously supposed to be soothing, but to me it's verging on being too dim. Most of the people I saw in the lobby would be unable to sit in the armchair and read a book without extra light. There are sliding doors out to the balcony, and another door that leads into a surprisingly small marble bathroom with a shower and bath. I eye the bed with relief; I've had a couple of bad dreams on the run-up to this trip where Toby and I ended up jammed into a single bed.

'I normally sleep on the left-hand side of the bed. Is that OK with you?' I ask him.

'Fine,' he says. 'I'm currently sleeping in a single bed at home, so it doesn't make a lot of difference to me either way.'

There's an awkward atmosphere as the reality of sharing a room and a bed dawns on us. I still hardly know him, and unpacking my case in front of him feels uncomfortably intimate. I wait until he's looking the other way before hastily transferring my underwear to 'my' drawer, and I'm reminded of boarding school as I place my pyjamas on the pillow on my side of the bed. Normally I just sleep in a long T-shirt and knickers, but that didn't seem appropriate so I've splashed out on some cotton PJs from M&S. Toby is obviously feeling uncomfortable too, so I curb my natural curiosity and avert my eyes while he unpacks.

'I might have a shower,' I announce, to break the silence. 'I always feel a bit grimy after travelling, and I need to change for dinner tonight anyway.'

'Good idea,' Toby agrees. 'I'll iron my shirt and trousers while you're in there and have a quick shower after you.'

I grab my dress, some clean underwear and my make-up bag, and retreat to the bathroom, locking the door behind me. There's a hook on the back of the door, on which I hang the dress. After I've stepped out of my travel clothes, I sit on the loo, feeling very aware that Toby can probably hear me weeing. Now that it's a reality, this pretending to be a couple suddenly seems like a really bad idea. It's not that I don't like Toby, I do. I'm just not sure I can stomach a week of us behaving like shy teenagers around each other. I stand up, flush the loo and stare at my face in the mirror.

'Pull yourself together, Mads,' I tell my reflection, firmly. 'This was your idea, remember? Grow a pair and make the best of it.'

There's the usual array of little bottles containing shampoo, conditioner and so on, and I scan the labels looking for the body wash. I turn on the shower and I'm relieved to see that the water pressure is good. There's nothing I hate more than trying to wash in a pathetic dribble. I turn the heat up and step in. After I've showered and washed the travel grime off, I dry myself and wrap a towel round me. It's at this point I realise that I have a problem. The steam from the shower has completely filled the room and I can't see a thing in the mirror. The extractor fan is running, but it's evidently not up to the job. Not only can I not use the mirror, the heat and humidity in here is making me clammy. I can feel beads of moisture forming on my top lip and forehead already. My clothes will cling to me if I try to get dressed in this, and I'll have no chance of getting any make-up to stick to my face, even if I could see what I was doing in the mirror. I look around for a dressing gown to cover myself up with, but can't see one. With a growl of frustration, I grab my clothes and fling open the door, still wrapped in the towel. Toby appears to have found an ironing board and iron and is carefully pressing his trousers. His eyebrows shoot up at the sight of me.

'Sorry,' I explain. 'I can't get ready in there, it's like a sauna!'

'I can imagine,' he replies, with a smile. 'You should have seen the cloud of steam that followed you! It was very dramatic. I'm nearly done, and then you can get changed in here while I shower. Does that help?'

'Yes, thank you.'

'If you want a dressing gown, they're in the wardrobe by the door,' he tells me. 'I came across them while I was searching for the ironing board.'

Toby hangs up his trousers, folds up the ironing board, and

peers tentatively into the bathroom. Declaring that the worst of the steam appears to have gone, he grabs a dressing gown and shuts and locks the door behind him, and I soon hear the sound of the shower. Hastily, I whip off the towel and get dressed. I've left my make-up bag in the bathroom, so I'll have to deal with that later. I check the time and send a message to Charley to ask how she is.

There's no desk in the room, so I sit carefully on the bed, turn on my laptop and open the Istanbul article. It's starting to take shape and I'm beginning to hope that I might get it finished while I'm in Courchevel, which would leave me more time to write up this trip and get it to Mark by the tenth of February. I'm in the zone when Toby finishes his shower, so I don't really notice him coming back into the room.

'I'm not wild about the little bottles of shampoo and stuff,' he complains. 'They're a bit fiddly, aren't they?'

It takes me a moment to disengage myself from Istanbul and work out what he's talking about.

'You sound like my dad,' I tell him. 'He gets really annoyed with them, because the writing is so small he needs his glasses to read the labels. He's always going on about how they should put different coloured liquids in them so, once you've read the labels, you can still work out which is which easily. Given the average age of the guests we've seen so far, I'm sure a good percentage of them have been washing their hair with body wash and vice versa.'

'It's probably the same stuff in both bottles anyway,' Toby remarks.

'You're probably right,' I laugh. 'Anyway, we've got an hour before we're due in the restaurant. Do you mind if I crack on with this for a bit? Once the bathroom has cooled down, I'll go and do my make-up and you can get dressed.'

Toby settles himself on the bed next to me, opens his own laptop and plugs the card from his camera into it. The pictures that he took while we were out exploring appear on the screen after a few seconds. I try very hard to focus on my article, but every so often I find myself pausing to watch him work. In one photo he carefully airbrushes out some skiers and it's slightly mesmerising to observe them slowly vanish until it looks like they were never there. I'm distracted by a ping from my phone. It's Charley, reporting in.

The midwife lied. Newborns aren't easy – they cry. All the time. Ed has suggested that maybe Amelia's not quite done yet and we should go back to the hospital and see if they'll put her back inside me!! She still isn't feeding that well and we're thinking of changing to bottle feeding to see if that helps, but I feel guilty as everyone says breast is best. How's the GBF?

There's a picture of Amelia, red-faced and angry looking. I type back:

Sod what other people say – do what works for you. Bottle-fed babies in the adverts always look happy, don't they? GBF OK. Slightly awkward sharing a room though!

I can see she's typing.

Adverts aren't real – but thanks. Room sharing was your idea, wasn't it?

Ha ha. Reality rather different from the idea.

I get up from the bed and wander over to the window, taking a surreptitious photo of Toby on the bed in his dressing gown over my shoulder as I go and sending it to her.

Her reply is instant.

He's HOT!

I think you should ask the doctor to look at your hormone levels. I'm worried about you.

The restaurant is exactly as I imagined it. Like the lobby, the walls are all wood panelled and there are oil paintings in heavy frames dotted about, each with a little light mounted above it to illuminate the scene depicted. There's a muted hum of conversation, and the clinking of knives and forks on expensive china. Waiters in dark suits and white gloves glide silently through the room. It's the sort of place my parents would love, but I find unbearably pretentious.

'Is your dad a travel writer too?' Toby asks, after we've been shown to our table and been given the menu.

'No, he works for Shell. Why?'

'Oh, it's just the way you were talking about him and the bottles in the bathroom. I wondered if he was a travel writer and you'd followed in his footsteps.'

'No, it's just he travels a lot for the company, so stays in a lot of hotels. He doesn't really understand what I do and keeps asking when I'm either going to get a proper job or get married.'

We're interrupted by the sommelier with a wine list the size of an encyclopaedia. We order a glass of house white each and he retreats, with a slightly disdainful expression. I don't hear him call us peasants, but I'm pretty sure he's thinking it. Toby and I turn our attention to the menu, which is totally incomprehensible. The main part is all in French, but even the English translations don't help much. In the end we order pretty much at random, hoping that we'll be lucky. I sneak a few pictures of the food as it arrives on my iPhone, trying to be as unobtrusive as possible, and Toby does the same.

'There's a reason I'm a travel writer and not a food critic,' I tell him as we make our way back up to our room at the end of the meal. 'I mean, it all tasted very nice, but I hate all the pomp and ceremony, with the synchronised lifting of the cloches, and the foams, and the little smears of stuff. It just makes me want to rush out and get a burger!'

'It was quite a weird atmosphere,' he replies. 'Almost religious, in a way. I found it slightly intimidating.'

'Exactly!' I agree. 'You shouldn't be intimidated by a restaurant. Well, at least we've done it and we can eat somewhere else tomorrow.'

Once we're back in the room, we take turns to use the bathroom to change and brush our teeth before climbing into bed. We lie there for a bit, as far apart as it's possible to be without either of us falling out, and another uncomfortable silence descends.

'Shall I turn off the light?' Toby asks, eventually.

'Yes,' I tell him, as I roll onto my side with my back to him. 'Goodnight, Toby.'

'Goodnight, Madison.'

8

JANUARY

This is hopeless. I reach for my phone on the bedside table and check the time. It's well past one in the morning and I'm still wide awake. Toby appears to be fast asleep; his breathing is deep and even, with the occasional little sniffle. I've tried lying on my right side, my left side, and my back, but I just can't get comfortable. It's the bloody pyjamas. The top is OK, but I'm very aware of the bottoms, particularly as they keep wrapping themselves uncomfortably around my thighs and digging into my crotch. They're also stiflingly hot. I've tried sticking my legs out from under the covers to cool them down, but then my feet get cold. If I want to get any sleep tonight, the pyjama bottoms are going to have to come off. I wriggle out of them, as carefully as I can so as not to disturb Toby, and place them on the floor next to the bed so I can put them back on as soon as I wake up. Hopefully he'll never know, and I've still got my knickers on so I'm not totally indecent. The relief is instant, and I soon drift off to sleep.

The room is still dark when I wake again. I lie still for a few moments, trying to work out if Toby is awake too. I listen for a while, but can't detect his breathing, and when I open my eyes and look at his side of the bed I realise why. There's no sign of him. Shit. I hope he hasn't woken up, seen that I've broken our agreement to stay covered up, and gone off in a huff. Or worse, gone home. I leap out of bed, stuffing my legs back into the pyjama bottoms, and check to make sure he hasn't taken all his stuff. His camera bag is gone, but his clothes are still in the drawer and his toothbrush is in the bathroom, so he hasn't gone home at least. But where the bloody hell is he? I check the time. It's just coming up to half past seven and it's still dark outside. What on earth could he be doing?

I decide to get dressed. If he's still not back after that I'll go and look for him. I ease myself into the thermal base layers and my salopettes and pop a jumper over the top. I'll put the rest of my ski clobber on just before we go out, otherwise I'll cook. I'm just tying my hair back when I hear Toby's card in the door. He's obviously been outside for a while, as his cheeks are flushed from the sudden warmth of the hotel and I notice that he's already fully kitted out in his ski wear.

'Where have you been?' I exclaim, with relief washing through me.

'Taking photos,' he replies, as if it's the most normal thing in the world. 'Dawn and dusk are the best time to take landscape shots – the light is amazing. I hope I didn't disturb you when I left?'

'No, not at all. I was just worried that...' I realise, as I'm forming the words, that he obviously didn't notice that I broke our agreement, so perhaps I don't need to mention it either. 'Oh, never mind. Are you ready for breakfast?'

The hotel breakfast is fairly standard continental fare, with a selection of pastries, cold meats, cheeses, fruits and yoghurts. There is a menu with hot options as well, but we don't have time for that if we're going to get Toby to his ski school on time. I fill a small bowl with fruit and yoghurt, while Toby makes a beeline for the pastries.

'I need the carbs if I'm going to be exerting myself,' he explains, adding a pain au chocolat to the two croissants already on his plate. 'Also, delicious as it was, that dinner last night wasn't really very filling, so I'm starving!'

'Not exactly healthy carbs though, are they?' I tease him. 'They're basically just fat with a bit of flour to hold them together.'

'I don't care,' he replies, adding butter and jam to his plate. 'I need this.'

Once Toby has grabbed some hasty second helpings and we've finished eating, we return to the room to finish kitting ourselves out, before retrieving our skis and boots from the storage room. Toby is particularly impressed that his boots are warm, and I explain that the boot racks are heated to help dry the boots out after a day on the slopes. We locate the ski school and I wish him luck, before heading for the Verdons gondola to do the green run that I've selected as my refresher run. The ski runs are all colour coded: green are the beginner slopes, then you work up through blue and red to black, which are for the most serious skiers. Although I've done my share of red and black runs over the years, I generally steer clear of them now; they tend to attract the kamikaze skiers, who whoosh past at dizzying speeds, often missing you by a whisker.

I'm glad to see the queue for the lift is fairly short, and soon I'm whisked to the top of the slope for my first run. My exit from the chairlift is a little ungainly, as I'm rather out of practice, but at least I don't fall over. It's not an especially long slope, and I take it gently, doing wide traverses and letting my body get the feel of being on skis again. It takes a couple of green runs before I feel that I've got my balance back and I'm ready to tackle something a little more interesting. This time I take the Jardin Alpin lift as far as I can, then transfer to the Biollay lift. From here I'm able to follow a series of blue and green runs all the way down into Courchevel Village, some 300 metres lower than the main part of the town where we're staying. I'd forgotten how much I enjoy this, the cold breeze and the bright sunlight, the gentle swish of the powdery snow under my skis, my body reacting almost instinctively to the bumps. The slope is not too crowded, so I've got plenty of room around me, and the scenery, particularly as I pass through the trees, is stunning. The sky is that deep, cloudless blue you only seem to get at altitude, and the snow is dazzlingly white.

In the village I stop for a coffee and an opportunity to write up some notes before catching the lift back up to the main part of Courchevel. I check my watch and see that there's just time for a short green run before Toby's class finishes, and I arrive just as they're wrapping up. Poor Toby looks absolutely miserable.

'I've spent most of the morning on my arse,' he complains as soon as we're out of earshot of the rest of the group. 'I fell off the lift more times than I can remember, and that was before the humiliation of falling over when I actually made it to the top. I managed one successful descent in the whole morning, and that was right at the end. I was going so slowly I probably could have walked down the slope faster. Explain to me how this is fun?'

'You'll get there,' I encourage him. 'It is hard at first, particularly as an adult. Were there any others in the group who were doing it for the first time?'

'We're all beginners,' he replies.

'And did any of the others find it any easier?'

'No, I guess not.'

'There you are then. Stick at it. Each day will get a little easier. What's the instructor like?'

'Good, actually. Very patient. He's British, works here every season.'

We saunter back to the hotel, drop off our skis and boots, and head for a local restaurant that was mentioned in the famil pack. Toby's eyebrows shoot up at the prices on the menu and I have to remind him that everything is expensive here.

'So, when did you learn to ski?' he asks, after we've placed our orders.

'As a child,' I reply. 'My parents were well-off, so I had a typically privileged upbringing. Boarding school from the age of eight, ski holidays every February half-term, decamp to the south of France, or Tuscany, or some other clichéd destination every summer. Don't get me wrong; I may sound jaded, but at the time I loved it, and it definitely gave me my desire to travel. I think I realised in my teens that there was so much more of the world I wanted to see outside the pristine hotels and villas my parents took me to.'

'Boarding school at eight?' Toby repeats in amazement. 'That's so young. I could never do that to a child.'

'I wouldn't do it either, but my parents thought it was normal in the UK. I cried myself to sleep every night for the first three weeks. I was also picked on because of my American accent, which made it harder. I was utterly miserable at the start, but things did get better, and I was quite enjoying it by the time I left to go to secondary school at thirteen.'

'You're American? I would never have guessed.'

'My parents are American, and I was born there. I've lived in the UK since I was small, though, and I'm a British citizen now. We have family in the US that we visit every few years, but I don't feel any affinity to the place. In my head I'm British.'

'You certainly don't have any hint of an accent.'

'Well, as I said, I was bullied for it at school, so I quickly learned to speak like everyone else to fit in. According to my friend Charley, I still revert to American when I'm talking to my parents. I have to say that I don't notice.'

'And your secondary school, did you board there as well?'

'Oh yes, but that was fine. I was used to it by then, and I was popular, which helped. When you don't have your parents around, you learn to be self-reliant at a young age. I realised that nobody else was going to stand up for me, that I had to believe in my own worth and stand my own ground. It was formative, for me anyway. Some of the other girls definitely weren't suited to it, and we had our fair share of dramas over the years.'

'What sort of dramas?'

'Eating disorders, mainly. At one point there was a secret club of around five girls in my house who used to sneak off after each meal to throw up together. There was a huge scandal when they were inevitably caught, and various people were brought in to give us talks on the importance of eating healthily. All these posters went up about how to spot the signs of anorexia or bulimia, and we were offered counselling if we needed it.'

'Sounds brutal,' Toby remarks.

'It was, in a way. I don't regret it though. Like I said, it taught me to believe in myself, and not to put up with bullshit.'

Our food arrives, and there's a brief silence while we start to eat. We've both ordered the *tartiflette* and it's delicious.

'So, you don't hate your parents for putting you through it?' Toby asks, after a few mouthfuls.

'Interesting question. I think my relationship with them is different than it would be if I'd stayed at home and gone to a day school. I love them, but I don't feel the need to run my life choices past them and get their approval, if that makes sense. As I've mentioned before, my dad isn't wild about my job; Mum never worked and they never expected me to, either. I was expected to find a nice, rich man, marry him and have babies.'

'I don't see you fitting very well into the "kept woman" mould,' Toby says, with a laugh.

'What do you mean by that?' I ask, slightly affronted.

'Nothing bad, it's just that it sounds like quite a submissive role, and I think we can both agree that submissive isn't a word that could be used to describe you.'

'I think I'd be bored if I didn't have a job, and I don't think I could respect a man who expected me to give up my independence,' I agree, after a pause to consider. 'If I'm brutally honest, I don't think I've met a man yet that I really respected, even my dad. He's a good man, but he lives for his work. I think Mum's been quite lonely over the years. I couldn't accept that kind of relationship.'

'Your Prince Charming is going to have to be the full package, isn't he? No feet of clay allowed.'

'Hah, after the number of frogs I've had to kiss, I'm starting to doubt he exists! Come on, eat up. We've got a spa to check out this afternoon.'

The rest of the meal is largely silent. I'm surprised how much I've told Toby about myself. I'm normally very cautious about what I share, and I have to know someone really well before I open up, but Toby is a good listener, and there's something honest and trustworthy about him that I like.

9

JANUARY

'What about you?' I ask Toby. We've both had massages in the spa, and we're now wrapped in our dressing gowns, lying by the indoor pool, which is deserted apart from us.

'What about me what?' he replies.

'I've told you my story. What's yours?'

'Pretty uninteresting,' he says. 'My parents aren't well-off, and I think I already told you they live in the same house that they bought when they first got married. I went to the local comprehensive, where I was ruthlessly bullied for being short. When I was in the sixth form, I started doing bits and pieces with Paul and found I was good at it. Things kind of went from there, and now photography is my bread and butter.'

'I'm guessing it doesn't pay that well, if you're stuck in a shared house,' I observe.

'It's probably like journalism,' he tells me. 'When you start out, you're barely making ends meet, but if you're good and you have the connections, the commissions start to come. I was lucky because Paul helped me a lot. You also have to be versatile. On top of the studio and location shoots I do for magazines like

Voyages Luxes, I get commissions for a lot of celebrity photo shoots and weddings for *Hello!* I do private work as well, and I also sell images online. It all adds up, and I work hard at it. I could have moved out of the house ages ago, but I wanted to be able to buy my own place and kit it out with the best equipment without borrowing any money. I have an aversion to debt, it turns out.'

'But look at a trip like this. How many images is Mark going to buy? Five or six, maximum? That's not going to make you a lot, surely?'

'You're right. If you want to make loads of money from a single image and a single publication, then becoming a paparazzo is probably your only option. Get a clear shot of a celebrity doing something revolting, or a high-profile criminal arriving at court, sell it to the papers, you can make serious cash. But, apart from the fact that it would make me feel grubby, that type of life absolutely relies on you being in exactly the right place at the right time, and you spend most of your time waiting around for something to happen. I don't think I was designed for hanging around in the cold for hours on end.'

'So why did you agree to come here?' I ask him. 'In case you haven't noticed yet, there's a lot of hanging around in the cold when you're skiing!'

He thinks for a moment. 'When Mark called me into that meeting room, you looked really tense. Totally different to how you were when we met in the lobby, and how you've been since. You reminded me of a friend of my dad's, who bet way more than he could afford on the outcome of a football match years ago. Dad told me they were in the stands together, and this guy was green, he was so anxious. Something told me that, whatever was going on in that meeting, you had a lot riding on the outcome, and I suppose I felt I wanted to help—'

'Oh God, I wish I hadn't asked!' I interrupt. 'If I'd have known you only agreed to come out of pity, I'd have told you where to stick it!'

'Hang on,' he admonishes me, 'I haven't finished. Yes, I might have felt a bit sorry for you, but I was also curious. The idea sounded interesting, and I thought it might be fun. I'll admit it hasn't been much fun so far but, although Mark will only buy a few of the images, I'll put the others on various stock image sites I belong to and sell them there, so I'll do all right financially out of it.'

'Thinking of which, I'm relying on you for all the boring shots that I normally do. Pictures of the rooms and so on.'

'Don't worry about that. I took one of the room while you were in the shower last night, and I took exterior shots of all the places we're staying, plus a few general ones of Courchevel, while you were having your lie-in this morning.'

'Cheeky bastard! I was up at a perfectly respectable time. It's not my fault you're an insomniac!'

'I told you, the light is best first thing in the morning or at the end of the day. At least the days are quite short here, so I didn't have to get up that early. It's not unusual for me to have to get up at three or four in the morning to be in place when the light is just right. Thinking of which, the sun is starting to dip, so I'd better get back out there.'

'What happened to your dad's mate?' I ask, as we're walking back towards the lobby. 'Did he win?'

'He won that time,' Toby replies. 'But, of course, the win just went into more bets, and he lost it all again soon afterwards. He nearly lost his house before his wife found out what he was up to and forced him to sign up to Gamblers Anonymous. They had to do some pretty heavy debt restructuring and stuff to keep the bailiffs away. I think my fear of debt probably comes from seeing what happened to them.'

'I would have thrown him out,' I remark.

He studies me for a moment. 'Would you though? If it was someone you really loved, and it was an addiction? Yes, if he'd refused to seek help then I can see there's nowhere else you can go, but everyone deserves a second chance, don't they?'

'I think you might be a nicer person than me. I'm very much a "one strike and you're out" sort of girl.'

'And how is that working out for you?' he asks, with a twinkle in his eye.

'Fuck off!' I shove him hard on the shoulder. 'Where is your army of admirers if you're so bloody wise about relationships?'

'Fair point. However, I like to think my lack of allure is related to my lack of height and the fact that I'm not massively outgoing, rather than my unforgiving nature.' He laughs, knowing he's got to me.

Back in the room I settle down on the bed to work and Toby sets off with his rucksack. I write my shorthand notes about the spa, and then turn my attention back to writing up the Istanbul trip. I'm in the zone again when Toby reappears, but I'm aware of him sitting down next to me and opening up his computer. After a couple of hours, I reckon I've pretty much got it. I just need to decide which pictures to send in with it, so I get out my iPhone and start scrolling through, sending any images I think might be worth using to my laptop.

'Can I see?' Toby asks, suddenly.

'What?'

'Your pictures, can I see them?'

'I suppose so. Don't be too critical though.' I hand him the phone and he starts scrolling through.

'What do you use to edit them?' he asks, after he's looked at a few.

'What do you mean? I just point the camera, take the picture and, if I think it goes with the article, I send it in.'

'Some of these could be good, with a little bit of editing. May I?' he asks.

I can hardly refuse. He goes to the app store and downloads an app, then opens up one of the pictures I took in the Grand Bazaar. It's a view down one of the thoroughfares, with shops and stalls on either side.

'OK,' he says. 'Let me show you. The first thing I'm going to do is crop this. Have you heard of the rule of thirds?'

'No.' I'm starting to regret this already as it sounds like we're going to set off down a nerdy rabbit hole.

'It's quite simple,' he explains. 'In your mind, imagine the picture is divided into three, both horizontally and vertically, like a grid. Got it?'

I look at the image and mentally try to overlay the grid lines.

'Yes,' I reply.

'OK, so the rule of thirds is that you should place the main focus of interest on one of the points where the gridlines intersect. So, in this picture, we've got a chap walking away from us, wearing a pink shirt. I'm going to crop the picture so that he's in the bottom right third.' He fiddles with the app for a moment. 'See?'

I look at what he's done and have to admit that it has really improved the picture.

'Now we can adjust the colouring and so on. There are lots of things you can adjust, and they're all on sliders, so you can just play with them until it looks the way you want.' He demonstrates, and within a few seconds the picture is unrecognisable as one of mine.

'That's extraordinary!' I tell him.

'It's not bad, is it? You can get some pretty impressive pictures with a phone these days. There are still some significant shortcomings compared to a DSLR, but...'

'A what?'

'DSLR. It stands for Digital Single Lens Reflex,' he explains. Seeing the look of utter incomprehension on my face he opens his rucksack to reveal not one but two full-sized cameras, lots of different lenses and various other bits of paraphernalia.

'Like this,' he says, fishing one of the cameras out and handing it to me.

'Good grief! Why do you need so much stuff to take pictures? Actually, don't tell me, I'll just trust that you do. I'll stick with my iPhone, thanks. Much less obtrusive, for one thing.'

'Fair enough,' he replies, taking the camera and putting it back in the bag. 'Do use that app though, it will make a big difference.'

* * *

The next morning, we have breakfast early, before it's properly light, so we can pack our bags and check out before Toby is due at ski school. When I hand over the voucher to cover the bill, the receptionist is evidently totally bemused, and asks us to wait while she carries out a whispered conversation on the phone. A smartly dressed man appears a few minutes later.

'*Bonjour, Monsieur, bonjour, Mademoiselle,*' he says to us, shaking our hands. 'I am Alain, the day manager. This is very new for us, not to know who is coming and when they will arrive. I trust you enjoyed your stay?'

'Very much, thank you,' I reply. 'The room was very comfortable, and we have been well looked after. Is it OK if we leave our baggage here and collect it later?'

'*Mais bien sur!*' He waves the concierge over. 'I will take care of *l'addition* – the bill – for you. Is there anything else we can do?'

'No, that's great. *Merci*, Alain,' I reply.

'In that case, I will wish you an enjoyable day, and I look forward to the review. *Au revoir!*'

The concierge takes our bags and issues us with tickets to present when we want to collect them. As we go to retrieve our skis and boots, I notice that Toby is even quieter than usual.

'Is everything OK?' I ask him.

'I'm not really sure skiing is my thing,' he replies. 'I didn't enjoy it yesterday and my legs are pretty stiff this morning, despite the massage. I have to confess I'm not brimming over with excitement at the prospect of a repeat performance today.'

'It'll be better today, trust me. While you were asleep, your brain has probably been whirring away, working out what it needs to do.'

'I hope you're right,' he replies, 'otherwise this is going to be a dismal experience.'

I feel slightly guilty as I leave him, face downcast, at the ski school, but it's such a beautiful day that I soon forget about it. I've decided to tackle a couple of red runs today, not because I enjoy them, but because I need to be able to write about them. There's just me and another man in the ski lift as we start our ascent. I glance at him briefly. He's middle-aged, with dark, greasy-looking hair, and he has the distinct beginnings of a paunch. As the lift begins to climb, I turn my attention to the view. A fresh layer of snow has fallen overnight and it's glistening in the sunlight. The sky is bright blue and the air is clear and fresh.

'English?' The voice rudely interrupts my reverie. Reluctantly, I abandon the view and face my companion.

'I'm sorry, were you speaking to me?' I ask, desperately hoping that the answer is no. I have a horrible suspicion I know where this is going.

'Yes. You are English, yes?' His accent indicates that he's Italian. I notice that his hair is suspiciously evenly coloured, without a fleck of grey. I suspect the colour comes out of a bottle.

'I am Aldo,' he continues. 'What is your name? Are you here on your own?'

I sigh and summon up my most dismissive expression.

'I am English and no, I'm not here on my own. My boyfriend is at the ski school,' I tell him. Of course that's not true but, after Toby's antics on the plane, I don't think he's in a position to object to me using him to get rid of Aldo.

'Ah, he is not a skier. But you, you ski well? You must come and ski with me, I will show you the best places. Your breath will be taken away.'

'I don't think so. Thank you, but I'd rather ski alone.'

'Are you sure?' He's looking me up and down with a lascivious leer on his face. 'You and me, we could have fun, you know? Your boyfriend, he doesn't need to know. I could make you very happy.'

He's so cheesy it's all I can do not to laugh out loud at him. Instead, I hold up one finger to pause him while I reach into my pocket and bring out my phone, pretending to take a call.

'Hello? Right, yes, I see. I'll ask him.'

I lower the phone and look at Aldo. 'It's some bloke from a seventies porno movie. He says you've stolen his chat-up line and he'd quite like it back. Apparently, he needs it for this woman whose washing machine he's just fixed, because she doesn't have any money to pay him with. What shall I tell him?'

Aldo's expression turns thunderous. Thankfully, further conversation is impossible as we've arrived at the top. I deliberately hold back so I can see which way he goes and stay away from him. He turns and calls out to me as he sets off. The breeze takes most of it, but I can still make out the words 'frigid bitch'.

'It was lovely to meet you too!' I yell after him as I set off down the slope. What an arsehole.

10

JANUARY

Toby appears to be in much better spirits when I arrive at the ski school to meet him.

'I think you were right,' he tells me, as we head off in search of lunch. 'I still fell over, but not as often, and I managed a couple of runs where I didn't fall at all. The instructor says we'll start looking at turns tomorrow.'

'Who are you, and what have you done with the miserable bastard I left here earlier?'

'Ha ha. How was your morning?'

'Well, the skiing was good, but some slimeball calling himself Aldo tried to come on to me. Even when I told him I had a boyfriend already, he still tried it on. Revolting.'

'I thought you said you were single?' Toby looks genuinely confused.

'I am. I took your name in vain. You owe me after your antics with that woman on the plane. Anyway, it's no big deal. I've come across his type plenty of times before. Deficient men compensating for their unattractiveness by showing off, whether with a flash car, ridiculous clothes or, in Aldo's case, alleged ski and sexual prowess.'

'Wow, that's harsh!'

'It's true, though. There's a type of man that thinks women are going to find them completely irresistible just because they've got a Ferrari, or a Rolex, or whatever it is. Most women I know don't give a shit about any of that stuff. If you're severely challenged in the looks department and you don't have the personality to compensate for it, no ridiculous car or fancy watch is going to save you. A private jet might soften me a little,' I add, with a smile, 'but I still don't think it would be enough to make me want to put up with some fat, sweaty, bald old man grunting away on top of me.'

'OK, that's an image I didn't need, particularly just before lunch,' Toby laughs.

'Don't get me wrong. I like nice stuff, but not when it's waved around as some kind of status symbol or expected to act as a fanny magnet that we poor women are supposed be completely unable to resist. Total turn-off.'

After lunch, we head back to the Mirabelle to retrieve our bags and then walk to our next hotel, La Residence. The drop from five to three stars is immediately apparent in the lobby, which is small and very spartan compared to the luxury of the Mirabelle. It's bright and clean though, which bodes well.

'I don't understand why *Voyages Luxes* is sending us to a three-star hotel,' Toby whispers, after we've rung the bell at the deserted reception desk. 'It seems off brand to me.'

'Yes, but this is Courchevel, so even staying here costs much more than the average three star. I guess they wanted to show different options. It's hardly a hostel, is it?'

Our discussions are interrupted by the arrival of the receptionist, who takes our details and, after a bit of tapping on the computer, informs us that our room is ready and hands over the key cards. I double-check our dinner reservation with her, and we head over to the lifts.

The room, on first impression, follows the same theme as the lobby. It is smaller and more spartan than the room at the Mirabelle, but it's much more modern and the window lets in lots of natural light. The bed is a standard double and the sheets look clean and crisp. Once again there is no desk, but there are two low-backed chairs by the window. We drop our bags on the floor and Toby wanders over to the window to look at the view. I turn slowly, taking in the rest of the room, and that's when I spot it.

'Umm, Toby, we have a problem,' I tell him.

'What's up?' he asks, still looking out of the window.

'Turn around,' I command, and he does. As he spots what I've seen, his eyes widen.

'Ah,' he says. 'Yes, that's awkward.'

Instead of a separate bathroom, the shower, washbasin and toilet are all in the room itself. There are frosted glass partitions, which I imagine are designed to protect a little bit of modesty, but frankly they're not going to leave anything to the imagination. On top of that, the sound of either of us using the toilet is going to be very clearly audible. Some things, no matter how intimate you are with someone, should remain strictly private.

'What are we going to do?' he asks.

My mind is whirling. I cross to the telephone by the bed and dial down to reception. I recognise the voice of the same receptionist and ask her whether all the rooms in the hotel have the same layout.

'*Non, Mademoiselle,*' she replies. 'The superior rooms are larger and have balconies, and the executive rooms are larger still, with desks for working and separate bathrooms with bath and shower.'

'And are any of the executive rooms available?' I ask her. I can hear her tapping at her computer and, after a moment or two, she comes back.

'*Oui, Mademoiselle*. We can certainly transfer you if you wish. It will be an extra two hundred euros per night. Is that OK?'

No, it bloody well isn't OK! 'I need to consult my boyfriend,' I tell her. 'I'll call back if we decide to move. *Merci*.'

'What did you find out?' Toby asks.

'The good news,' I tell him, 'is that they do have some rooms where the bathroom is separate. The bad news is that it'll cost an extra four hundred euros for the two nights.'

'I can go halves with you, if that helps?'

I sit on the bed and ponder our predicament. Toby sits in one of the chairs by the window, waiting for me to decide our next move.

'I don't think it does,' I say, eventually. 'We're not sticking to the brief if we upgrade. The whole point is that we're supposed to stay in standard accommodation to experience it as the majority of the public would. I doubt the hotel or *Voyages Luxes* would cover the extra cost either, because it's not what they signed up to. I think we're stuck with this room.'

'OK, well I can go for a walk up and down the corridors or somewhere while you're showering or whatever, and then you can do the same when I am.'

'Yes, but what about getting up in the morning, or getting ready for bed? That means one of us is prowling around out there in our pyjamas, and I think that might raise an eyebrow or two with our fellow guests. Plus, what if I need to wee in the middle of the night? Am I supposed to wake you up and throw you out while I go? I can't see that one working. God, what if one of us needs to poo? I really don't think I could cope with listening to, let alone smelling your bowel movements, and I'd rather stick a cork up my arse than have you listening to mine.'

'Who on earth thought this was a good design?' Toby wonders out loud.

'I have seen it once before, actually,' I tell him. 'The Park Inn in Alexanderplatz, Berlin. I remember thinking it a little odd at the time, but I was on my own, so the full implications didn't really hit me.'

'So, what's the plan?' he asks.

'I don't know. Let me think some more.'

I try to work out every option that we have, but they all come to dead ends. We have no balcony, so we can't wrap up warm and go out there. We can't upgrade. We could pretend to have had a massive row and reserve a second room, but the cost would probably be even more prohibitive than upgrading. In the end there's only one way I can think of to make this work, but it goes against everything that Toby and I agreed, and it makes my palms sweat just thinking about it. Fiercely, I wrack my brains one last time for a viable alternative, but nothing else comes. I decide to lead Toby up to it gently, buying myself extra time in the process, in case there's a solution I've missed.

'I think the fundamental problem we have here,' I begin, 'is that the people who normally stay in these rooms are actual couples.'

Toby is looking at me earnestly. 'Yes…' he says.

'So, for them, being undressed around each other wouldn't be an issue.'

'No,' he agrees.

'So…' I pause, giving my frantic brain one last chance to come up with anything else before I press the nuclear button. 'We either upgrade, which will hit me much harder in the wallet than I can stomach and also takes us off the brief, or…'

'Or what?'

'Or we have to learn to be comfortable being undressed around each other,' I say quickly, trying to make it sound like the most natural thing in the world.

Toby's face is a mask of horror. 'You're not suggesting what I think you are?'

'Have you got a better idea?' I ask him. 'Believe me, this is not my idea of fun, and I've tried to think of an alternative, but I can't see one.'

I can see him going through the same mental exercises that I've just been through, and drawing a similar blank. His voice, when he speaks, is barely above a whisper.

'So, how do we do this?'

I've been using his processing time to consider just this question, so I'm ready for it.

'When I was at university, one of the girls I shared a house with was studying Psychology,' I tell him. 'Bear with me – there is a point to this. One evening we were talking about phobias, because I was terrified of spiders, and she explained to me that there were essentially two ways to confront them: systematic desensitisation and flooding.'

'Go on.' I think he realises I'm playing for time. I suspect he is, too.

'Systematic desensitisation works by building you up slowly. You might start by looking at pictures of spiders in books, then move on to maybe handling a Perspex cube with a dead spider inside it, then a cube with a live spider inside it, and so on. It's a series of tiny steps; once your anxiety decreases enough at each step, you move to the next, until you're able to have tarantulas wandering over your hands without even breaking a sweat.'

'I get that,' he says, 'and the other one?'

'Flooding is the opposite. Have you ever seen *I'm a Celebrity...
Get Me Out of Here*?'

'No, sorry.'

'OK, never mind, it was just a good illustration. Flooding is
essentially ripping the Band-Aid off. By forcing you to confront
your phobia at an extreme level, dealing with it at a normal level
seems like a walk in the park. So, with the spider example, instead
of the slowly, slowly approach, you might be shut in a room with
thousands of spiders of all shapes and sizes. Or, if you're scared of
heights, you might have to jump out of a plane. After that, assuming
the stress hasn't killed you, a single spider or a ladder doesn't seem
so scary. On the TV show the celebrities can win food and stuff by
being locked in small spaces and having thousands of creepy-
crawlies dumped on them, or rats crawling over them. That would
definitely count as flooding if you're phobic about creepy-crawlies.'

'How does that apply to us?'

'Well, if we went down the systematic desensitisation route
then we'd each have to remove one piece of clothing at a time and
wait until we were comfortable before moving on. Besides feeling
like a really weird game of strip poker, which is a game I hate by
the way, it would take hours and I want to get on with some work.'

'So you want to go down the flooding route, I assume.'

'Exactly. I propose that what we do is stand back to back, take
everything off and then, when we're ready, we turn around and
face each other. Once we're comfortable seeing each other naked,
we get dressed and it's done. What do you think?'

'Are you sure this is the only way?'

'Have you got a better idea?'

'No.'

'Well then. Come on, let's get it over with.'

Suddenly, Toby bursts out laughing.

'What's so funny?' I ask him, bemused.

'Are you always this romantic?' he asks.

'Oh, shut up and get your kit off!'

We dutifully turn away from each other as if we're preparing to fight a duel. I feel incredibly self-conscious as I remove my fleece, salopettes and vest. I can hear Toby rustling behind me, and I hope furiously that he's doing the same, and I'm not going to turn around and find him still fully clothed. I don't think I could bear the embarrassment. It takes all my will to remove my bra and step out of my knickers. I make sure I place them very close to me on the floor so I can put them on quickly when this ridiculous exercise is over. Finally, I remove my socks.

'I'm ready,' I say.

'Give me a couple of seconds.' I hear some more rustling of cloth before he says, 'OK. I'm ready too.'

'On the count of three then. One... two...' my heart is in my mouth as I start to turn, and I can feel myself blushing furiously '...three.'

My first feeling is relief. Toby is as naked as I am, and also has high colour in his face. We stand there for what seems like an age, but our embarrassment only seems to be getting worse. Although I'm trying to focus on his chest, which is surprisingly masculine and has just the right dusting of hair, I'm acutely aware of his penis. There's nothing unusual about it, it's a perfectly average penis, it's just that I never expected to find myself standing in a room being confronted by it. I wonder what parts of me he's focusing on. My B-cup boobs are perhaps on the small side, but I don't mind that. At least they won't give me backache or drag along the floor when I'm older. I'm also not a fan of extreme pubic topiary – no Brazilian or Hollywood waxes for me, thanks – but I do keep things neat and tidy down there. I don't think any of that will be of any interest to Toby though.

'Maybe we should each do a pirouette,' I suggest, after what feels like forever, but is probably no more than a minute or so, 'and then we could start getting dressed again?'

'Good idea,' he replies. 'After you.'

Slowly, I turn my body round until I'm facing him again. When I'm done, he starts to turn, and I study him as he does. He is compact, but he obviously keeps in shape because he's pretty muscly. His back is broad at the shoulders, narrowing down to his waist, and he has a very pert, nicely shaped bottom. Once we're facing again, we start to get dressed, in a kind of strange reverse striptease. It's almost choreographed; he pulls on his Calvin Klein briefs as I step into my knickers, and soon we're fully clothed.

'OK!' I say, rather too brightly. 'That's that. No more mystery, and we should be fine in here now. There's just one thing.'

'What?'

'The loo. I think we should agree a "no solids" rule. I think there's a loo downstairs near the restaurant, so if either of us needs to poo we should go down there.'

'Good idea. By the way, I liked your knickers,' he says, with a twinkle in his eyes.

'*What?*'

'Nice colour. They bring out your eyes,' he adds, and starts laughing. Instantly, the last threads of tension are broken.

'Sod off!' I tell him, through my own laughter.

11

JANUARY

Our dinner in the restaurant at La Residence is a good-natured affair. It's much less fussy than the Mirabelle's, and that suits us both. There's still a little bit of awkwardness when we get changed for bed, but at least I no longer feel the need to wear the irritating pyjama bottoms until Toby's asleep. The top is pretty long, so I'm not flashing my knickers when I walk around the room and, given what we've seen of each other now, I don't think showing my knickers to Toby is going to worry him unduly anyway.

In the morning, we take turns in the shower. I can't help observing him surreptitiously as he washes. The light frosting on the cubicle glass really doesn't disguise anything, and I can make his form out very clearly. He really is well proportioned, if compact. If he were taller and attracted to women, he'd be very much up my street. When my turn comes, I watch him from within the shower cubicle to see if I can catch him looking at me, but he shows no interest whatsoever, turning away and opening his laptop. The shower cubicle is very small, so I've had to leave my towel on the floor outside. I keep an eye on him as I step out and dry myself, but he's obviously absorbed in what he's doing, and he doesn't even glance round.

After breakfast, I drop him at the ski school and continue my exploration of the ski runs. Thankfully, there's no sign of Aldo and I have a very pleasant morning. I arrive around ten minutes before the end of Toby's lesson and take a few pictures of him as he slowly snowploughs down the slope. I can see he's starting to get the hang of turns too, and he doesn't fall over once, unlike a couple of his classmates. The instructor declares him ready to practise on his own, as long as he stays on the nursery runs, so we spend a happy afternoon pottering up and down together. I can see his confidence growing, although his turns are very tentative.

'There is a point during every turn,' he explains, when I ask about it, 'where you're facing directly down the slope. I don't like that bit.'

'As long as you know how to slow it down and stop if you feel uncomfortable, you'll be fine,' I tell him. 'Are you enjoying it more now?'

I have to wait until he's completed his latest turn before he answers. 'I'm starting to enjoy it more, although I'm still not sure it's going to be my new favourite thing to do.'

After a couple of hours on the slope, we head back to the hotel to work, and then head out to a bar that's recommended in the famil pack. It's busy, but I spot a few free tables at the back and we start to thread our way towards them. We haven't got very far before I notice a horribly familiar figure leaning on the bar, talking to a distinctly unimpressed-looking young woman.

'Hold my hand and look like you adore me,' I command Toby, grabbing his hand.

'What's got into you?' he asks, as I pull him close.

'Ten o'clock. Slimy bloke talking to the redhead.'

Toby's gaze follows my instruction. 'What about him?'

'Aldo.'

As if on cue, Aldo turns his head and spots us. I can feel his eyes following us as we make our way to one of the spare tables and sit down opposite each other. Toby lets go of my hand, but the noise level in the bar means that we have to lean our heads close to hear each other, so I'm sure the illusion of a loved-up couple is still convincing. A waiter appears, seemingly from nowhere, and we place our orders.

'She must be half his age,' Toby observes. 'What is he, late forties?'

'She doesn't look very keen, does she?' I reply.

At that moment Aldo reaches out, tucks a lock of hair behind the girl's ear and whispers something into it. Her eyes widen in shock and then she delivers a hefty slap to his cheek, before throwing what's left of his drink in his face and pointedly turning away from him to talk to another young woman on her other side. Thankfully for him, most of the people in the bar are too engrossed in their own conversations to notice, but we can't help laughing. We watch as Aldo wipes his face with a napkin and starts scanning the room, obviously looking for his next victim.

'His technique obviously isn't improving. I almost feel sorry for him,' I say. 'I wonder when was the last time he actually had any success?'

At that moment, a very brassy-looking blonde, with absurdly plumped-up lips and suspiciously large and perky breasts, comes into the bar. She's wearing a silver-coloured jumpsuit that leaves very little to the imagination, particularly as she's positioned the zip deliberately low, maximising the amount of cleavage on show. I guess she's still just about in her twenties, but she reminds me a little of a clown; despite the gaudy costume jewellery and heavy make-up, there's a world-weary sadness in her eyes. Aldo's eyes, on the other hand, are out on stalks.

'Uh-oh,' I say. 'New target identified.'

Sure enough, Aldo sidles up to her and engages her in conversation as soon as she sits down. To our surprise, however, she lets him buy her a drink, and it's not long before she seems to be flirting with him just as hard as he is with her. After just one drink they leave together.

'Well, his luck seems to have changed. Maybe she likes his rather pornographic chat-up lines,' I observe.

'Unless her attraction to him has a price tag attached to it,' Toby counters.

'Prostitute, you mean?'

'Well, I'm no expert on these things, but to leave with him after just one drink seems a little suspicious to me.'

'That's surprisingly judgemental, coming from you. She could be his daughter, for all we know.'

'I don't think so. Not the way his eyes were locked onto her cleavage.'

'Fair point. Now that the entertainment has gone, shall we finish up and go to get something to eat?' I ask.

* * *

Although Toby and I manage much better with our night-time and morning bathroom rituals, we're both palpably relieved to check out of La Residence the next day. The receptionist doesn't bat an eyelid when I present her with the voucher, and happily agrees to store our bags until the afternoon.

'Do you think she clocked who we were?' Toby asks as we head towards the ski school.

'Dunno. She did seem suspiciously blasé, but I can't see how she could have known who we were. It doesn't matter though, we certainly didn't get any special treatment, did we!'

In comparison to La Residence, our apartment in Les Suites de Bellevue feels massive. We both sigh with relief when we spot that the bathroom is properly self-contained. The main room contains the sitting area, a small dining table and a kitchenette, with doors off to the bedroom and bathroom. The sofa converts into a bed and Toby gallantly offers to sleep on it to give me back a bit of privacy, but it doesn't look terribly comfortable when we pull it out, so in the end we agree to continue sharing the bed. I'm so relieved not to have to shower in front of him any more that sleeping next to him doesn't feel like a problem at all. He's a tidy sleeper, he doesn't steal the duvet or encroach onto my side of the bed, and he only snores occasionally and very lightly, so it's no hardship to share a bed with him.

The next day is our last full day. Toby is determined to see if he can master parallel turns in the ski school, and I spend some time checking the map against my notes before catching the ski lift, to make sure that I've covered a good cross-section of the available runs. In the afternoon I persuade him to tackle a blue run with me, which he professes to enjoy, even though his speed on skis hasn't improved much, so it takes an age to complete it. I've made a start on the write-up, and Toby and I have agreed which pictures he'll submit to go with the finished article. Despite his protestations about not being much of a writer, he's also managed to provide me with his impressions of both the resort and the ski school on an email, which I'm planning to include in a 'he thought... she thought' format. I'm confident that Mark will like the article when I submit it to him. Overall, apart from the bathroom issue, I think the trip has been a great success.

As we've covered all the bars and restaurants that were requested in the famil packs, we decide to head back to our favourites for the final evening.

'So, how has this trip been for you?' I ask Toby, once we're settled at a table with our drinks.

He takes his time considering my question, but I'm used to this now, so don't feel so impatient as I wait for him to respond.

'It's been interesting. I've enjoyed it,' he states, eventually.

'Would you be happy to do it again? I don't know what Mark has in store, but I think the trip to the Bellavista is definitely on the cards.'

'Yes. I couldn't do it too often, as it would interfere with my proper work, but as an occasional thing it would be fine. What about you?'

'I'd be lying if I said I hadn't had my reservations before the trip, especially as I'm used to doing this on my own, but you're surprisingly easy to get along with, Toby Roberts. I reckon I could put up with you again.'

'Oh, stop,' he replies, his eyes twinkling with amusement. 'The begging is just embarrassing!'

* * *

On the long transfer back to Geneva for our flight home the next day, I exchange a few messages with Charley. It seems things with Amelia are starting to settle down, although she still screams a lot, and she sends me a couple of pictures of her. To my untrained eye she doesn't look particularly beautiful. She's got that slightly myopic, bewildered look that all newborn babies seem to have and, try as I might, I can't see any particular resemblance to either Charley or Ed in her facial features. Nevertheless, I make all the right cooing noises, and we agree that I'll pop in to meet her the following day. I notice that Toby seems tense and is checking his phone every couple of minutes.

'What's up?' I ask him.

'What do you mean?'

'You keep checking your phone. Is anything wrong?'

'No, it's completion day on the studio. I'm waiting for the email from the solicitor to say that it's all gone through and I can collect the keys tomorrow. I've spent so long saving up for this, I can't quite believe it's really happening.'

Just then his phone pings and he can't unlock it fast enough. After reading the message he turns to me and gives a little fist-pump.

'It's gone through then?'

'Yup. I'll collect the keys in the morning. There's so much to do now. Although it's currently a photo studio, the guy that owned it just filled it with crap stuff. I've ordered a skip to chuck it all into, and I will have to redecorate before I start installing the equipment I've bought. I also want to put in a dressing room and redo the kitchen, so it's going to keep me busy. I've got loads of spreadsheets with plans and costings on, and I'm really excited about bringing them to life.'

'How long do you think it'll be before you're up and running?'

'I've given myself two weeks for the studio. I need that to be operational as soon as possible, as I'm basically losing money until it is. I've got shoots booked in, and a grand opening as well, so that should keep me focused.'

'Can I see it?'

'Sure. I'll pick up the keys first thing, and I've hired a van to move my stuff from the house into the flat. I should be all finished by late afternoon. Why don't you drop in around six o'clock if you're free? I might even manage some champagne, although we'll probably be drinking it out of mugs.'

'I'll look forward to it. Let me bring the champagne though. I'll come by after I've seen Charley and the baby.'

* * *

Toby's car is parked in the same area of the car park as mine, so we don't say our farewells until the bus has dropped us. I throw my case in the boot and set off towards home, stopping at the supermarket for bare essentials on the way. I'm always pleased to get back to my little flat after a trip, and this time is no different. I unpack the shopping and my suitcase, and stick a load of washing on, before pouring myself a 'welcome home' glass of wine. I have a rule that I don't work on the first night back from a trip, so I make myself a salad and settle down in front of the TV. Looking at the schedule, my eye is drawn to a programme where a wealthy family and a family on benefits swap holidays, so I watch that while I eat and drink. It's not long before the travel catches up with me and I sink gratefully into my bed. At first it feels odd without Toby next to me, but the feeling soon passes as I drift off to sleep. My final thought is that I'm looking forward to seeing him again tomorrow. I've enjoyed his company much more than I was expecting to.

The next morning is filled with mundane chores, like sorting out the laundry after my back-to-back trips and properly restocking the fridge, so it's mid-afternoon by the time I pull up outside Ed and Charley's house. The first thing that I notice is that her jolly blue Fiesta, which she adored, has been replaced by something bigger and probably better suited to carting around baby para-phernalia. No such compromises for Ed, I note, as his completely impractical Porsche is parked alongside it. I've got the presents I bought for them in Istanbul in a carrier bag, as well as a bottle of champagne and a lasagne to go in the freezer.

I ring the bell and listen. I can't hear any crying, which has to be a good sign. After a few moments, Ed flings open the door and envelops me in a hug.

'Madison! Lovely to see you. Do come in. Charley's just feeding Amelia, so you've arrived at a good time.'

I hand over my bag of gifts and follow him through to their sitting room, where Charley is perched on the sofa, bottle-feeding the tiniest, most perfect-looking human being I think I've ever seen. Somehow, Amelia manages to look completely different in the flesh, even though she's obviously the same baby I've seen in the photos. I'm not at all maternal, so the sudden rush of love I feel, both for Charley and her baby, catches me completely by surprise. For a moment I'm overwhelmed by the magic of the scene before me, lost in wonder that Charley grew this tiny new person inside her. I can feel my eyes filling with tears. Charley glances up and smiles at me. She looks tired and pale, with dark shadows under her eyes, but she is also radiant with happiness and pride. I want to wrap my arms around them both, but I think that's probably impractical, so I stand there foolishly, unsure what to do with myself. Ed has vanished into the kitchen with the bag.

'Come and sit next to me,' Charley instructs. 'She's nearly finished, and then you can have a cuddle if you like.'

I gently lower myself onto the sofa next to her. I don't want to risk disturbing Amelia, who has her eyes closed as she sucks intently on the bottle. While Charley finishes up, I look around me. Although most things look the same, there is plenty of evidence of how much the baby has changed everything for them. There is a pile of freshly laundered babygros on the stairs, obviously waiting to go up and be put away, and the dining table appears to have been converted into a nappy changing station, with a pile of nappies, a mat, and a large tub of Sudocrem on it. There's a little recliner chair on the floor next to the sofa, with a mobile above it. Charley eases the teat out of Amelia's mouth, causing her face to wrinkle with displeasure, and then gently places her over her shoulder, rubbing her back until she emits the most unladylike burp. I can't help but laugh.

'There you go, Amelia. Go and have a cuddle with your Auntie Mads,' Charley says, and hands her over to me. I remember to support her head and, after a couple of slightly awkward manoeuvres, manage to nestle her into the crook of my arm. She doesn't make any noise, but her eyes are wide open, her lips are moving gently, and her fingers are curling and uncurling constantly, as if she's only just discovered them and is testing them out.

'Oh, Charley, she's absolutely adorable!' I exclaim.

'Mm. Don't be fooled. She looks like butter wouldn't melt now, but when she gets a scream on, she can be a right little madam, can't you, sweetie?' She leans in towards the baby as she addresses her, and Amelia's eyes lock on to her mother.

'Madison's brought us champagne and a lasagne,' Ed announces, returning from the kitchen with two mugs of tea, which he sets down next to us.

'You didn't have to do that,' Charley tells me. 'It's very kind though, thank you.'

'I just thought it might help to have a meal you didn't have to cook,' I explain. 'There are some presents too. Nothing big, just a couple of things I picked up while I was away.'

Ed brings in the small parcels and they start to unwrap them. Charley is delighted with the pretty bracelet I've got her, and Ed professes to love the silk tie I've bought. For Amelia I've bought a simple gold necklace that she can wear when she's older, with a blue pendant on the end.

'What's this?' Charley asks. 'It's very pretty.'

'It's a Turkish evil eye pendant,' I explain. 'It's supposed to ward off evil spirits. People in Turkey hang them in their homes, wear them, even put them on their pets. It's supposed to keep her safe, if you believe in that kind of thing.'

'What a lovely idea. We'll hang it in her room. Thinking of which, we have a question we'd like to ask you. Ed?'

Ed clears his throat. 'Yes. We wondered if you would like to be Amelia's godmother?'

'Of course, I'd love to!!'

'Excellent,' Ed declares. 'We haven't organised a date for the christening yet, but once we have some idea from the vicar, we'll let you know.'

I spend a happy couple of hours with them, catching up on their news and filling them in on my trip with Toby. Amelia drifts off to sleep in my arms, and I find that I keep glancing down at her, marvelling at her perfection. When the time comes for me to leave, I gently hand her back to Charley, and almost tiptoe out of the house so as not to wake her.

There's still a bit of time to kill before I'm due to meet Toby, so I decide to explore Sevenoaks and find him a studio warming gift if I can. I've already bought the champagne I promised; I picked it up at the same time as Ed and Charley's, but I'd like to give him something a little more permanent as well. On one street I come across a hardware store, with bins and brushes displayed on the pavement outside. Looking through the windows, it quickly becomes clear that they sell all kinds of things for the home, so I wander inside. It turns out to be a real Aladdin's cave, with lots of different rooms displaying everything from DIY stuff to kitchenware. Remembering Toby's comments about drinking from mugs, I buy him two pint glasses, two tumblers, two wine glasses and two champagne flutes.

I follow his directions and find the studio in a somewhat down-at-heel parade of shops near the station. It looks unloved; the sign above the door is cracked and peeling, making the swirly writing difficult to decipher. Eventually, I work out that it says 'Dave Myers – Exquisite Memories'. In the window are a series of faded portraits, pet photos and wedding shots. I wouldn't describe the photos as exquisite – clichéd and dated would be more accurate. One, featuring a faded image of a woman with big hair and shiny clothes, looks like it might have been there since the eighties. Next door on the left is a dingy-looking greasy spoon café calling itself Nora's

Diner. Large signwriting on the window advertises its 'All Day Break-fast's' and 'Traditional Roast Diner's'. I resist the urge to go inside and explain how plurals work or point out the unfortunate spelling mistake. On the other side of the studio is a dry-cleaner, which seems to be thriving, if the large number of garment bags visible through the window and strong chemical smell are anything to go by.

The studio door is locked, so I ring the bell next to it and wait. Toby appears after a few moments and lets me in. He's dressed in overalls, which are covered in white dust, and there's also dust on his face and in his hair. For someone who is normally so fastid-ious about his appearance, it's a bit of a shock.

'It's OK, don't dress up on my account,' I snigger.

'Ha ha. Be careful what you touch when we get in there. Everything's very dusty and dirty.'

We pass through the front area (desk, couch for waiting customers, table with ancient magazines, more clichéd photos in frames on the wall) into the studio at the back.

'Bloody hell, Toby, it's massive!' I exclaim, looking around at the enormous room.

'Not bad, is it?' he replies, with pride evident in his voice. 'It needs a lot of work, but I could see the potential as soon as I saw it. I'm going to completely gut the place and start again from scratch. Paul came and helped me move, and then we couldn't resist making a start on the studio. We've made good progress already.'

At that point Paul appears through a door at the other end of the studio. He's also wearing overalls and is covered in dirt, like Toby. I feel suddenly out of place, like I'm distracting them from their work but, as Paul spots me, his face breaks out into a huge smile.

'Hello again, Madison. Toby's been telling me how much he

enjoyed the trip with you, even if he's not sure he's a born skier,' he says to me, before turning to address Toby. 'That skip is already half full. I reckon we'll fill it tomorrow. Have you got a replacement lined up?'

'Yes,' Toby tells him. 'It should be here first thing on Monday morning, and I've got regular changeovers booked through the week.'

'Well, if you boys fancy a quick break, I've got some champagne in here to celebrate,' I tell them.

'That sounds brilliant!' Paul enthuses. 'I'll just go and wash out the mugs. Toby hasn't got any glasses yet,' he adds, by way of explanation.

'Don't worry, I've thought of that.' I reach into the bag and pull out the bottle and the carefully wrapped glasses, setting them on the side in the kitchen area. 'I've only got two champagne flutes I'm afraid, but I'm happy with one of the wine glasses.'

Toby does the honours, and we drink a toast to his future success. The champagne is still reasonably cold, and it slips down easily.

'So,' I say, after a couple of sips. 'Give me the tour.'

Toby, Paul and I wander round the studio together, as Toby outlines his vision. Pretty much everything currently in here is going in the skip, apart from a hideous double bed in one of the corners. The frame is made from ornate wrought iron and it's currently sporting black satin sheets.

'Are you going to be shooting porn in here, Toby?' I ask, indicating the bed. He doesn't seem the sleazy type, but maybe I've got him wrong.

'No!' he laughs. 'I know it looks tacky, but it's one of the few things that Dave Myers, the previous owner, got right,' he explains when he sees my raised eyebrows. 'You'll just have to trust me that it will look good with the right lighting.'

'But what are you going to use it for?'

'Boudoir photography. It's surprisingly popular,' he continues, obviously picking up on my scepticism. 'Brides-to-be often like to have some sexy photos to give their new husbands. It's quite a trend. It's popular with models too, as it shows their versatility. The black sheets look tacky in real life, but they're barely visible in the photos, which means the model really stands out. I can also change the black sheets for white and do nightwear shoots for magazines.

'Now, over here is where the main studio area is going to be. I've got a big infinity wall arriving at the end of the week, and we'll have a whole variety of different backgrounds available too.'

'What's an infinity wall?'

'It's a background wall that curves into the base, so there's no join visible between wall and floor. It makes the model, or the object, appear to float because there are no reference points in the background,' he tells me, as we walk towards the door that Paul came through earlier. It leads into a small corridor, and Toby ushers me through. There's an open door in front of me, which is obviously the back entrance. I can see that there are two car parking spaces behind the building. One of them is currently occupied by the skip and Toby's car is jammed into the other. To the right, there's a door marked 'Private'. Toby unlocks it to reveal a staircase.

'This is the way up to the flat. Would you like to see?' he asks.

'Absolutely, lead on!'

The flat is even more unloved than the studio. It's not damp or anything; in fact, it's surprisingly warm in here, given the cold winter weather outside. It's just very tired and dated looking, with textured ceilings and floral borders in abundance. There's a good-sized sitting room, master bedroom with a horrible avocado green en suite, another bedroom, an equally horrible bathroom with pink units, and a dated pine kitchen. The carpets are tired and threadbare, which is a relief as it looks like the original patterns would have been migraine inducing. There's almost no furniture; the master bedroom has a single mattress on the floor, and there are a couple of folding chairs and a table in the sitting room. Toby is full of enthusiasm, telling me about how he plans to modernise it and furnish it. It sounds like it will be lovely when it's done. One thing niggles me though. Although it's reasonably spacious, I can see that it's nowhere near as big as the studio below. Toby sees my confusion and explains.

'There are two flats. The other one is accessed from the front of the building and is let out. I own the freehold of both, so I'll get some income from the rent. I haven't met the couple that live in there yet, but they've been there for nearly three years and have been no problem, according to the records.'

We wander back downstairs and, after draining my glass, I start to gather my stuff.

'Why don't you stay and have dinner with us? We're going to get fish and chips from across the road if you fancy some,' Toby says.

'Tempting offer,' I reply, 'but I need to get the write-up to Mark, so I ought to get back and do some work.'

'Another time, perhaps.'

'Yes. I'd really like that,' I say.

13

FEBRUARY

The week turns out to be manic. As well as writing up the Courchevel trip, I've got my regular Sunday column to do and I lose two days in the middle as I have to fly up to Scotland to experience a whisky distillery tour for one of the airline magazines. This proves to be a bit of a struggle, as I really don't like whisky, but I think I manage to capture the passion of the distillers and I take the tasting notes so that I can rehash them in the article. I use the techniques Toby has taught me and run my photos through the app, and I have to say I'm pretty pleased with the results.

By Friday evening, I reckon I'm on top of it. The Courchevel article is in ahead of schedule, I've managed to put together suggestions for people who have written into the Sunday supplement, and the Scotland article is also done and submitted. Ed rang midweek with a date for the christening in May, which thankfully coincided with a clear patch in my diary, so that's all sorted as well. I decide to ring Toby to see how he's getting on.

'It's going really well,' he tells me, after we've exchanged the usual pleasantries. 'All of Dave's crap is gone, I've given the place a really good clean and I'm currently painting it. I've got the electrician arriving on Monday to put in a load of extra sockets, so I need to be done by then.'

A thought occurs to me. 'Do you need a hand? I'm on top of my work now, so I can probably come and do some decorating over the weekend if that would help.'

'That would be brilliant, if you can really spare the time. Paul's helped as much as he can, but obviously he's got his own studio to look after. He's got shoots booked in solidly over the weekend, so it's just me on my own at the moment.'

* * *

I'm up early the next morning. After rummaging around in the wardrobe for a while, I find an old pair of jeans and a top that I haven't worn for years, as well as a pair of trainers I bought ages ago when I had a brief, mad idea that I might take up running. I put my hair up into a messy bun to keep it well away from any paint, and don a baseball cap for extra security. The end result is not beautiful, but I'm ready for a day of decorating.

Toby explained on the phone how to get round to the back of the studio and, as instructed, I park across the back of his car and the latest skip. It's a tight squeeze, but I just manage it without sticking out beyond the line that denotes the end of his parking area. The studio itself, once I get inside, is transformed. All the stuff that was in here, apart from the hideous porno bed, has gone and it's immaculately clean. The new infinity wall completely fills one corner and the smell of fresh paint hangs in the air. A brand-new dressing room has been created next to the kitchen area, which has new units and an enormous coffee machine. Even the toilet has smart new sanitary ware, although the walls are yet to be repainted and the mirror is on the floor, resting against the wall. There's still a way to go, but I can see that no expense is being spared, and the end result is going to be both stylish and functional.

'Would you like a coffee before we start?' Toby offers, advancing on the machine. 'The closest decent coffee shop I could find was at the station, so I invested in this. I reckon it's got enough options to keep even the fussiest Londoner happy.'

'Does it do flat whites?' I ask.

'Naturally.'

Toby puts a mug under the dispenser and pushes a button. After a lot of whirring and shooshing, it starts to dribble coffee and steamed milk into the mug, beeping proudly when it finishes. Toby hands me the mug with a flourish, before repeating the process for himself.

'This is actually pretty good,' I tell him, after taking a sip.

'It's not bad, is it? The machine was a bit more than I wanted to spend, but the guy assured me it was worth it. It's plumbed in for water, so all I have to do is make sure I keep it topped up with beans and milk powder, clear out the waste when it tells me, and give it a clean every so often.'

Toby turns on a radio and sets me to work painting white gloss on the doors, door frames and skirting boards, while he continues with the studio walls. I find the background noise from the radio and the monotonous work very relaxing, and soon I'm into a rhythm. After a couple of hours, Toby downs tools and comes to check how I'm getting on.

'You're a much neater painter than Paul,' he observes, after checking a couple of the door frames. 'Quicker, too. Don't tell him though, he'll only get all sensitive about it.'

'Really? He doesn't strike me as the oversensitive type.'

Toby laughs. 'No, not really. He's been really good and given me a lot of help this week, but I don't think painting is his thing. I suspect he got more paint on himself than he did on the walls.'

After a quick coffee break, we settle back to work and, by lunchtime, I've pretty much covered all the woodwork and my stomach is growling. Toby has moved on to painting the dressing room but, because there is no proper light in there yet, it's difficult to tell how it's going to look. He's been using one of the old studio lights on an extension lead, which is fine for illuminating the bit he's working on, but it leaves the rest of the room in shadow.

'How brave are you feeling?' he asks.

'Why?'

'We have two choices for lunch. Either you can come up to the flat and I'll make you a sandwich, or we can go next door to the café. It's pretty dismal in there, but the baked potatoes are harmless enough.'

A hot baked potato sounds much more tempting than a sandwich after all my hard work this morning, so Toby locks up the back and we walk out of the front door to the café next door. As we pass through the shop front, I notice that the faded pictures and gaudy furniture have gone, and the windows have been covered with paper.

'It means I can set everything up without anyone seeing what it looks like. Then, when I'm ready, off comes the paper for a big reveal,' Toby explains, when I ask about it. 'To be honest, I'm not completely sure what I'm going to do with this space. I'm not going to be accepting walk-in clients, so I don't need an area for them to wait, but I want it to look inviting.'

The inside of the café is every bit as grim as the outside promises. My nostrils are assaulted by the smell of stale fat as we walk in. It's not particularly busy, even at lunchtime, and most of the clientele seem to be elderly. We find a table in the corner and Toby hands me a laminated piece of paper with the menu on it. I guess the same person has written the menu as is responsible for the signwriting on the window, as the spelling and grammar are equally atrocious. I skim through All Day Breakfast's, Burger's and Salad's until my eyes finally alight on Baked Potatoe's.

'I wonder how many salads they sell?' I say to Toby. 'It doesn't strike me as the sort of place you'd naturally pick out for a delicious salad.'

'Perhaps you should try one,' he replies. 'Let's see, you could have tuna, egg, tuna and egg for an extra one pound fifty, or chicken. Pretty exotic stuff, don't you agree? In fact, I think I can hear Gordon Ramsay trembling with fear at the prospect of Nora's diner stealing his Michelin stars.'

I laugh. 'I'm not sure my palate is sophisticated enough for such delicacies,' I tell him. 'I think I'll have a baked potato with tuna mayo.'

'I'm not sure where the sommelier is,' Toby continues, warming to his theme. 'It's a shame, because I've heard the wine cellars here would put the Mirabelle's to shame. Can I tempt you to a cup of tea or coffee instead?'

I study the list of drinks and decide that a Diet Coke is probably the safest option. Toby goes up to the counter to order, and I continue my observation of the café. On one wall is a large blackboard with 'Specials' written at the top. The board itself is blank. I wonder how long it's been since they had anything to write on there. There's a pretty young girl serving behind the counter. She can't be more than sixteen, so I imagine this is a Saturday job for her. She seems happy in her work and smiles widely at Toby as he places our order. The tables, which are fixed to the floor, are covered with chipped Formica, and each table has salt and pepper shakers, bottles of vinegar and red and brown squeezy bottles for the different types of ketchup. Everything feels very slightly sticky, which is not a pleasant sensation. It has the air of a place that might have been loved once, but has been neglected for a long time.

The baked potatoes, as Toby promised, are not too bad. The skins aren't crispy, so they've obviously been microwaved, but they're a decent size and generously filled. I offer to pay my share when we finish, but Toby is having none of it, insisting it's the least he can do in return for my help with the painting.

The afternoon follows much the same pattern as the morning. I've moved on to painting the toilet; Toby has chosen a neutral bluey-green colour for the walls, which is a huge improvement on the bubblegum pink that was there before. Toby continues in the dressing room and, by the end of the day, both rooms have had their first coats of paint. I have got a few spatters of white paint on me from painting the ceiling in the toilet, so I'm glad I remembered the cap to protect my hair. Promising to be back bright and early the next morning, I head home to soak in a long, hot bath.

* * *

By Sunday evening, the painting is finished and the studio looks very smart. We've refreshed the paint in the entry area as well. Toby has decided to dress it rather like an art gallery, with large scale prints of some of his work, so we've painted everything in white as a neutral backdrop.

'What about that fish and chips I promised you?' he asks, after we've tidied the painting stuff away.

'I'd like that,' I reply, and we wander across the road to Tony's Fish Bar. It's obviously popular, as there's a bit of a queue, but there are several people working behind the counter and on the fryers, so we don't have to wait long. We eat it out of the paper, sitting cross-legged on the floor of the studio. The fish batter is light and crunchy, and the cod steams and flakes underneath. It's delicious, and I groan with pleasure as I bite into it.

'It's good, isn't it?' Toby says. 'A bit of an improvement on the café, anyway.'

'It's excellent,' I reply. 'Give me this over the ponced-up stuff we had at the Mirabelle any day. Food like this is why I could never go back to America.'

'I'm sure they have fish and chips in America, don't they?'

'They do, but it's just not the same somehow. Sometimes it comes with skinny fries, which is patently wrong, but even when they get the chips right, it just isn't quite there. I can't put my finger on it, but there's definitely something missing. To be fair, it's not just an American problem. I've tried fish and chips in all sorts of countries, and none of them are like we get here.'

'Do you think you'll always be a travel writer?'

The question catches me by surprise, and I take a moment to think before answering. 'I loved it in my twenties, in fact I used to pinch myself sometimes because I couldn't believe I was able to visit all these amazing places and get paid for it. But the insecurity of it becomes wearing after a while. You're only ever as good as your last piece, you know? And, if you make a mistake...' I tail off, remembering how closely I came to losing it all at the beginning of the year.

'Have you ever made a mistake?' Toby asks.

'I don't know,' I reply. 'That's what we're hopefully going to find out when we go to the Bellavista.'

'Ah, yes. I'd forgotten about that.' He puts on a film trailer voice. 'Lucy Swann, aka Madison Morgan, gets her fingers burned by TripAdvisor. Is this the end for her, or will photographer Toby Roberts ride to her rescue?'

'Piss off, idiot! Anyway, it was a close shave, and I suppose it's got me wondering whether I should start looking for something with a bit more job security.'

'Such as?'

'I don't know. I like the industry so, if an editing job came up, I might apply for that. I've probably got another couple of years of this in me, so we'll see what happens.'

When we've finished eating, I gather my stuff together and get ready to go.

'Are you around next Saturday evening?' Toby asks.

'Why, are you after more slave labour?' I laugh.

'No, it's the grand opening. It's a black tie do, and I've invited various people from the industry, other photographers, editors, friends. I'd love it if you could come, particularly after all the work you've put in.'

I consult the diary on my phone. I'm off to Iceland on Sunday evening for four days, but Saturday is currently free.

'Saturday's fine. I'll look forward to it.'

* * *

Later that evening, as I'm soaking in the bath with a well-earned glass of wine, Charley rings.

'Ed's feeding Amelia and I'm desperate for adult conversation,' she confides. 'Tell me of life in the normal world, where everything doesn't revolve around the contents of nappies, or sleep patterns.'

I fill her in on my weekend and my invitation for next Saturday.

'You spent the whole weekend painting his studio for him?' she asks incredulously.

'It was relaxing, in a weird kind of way. You kind of lose yourself in it. I haven't done any painting and decorating since I bought my flat, and I'd forgotten how much I enjoy it. Toby was good company too, so it's been a nice weekend.'

'GBF?' she asks.

'He's definitely getting there,' I reply, with a smile.

14

FEBRUARY

The front of the studio is unrecognisable when I arrive for the grand opening. Only the depressing presence of Nora's café next door and the chemical smell from the dry cleaner's provide any clues that this is the same place. The cracked sign with the swirly writing has gone, replaced by a stylish modern one with 'Toby Roberts Photography' written on it. The paper has been removed from the windows and, at first glance, it does look a little like an art gallery. There are huge prints of some of his photos lit by bright overhead lights in the area at the front and people are milling around with glasses in their hands, chatting and admiring the artwork. The entrance is guarded by an attendant and, as he searches the list for my name, I notice a sign next to the door that says 'By Appointment Only'; there is a phone number and website address, which I tap into my phone so I can have a look later.

I feel like I've stepped into another world once I'm inside. I imagine that most of the people here are in the fashion industry; they're tweaked and plucked to perfection and some of them have interpreted the phrase 'black tie' very loosely, with brightly coloured jackets and shirts. I notice lots of air-hugging and air-kissing as they greet one another with loud cries of 'Daaaahling!' I accept a glass of wine from a passing waiter and start to circulate. Although there are a few faces I recognise, mostly models that I've seen in magazines, I don't know anyone well enough to strike up a conversation, so I'm relieved to spot Paul in the kitchen area, looking surprisingly smart in his DJ.

'Are you hiding out in here?' I ask as I join him.

'Maybe, just a little.' He smiles. 'This is very much Toby's crowd, not mine. I think most of them have come down from London. I've met a few of them when they've been at my studio and they've all been vile. Do you know why they all call each other "darling" in that incredibly annoying way?'

'It's a fashion thing, isn't it?'

'It's because they're all so full of their own self-importance none of them can be arsed to remember anyone else's name. Some of them are probably so full of coke that they'd struggle to remember their own names.'

'There's something I don't understand,' I tell him, when I've finished laughing. 'If the fashion industry is centred around London, why would they bother coming all the way to Sevenoaks, or Maidstone? Wouldn't it be easier to use a studio in London?'

'Good question. It's partly cost, because studio space is much more expensive in London, but it's also travel time. Toby's played a blinder with this place, because it's probably faster to get here than it is to cross London in some cases. Also, if you're high profile, you're much less likely to get papped out here in the wilds of Kent than you are in London. Travel down in a limo with blacked-out windows, come in through the back door, do your shoot, back in the limo. No paparazzi and much less stress.'

We're interrupted by a stick-thin creature, who I imagine must be a model of some sort. She's not one I recognise, but she has the classic androgynous look that is so popular with fashion magazines at the moment. She's talking into her phone and, although she notices us, we obviously don't register as remotely important as she turns her back on us to continue her conversation. We can't help but listen in as she's practically braying into the handset. She has an annoying upward inflection, which makes every sentence sound like a question.

'Yah,' she's saying, 'I'm at Toby Roberts' new place? Yah, like no idea? Yah, had to get, like, a train? Total nightmare. Yah, toe-dally fucking provincial, right? I didn't want to come, but my bitch agent said I, like, had to?'

At that moment I spot Toby in the crowd. He looks up and gives me a little wave, and I wave back. The model obviously thinks he's waving at her, as she instantly drops her call and totters over to him.

'Tobe!' she screeches. 'Looove the new place. Yah, when Lisa told me about it I was like, I've toe-dally got to see it for myself, you know?'

We don't hear the rest of the conversation, but from her animated air-kissing and gesticulating, I imagine she's not telling him how 'toe-dally fucking provincial' she thinks his studio location is. After a while, he disentangles himself from her and comes over to us.

'Tobe!' I cry, and exaggeratedly air-kiss him, before dissolving into a fit of unladylike snorts of laughter. Thankfully he's laughing too.

'I know. She is awful, isn't she? But the designers and editors adore her because she's a natural and, believe it or not, she works her socks off in front of the camera. As long as she doesn't speak, she's fine. Have you had a chance to look around yet? What do you think?'

I admit that I haven't got any further than the kitchen, and

Paul offers to show me the rest so that Toby can get back to his audience. I feel like I know most of it intimately from the previous weekend's painting, but the dressing room is a revelation. It's light and airy, painted in a neutral shade of grey. There is a mirror that runs along the entire length of the right-hand wall, with lights and plug sockets at regular intervals. Below the mirror is a wide shelf with four comfortable-looking castor chairs pushed underneath it. On the wall at the end are two more mirrors, full-length this time, and there is a clothes rail running all the way along the left-hand wall. I'm no expert, but it looks like it has everything a model or a make-up artist would need. As we make our way round the main studio, I'm surprised to note that there don't appear to be any photographic lights or anything.

'They're all piled up in the flat, in their boxes,' Paul tells me. 'The last thing you want is one of this lot tipping their champagne into one. He'll bring them down before he starts work on Monday. He's also covered over the bottom of the infinity wall to protect it from scuff marks, if you look.'

Suddenly, I spot a familiar figure and my heart rate quickens. It's Mark, the commissioning editor for *Voyages Luxes*. Hopefully he will have read my Courchevel piece by now, and I'm desperate to know what he thinks of it. My chances of getting to set the record straight about the Bellavista, and probably any future work, depend on him liking it. I make my excuses to Paul and go over to him.

'Hello, Mark,' I say, trying to keep my voice natural. I realise that my palms are sweating a bit, and I grip my glass a little tighter to stop it from slipping out of my hand. The last thing I need right now is to smash a glass and cover him in wine.

'Hello, Madison, how are you? I wasn't expecting to see you here,' he replies, warmly. This is a good sign, and my heart slows a little. Either he hasn't read it yet, or he likes it.

'I'm fine, thank you. I was just wondering if you'd had a chance to read my Courchevel article?' I ask him.

'Read it. Loved it. Showed it to Oliver, who loved it too. The whole "she thought... he thought" thing was brilliant, and it was an inspired idea to book Toby into the ski school for a beginner's perspective. His photos are stunning too, but that's no great surprise. Of course, the moment we publish, our competitors will be looking to copy it, but I reckon we've stolen a march on them for now. Great stuff, Madison. I'm talking to hotels in Corfu with a view to you travelling in April. Are you and Toby happy to work together again?'

'Yes, no problem.' I tell him, trying to hide my relief. 'Let's just hope he can fit me in.'

'I'm sure he'll find time for my favourite freelancer!' Mark assures me, wrapping an arm around my shoulders. Any reservations I might normally feel about the familiarity of the contact are far outweighed by my relief at being back in favour, and I smile widely at him.

We agree that I'll book flights on dates that suit both me and Toby, and he'll send me the list of hotels as soon as he's firmed it up. We discuss some other possible assignments, and he promises me that he'll be in touch with other concrete proposals soon.

As the evening wears on, the crowd begins to thin out until there are just a few stragglers left. The London contingent have disappeared, mainly by train, although I did spot one or two black limousines gliding off into the night. The waiters are now rinsing the glasses and loading them into crates, and Toby and Paul are collecting up discarded napkins and other detritus into black sacks. Without thinking, I kick off my heels and grab a broom from the store cupboard.

'You don't need to do that!' Toby calls, when he spots me sweeping up.

'It's OK, I don't mind,' I tell him.

After another half an hour the final stragglers have left, the waiters have finished packing up, and the studio looks like the party never happened.

'Did you have a good time?' I ask Toby.

'It was productive,' he replies. 'I actually find these kinds of things exhausting, but I got a lot of bookings out of it, so the studio is off to a good start. Someone also suggested I should do studio lighting and posing courses, which I hadn't thought of.'

'How can you not have thought of it?' Paul asks, incredulously. 'You cut your teeth doing stuff like that with me. It's a money-spinner too. Get eight or ten people in, charge them a hundred, hundred and fifty each, and you've got a healthy profit even after you've paid the model.'

'I'll think about it. I'm not sure that teaching is my thing,' Toby replies. 'Maybe I can rent the studio out to someone else, and they can do the teaching.'

'Not as lucrative though, mate,' Paul counters. 'All you'll get then are the hire fees.'

'He's got a point,' I chip in. 'And you were a pretty good teacher in Courchevel. My photos are loads better already, and that was after just a few minutes of your time.'

'I said I'd think about it, OK?' Toby replies, smiling. 'Stop ganging up on me!'

'Talking of Courchevel, I had a chat with Mark earlier,' I tell him.

'Oh yes?'

'He loved the article, the CEO loved it, and they want more. How do you feel about that? He asked whether we could do Corfu in April.'

'Does that mean I'm definitely going to see the famous Bellavista?'

'Yup. In all its glory.'

'Will all the rooms have separate bathrooms? My therapist will want to know,' he says, and his eyes twinkle with mischief.

'What's all this?' Paul asks.

Toby and I fill him in on our stay at La Residence, and he guffaws. 'I'd love to have seen that!'

'What are you, some kind of voyeur?' I ask.

'No, it's just the thought of Toby having to cope with a naked woman without the comfort blanket of his camera to hide behind.' He turns to Toby, still laughing, and puts his arm round his shoulder. 'Are you OK? Do you need to talk about it?'

'Piss off!' Toby replies, good-naturedly. He gets his phone out of his jacket pocket and we compare diaries. With a bit of humming and hawing, we manage to find a week in April that we can both do.

As I drive home, I reflect on the conversation at the end of the evening. Toby is a very closed book where his private life is concerned, and I'm starting to wonder if he hasn't openly come out of the closet yet. Paul obviously knows, or has worked it out though, because he found the whole idea of Toby being naked with me hysterically funny. From what I know of Paul, if he thought there was even the faintest possibility of chemistry, he would have taken a very different tack.

15

APRIL

It's nearly noon when the taxi drops us at the Bellavista. The sun is high in a cloudless sky and the temperature is warm without being stifling. Nevertheless, my heart sinks as we grab our bags from the boot. The reception desk is housed in a stand-alone building next to the drop-off area, and there's a track leading past to the main hotel car park, with the hotel itself behind that. The surface of the drop-off area and the track to the car park is made up of broken blocks of concrete, giving the impression that the place is unfinished. The smell of raw sewage hanging in the air doesn't help.

'It's coming back to me,' I say to Toby. 'When I was here before, they promised that this whole area would be resurfaced before they opened to the public. So much for that then.'

'What is that awful smell?' he asks.

'Sewage. The drains in Corfu are a bit hit and miss. Let's hope it clears soon.'

As we approach the reception door, my eye is drawn to a woman standing just outside, having what appears to be a heated argument with whoever is on the other end of her phone.

Curiosity gets the better of me and I dawdle deliberately to eaves-drop on a bit of the conversation. Straight away I can tell from her accent that she's from the North of England, and it seems she's less than enamoured with the hotel.

'And I'm telling you, Julie, that I won't stop here another night,' she shouts into the handset. 'I don't care what you have to do, you've to find us somewhere else.'

There's a pause while Julie obviously tries to mollify her, but she's having none of it.

'No, Julie,' she continues in the same belligerent tone. 'The curtain came away in my hand when I tried to close it, and it wasn't even a blackout curtain. It was so thin we had to get changed with the lights off, otherwise people would have been able to watch. And the bedclothes were damp, Julie. Damp!'

Toby tugs my arm, and I follow him reluctantly towards reception. My reluctance stems partly from the fact that I want to hear the rest of what the lady has to say, and partly because I'm increasingly worried about what we're going to find. The hotel wasn't interested in taking part in the mystery shopper scheme, so Mark managed to persuade the bean counters at *Voyages Luxes* to fund our two nights here. I don't know how he did it, but he's obviously as keen as I am to get to the bottom of the disparity between my review and the reports on TripAdvisor. We have already stayed in two very pleasant four-star boutique hotels on the island, and the Bellavista is our last one before we head back to England. So far, I've enjoyed spending time with Toby again; we haven't seen much of each other since his studio opening because he's been up to his eyeballs with work, but we've chatted a couple of times on the phone and I was delighted when I arrived at the airport to find him already there waiting for me. I always think that the sign of a really good friendship is when you don't see someone for a while but, when you do, you pick up the conversation as if it was only minutes since you chatted last. Seeing Toby again feels a bit like that.

The reception area is quiet, with just one receptionist behind the counter. She eyes us slightly suspiciously as we approach. I give her our names and she spends a long time trying to find our reservation. Just as I'm starting to fear that we're not booked in after all, she gives us a form to fill in, and bracelets to identify us as all-inclusive guests. Without even a hint of an apology, she tells us that our room isn't ready, that we can leave our bags, and we must come back at three o'clock to collect our key. Thankfully, Toby and I thought ahead this morning and we're both wearing swimming costumes under our clothes, so I ask for a couple of swimming pool towels.

'Twenty euros deposit for each towel,' the receptionist informs me, curtly. Either she hates her job or she's having a really bad day. I'm trying hard to give her the benefit of the doubt, but her rudeness is starting to grate on me. I hand over the money and we head off to kill some time by the pool.

The hotel is built into the side of a hill and has two swimming pools. The one at the bottom of the hill has a dozen or so sunloungers around it, which are all occupied, so Toby and I head up the stairs to the one at the top. This is definitely the better pool; it has an amazing view out over the bay below and there is also a bar up here, but again the sunloungers are all occupied, apart from a couple of broken ones in the corner.

'Let's have an early lunch and go to check out the beach,' I suggest.

The buffet in the restaurant appears to be divided into sections. There is an 'international food' area, which is serving rather lacklustre looking spaghetti Bolognese and chips. A little further along there are some Greek specialities; today it seems to be either grilled chicken or fish, with rice. Towards the end there is a large selection of salads, and I make a beeline for these. I load my plate with dolmas, Greek salad and olives and we find a table overlooking the bay to sit and eat.

'I wonder what we do for drinks?' Toby muses.

'I think you have to get them from the bar over there,' I tell him, pointing towards a rather disconsolate-looking woman standing behind a counter. The selection of drinks doesn't look very inspiring from here, so it looks like I got that bit right in my initial review, at least.

'I'll go,' Toby offers. 'What would you like?'

'I think I'll have a Diet Coke,' I reply.

When he comes back with the drinks, we tuck into the food. Toby has opted for grilled chicken, rice and a little bit of salad on the side.

'It's barely lukewarm!' he complains after a couple of mouthfuls. 'I know the Greeks don't like hot food, but this is ridiculous.'

He offers me a piece of chicken and he's right. Thankfully, the salads are more of a success. As we eat, I watch the other guests file in and make their choices. I'm surprised to see that most of them opt for the spaghetti Bolognese with chips.

'That's interesting. Hardly anyone is trying the Greek food,' I remark to Toby, who has his back to the buffet and can't see what's going on. 'What's the point of coming to a place like this and not trying the food?'

'Perhaps they have, and decided the spaghetti was a better bet,' he replies. 'If the Greek food is all like this, I might end up going for it myself.'

'It's not a very promising start, is it? First the receptionist and her attitude, then the lack of sunloungers, and now this. It's like a totally different hotel to the one I stayed in before.'

After lunch, a five-minute walk brings us to the beach, where a sign informs us that we can hire two sunbeds, a small table and an umbrella for five euros. It's beautiful, a wide swathe of golden sand leading down to the sea, which is lapping gently at the shoreline. There are a variety of small tavernas and restaurants nearby, most of which seem to be doing a brisk trade. The beach itself is not especially busy, and we spread our towels out on a couple of loungers, strip down to our swimsuits, and make ourselves comfortable. After a few minutes a woman comes to take our payment.

'This beach is lovely,' I tell her. 'Does it get very busy here?'

'At the weekends it is more busy,' she replies in accented English. 'But there are always places to sit. If you cannot find somewhere you come to me, and I will find somewhere for you.'

I thank her and hand over the money. Once she's gone, I turn to Toby.

'Fancy a swim?'

We head down to the water's edge. As we walk deeper into the sea, the water becomes crystal clear and we can see small fish swimming around our legs. The sea is cool and refreshing and, after swimming around for a bit, Toby and I turn on our backs to float.

'This is a nicer place to be than either of the hotel swimming pools,' he says. 'If I were on holiday, I'd come down here rather than stay up at the hotel, wouldn't you?'

'Mmm,' I reply. 'The problem is that, if you've booked all-inclusive, you might baulk at the prospect of having to shell out each day to hire the loungers here.'

'Fair point,' he concedes, 'but five euros per day is hardly bank-breaking, is it?'

After a while, we walk back to our little area and towel ourselves dry, before taking up position on the loungers. I make some notes on my notepad and then take out my book. I don't actually read much of it, but it's a useful prop to allow me to observe the other beach users candidly from behind my sunglasses. There must be other hotels in the area, because a lot of the other people on the beach are families with children of varying ages, and the Bellavista is adult only. I listen carefully and hear a mix of languages; there are a few other English people, but mostly Italians and Germans.

I watch a girl and a boy to our right for a little while. They are obviously brother and sister as they both have blonde hair and similar facial features. They're building a sandcastle and have dug out a moat around it. They take turns running down to the sea to fill up their bucket, before carefully pouring the water into the moat. It drains away instantly, of course, but they don't seem to mind. Their mother is toasting herself in the sun, and their father is keeping an eye on them from his position in the shade a little further away.

To our left there is another family with older children. The elder daughter must be sixteen or seventeen; she's lying on her back, wearing the skimpiest bikini that barely preserves her modesty and reading a magazine while she sunbathes. The boy is probably in his early teens; I can hear that his voice has broken when he speaks, but he's got that slightly awkward, beanpole look that teenaged boys have when they're going through a growth spurt. He's playing frisbee with the younger daughter, who I reckon is about ten. She's wearing a black, one-piece swimsuit and is very slightly chubby, as if someone has attached an air hose to her and inflated her a little. I remember when I was like that, just before I hit puberty and shot up. 'Puppy fat', my mum used to call it.

Movement from the teenager draws my eye back to her. She's turning over to tan her back. As she does so she unties the top of her bikini to ensure an even tan with no white marks. Another young woman in an equally skimpy bikini wanders past, with a man I imagine is her boyfriend in tow.

'Have you ever wondered,' Toby remarks, 'why it is that people feel quite happy wandering around in public wearing next to nothing when it's called swimwear, when they'd be terribly embarrassed if they were wearing underwear that covered up the exact same amount?'

'What do you mean?' I ask him.

'Well, take that girl over there,' he says, indicating the teenager. 'What do you think she'd say if someone asked her to walk into a room full of strangers wearing just her underwear? But, because we're calling that tiny piece of cloth a bikini, she's quite happy to be parading around in it, even though she's probably more exposed.'

I consider his point for a moment.

'What about your "boudoir brides"?' I ask him. 'They obviously don't have a problem getting their kit off in front of a stranger.'

'They do, actually. Very occasionally they're OK from the beginning, but with most of them I have to start fairly modest and work up. I never shoot anything tacky, but it has to be sexy, you know? It takes a while to build up their confidence and get them to trust me. They aren't like models, who are used to being told what to wear and do, and often they'll have body image issues that I have to work around. It can be a real challenge, but it's worth it to see their faces when they see the pictures. For many of them it's a real achievement, and it gives them a hell of a confidence boost.'

'I think I'm lucky,' I reflect. 'I'm not wild about my ears, because they stick out, but at least I can hide them under my hair. Other than that, I think I'm fairly happy with my body. I guess slightly bigger boobs wouldn't go amiss, but I'm not especially anxious about them. Do men have issues like that?'

He thinks for a while. 'I think a lot of men are probably anxious about their penis size, although you'd never get them to admit it. At the gym I go to there are two types of bloke. The first type goes into the changing rooms and strips down, waving their tackle for all to see, but I've always suspected they partially arouse themselves first to make themselves look more impressive. The second type, which is me by the way, faces into a corner and gets changed under a towel, so we don't get judged as inadequate by the willy wavers.'

'But, Toby, not to put too fine a point on it, I've seen your penis several times now and there's nothing wrong with it. It looks perfectly serviceable to me.'

He blushes profusely. 'You're very kind, I'm sure. I'm still not going to be waving it around at the gym.'

'It's not surprising that so many women suffer with body image issues,' I continue, 'given the way we're objectified and told we have to be perfect, otherwise nobody will ever fancy us. It's definitely much worse for women than men, don't you think? Men don't seem to have the same hang-ups. Do you remember Aldo, from Courchevel?'

'The one with the prostitute?'

'We still don't know that's what she was, but yes, that's him. Even though he was deeply unattractive, he was still somehow convinced he was God's gift. There are an awful lot of men like him out there, and I've been unlucky enough to meet quite a few of them.'

'Hm. I'll admit I know next to nothing about women, but I still reckon she had "for rent" written all over her.' He smiles. 'He probably had to swipe his credit card down her cleavage to gain access.'

'I'm not even going to ask where he had to enter his PIN number,' I snigger.

As if on cue, a man walks past carrying a couple of beers. Even though he's probably in his fifties, and old enough to be her father, I see his eyes roam appreciatively over the prone body of the teenage girl. After he's checked her over, he shifts his gaze to me, but looks away quickly when he sees that I'm watching him. He is not attractive. His shoulders and face are pink with sunburn and sweat is beading on his forehead. His most prominent feature is his belly, which stands out proudly, as if he's swallowed a beach ball. Underneath the belly I can just make out a very small, tight pair of swimming trunks, which leave absolutely nothing to the imagination. I don't want to be cruel but, if he ever went to the gym, he'd definitely want to get changed facing the wall. Despite his obvious shortcomings, he strides confidently across the sand, eyeing up the females as if he's an alpha male trying to decide which of us will be lucky enough to be chosen to mate with him.

Toby sees him too, and I laugh quietly. 'I rest my case, your honour,' I say to him.

16

APRIL

When we get back to the hotel at around five o'clock, we're greeted by a scene of absolute chaos at reception. There are people with suitcases milling around outside, and a long queue has formed at the desk indoors. I can see our bags, stacked with a load of others in the corner of the room.

'So much for secure storage,' I mutter to Toby. He rushes over to check that his camera bag is unmolested, and the relief on his face as he hoists it onto his back is palpable.

There are now two people behind the counter, but the second one doesn't appear to be doing anything apart from handing pieces of paper to the same receptionist we met earlier. She looks harassed and is gesticulating a lot when she speaks. The queue is moving agonisingly slowly, and people don't seem to be leaving once they've completed the check-in process. Instead, the group milling around outside appears to be getting larger and larger.

Our turn comes at last, and I explain that we've already checked in and we just want to pick up our keys. The receptionist shuffles through her papers, and then barks an order at her sidekick, who retrieves two keys from the rack on the wall. She hands them to the receptionist, who shoves them at us.

'Wait for the porter. He will show you your room,' she orders.

I look at the large group outside, who I now realise are probably all waiting for the porter, and decide against that idea.

'We only have a couple of small bags,' I say to the receptionist, 'why don't you just tell us where our room is, and we'll find it.'

'Wait for the porter,' she repeats, more insistently. 'He will show you.'

'Why can't you just tell me where it is?' I press. I can see my intransigence is annoying her, but I have no intention of backing down. I've never been in a hotel anywhere where they have refused to tell me how to find my room.

She obviously senses that I'm not going to let this go, as she grabs the keys back off me and turns them around so she can read the room number.

'Room 38. Ground floor. Go across the car park and you will find it,' she tells me, bad-temperedly.

I rustle up my sweetest smile for her. 'Thank you.'

The room is another aspect of the hotel that is nothing like my previous visit. I have a memory of a bright, airy room with a comfortable king-size bed and a separate seating area. This one is a characterless box, and the only natural light comes from the glass-paned sliding doors that open onto the car park. As we're on the ground floor, our only choice is either to leave the curtains open, in which case every passer-by will be able to see in, or close them and plunge the room into darkness. Thankfully, they do at least appear to be thicker than the curtains my Northern friend from earlier had described. Toby is flicking light switches, but nothing is happening. I wonder if this is a trick, whether there is some hidden switch that the porter flicks as you tip him, to give you electricity. As if by magic I spot him walking back towards reception, and hurry to intercept him.

'Excuse me,' I say politely, 'can you tell us how to make the lights work in our room?'

'Power cut,' he replies, without breaking his stride. 'No electricity in hotel. Try later.'

'Why couldn't the receptionist have told us that?' I ask Toby once I'm back in the room. 'She must have known. And why is everyone here so bloody surly and rude?'

'It gets better,' he replies. 'Check out the bathroom.'

I push open the door of the bathroom, but it jams against the shower cubicle before it's fully open. It's very dark in there, but I can just see the basin, with a mirror over it. There's no sign of a toilet.

'If you're looking for the toilet, it's behind the door,' Toby informs me. 'You have to go in, close the bathroom door, and then wriggle your way down the gap between the shower cubicle and the wall.'

'That's ridiculous,' I reply. 'I've never seen a bathroom so small.'

I realise that I do actually need to wee, so I close the door and am instantly plunged into total darkness. With a couple of muttered oaths, I stick my hands out in front of me and feel my way down the wall until my shins hit the hard surface of the toilet bowl. Slowly, I turn around, ease down my shorts and bikini bottoms, and gingerly lower myself until I come into contact with what I hope is the seat. While I'm going, I feel around to see if I can locate the toilet roll, but without success.

'Did you see where the loo roll was?' I call out. 'I can't find it.'

'It's on top of the cistern,' Toby replies.

I feel round behind me and I'm relieved when my hand lands on the familiar shape. I wipe myself, pull up my bikini bottoms and shorts, and even manage to locate the basin and something that I dearly hope is soap to wash my hands in, all in the pitch black. I've just found the door handle and managed to make it back into the bedroom without incident when the lights come on.

'This place is idiotic. I can't believe they managed to fool me so comprehensively last time,' I remark an hour or so later, as we're getting changed out of our swimwear for the evening. I no longer feel uncomfortable being undressed around Toby, and he continues to take absolutely no interest in me. He also seems totally unfazed by it now, and happily parades around without a stitch of clothing on. I can't say I mind, as I have to admit to myself that I quite enjoy the view.

Once we're dressed, we make our way up the stairs to the pool bar at the top of the hotel. I look around at the other rooms and spot the one I think I stayed in last time. It has a nice balcony looking out over the pool and I can see the seating area through the large window. The sun is starting to set, and Toby takes a few photos out across the bay while I get the drinks. There are plenty of sunloungers available now, and we park ourselves on two. Toby professes that his beer is fine, if a little watery, but my gin and tonic is foul. I don't know what they're using for gin, but it tastes like paint stripper and I set it aside after a couple of sips. There's a convivial crowd by the bar drinking what look like cocktails, so I decide to chance my luck with one of those instead. This time the bar keeper pours from a variety of unrecognisable bottles, before topping it off with some unnamed fruit juice and lemonade. Cautiously, I take it back to the sunlounger and take a sip. It's almost unbearably sweet, with a harsh undercurrent of cheap alcohol.

'Taste this,' I say, offering it to Toby.

He eyes it suspiciously. 'What is it?'

'It's what that group at the bar are drinking. It's called a Corfu Sunset, apparently.'

'It doesn't look much like a sunset,' he observes, peering at the bright pink liquid.

'No. Taste it though, and tell me what you think.'

Toby takes a sip and I see his mouth wrinkle in disgust.

'Ugh, what the hell is in that?' he asks, after swallowing hurriedly.

'I have no idea. I can't even work out whether it's better or worse than the pretend gin and tonic: they're both foul. I think I'd rather pay and have a drink I recognise.'

Once Toby has finished his beer, we saunter down to the restaurant to sample the dinner offering. It looks much like the lunchtime one, except the Greek hot dishes have been replaced with a moussaka and some grilled pork. Toby goes to get some wine and I secure the same table we sat at earlier.

'Don't expect much from this,' he tells me, handing me my glass of red. 'It's chilled and it came out of a dispenser.'

'That's a classic way of toning down cheap wine,' I tell him. 'Serve it cold and it mutes the flavours. If you served this at room temperature it would probably dissolve the lining of your mouth.'

The wine is rough but, unlike the drinks at the pool bar, it is just about drinkable. We leave our glasses as a marker that the table is occupied and explore the buffet. After his experiences at lunchtime, I'm not surprised when Toby reappears with a plate of spaghetti Bolognese and some chips. I decide to be brave and opt for moussaka with a side helping of Greek salad.

'This isn't too bad, actually,' I tell Toby, after a mouthful of moussaka. 'It's not hot, but it's a lot warmer than the chicken you had at lunchtime. How's the spaghetti? Does it go well with chips? Seems like a carb overload to me.'

Toby sighs. 'I seem doomed in my choices. The pasta is all

sticking together, and I have a nasty suspicion the Bolognese is made from dog food. The chips are OK though.'

* * *

The next morning, Toby is up early. I'm used to this now; I know he likes to catch the light, so I don't think anything of it. I squeeze my way into the shower and I'm just about ready for breakfast when he returns with a mischievous glint in his eye.

'What have you been up to?' I ask him.

'I've been laying on a bit of entertainment,' he replies. 'I was up at the top pool, taking some photos at around six o'clock, and all these people appeared, laid out their towels on the sunloungers, and then disappeared again. There are lots of signs saying that you can't reserve sunloungers and that towels will be removed, but nobody was actually doing it, so I did. I piled them all up by the bar. Should be fun later.'

After breakfast, we make our way up to the top pool. Sure enough, there is a pile of towels by the bar, but more people must have been up here since Toby, because most of the loungers have towels on them again. We settle down on two of the few remaining free ones and watch to see what happens. We don't have to wait long before guests are removing the new towels and replacing them with the originals, or having heated arguments with the new occupants of the loungers they thought they had reserved.

'I've always wanted to do that,' Toby admits, after an hour or so of chaos. 'I think it's bloody selfish to reserve loungers if you're not actually using them. Shall we go to the beach now?'

'It wouldn't be such a problem if the hotel provided enough for everyone, though, would it?' I say as we start walking down the road.

'Yes, I thought that too, but they don't have the space to do that around either pool, do they? I guess that's a limitation of building a hotel on the side of a hill.'

We spend the rest of the morning very pleasantly on the beach, and Toby practically begs to have lunch at one of the tavernas. Given his poor luck with the offerings in the hotel restaurant, I take pity on him and allow him to choose. We end up having a very successful lunch of calamari, souvlaki and baklava to finish, all washed down with ice-cold Mythos beer.

'That was much more like it,' Toby declares as we make our way back onto the sand. It feels odd to me to be spending a whole day on the beach. Normally, I'd be out trying all the various excursions but, as I've been here before and I'm definitely going to be writing this up as one to avoid, there doesn't seem to be a lot of point. I do make a note of the name of the restaurant where we had lunch; I'll include that as an alternative to eating in the hotel.

In the evening, Toby suggests we try a bar he saw on his early morning explorations. It's certainly popular; most of the outdoor tables are already occupied when we get there. Toby has another beer and I order a negroni as a treat. The cocktail is a delight after the dubious offerings from the hotel bar, and I savour every sip.

Toby is on good form, and his eyes sparkle with enthusiasm as he tells me about work he's got coming up. I already know that the studio is a great success, but he's also got plenty of weddings and other shoots booked in over the summer. He tells me that he's finally finished decorating the flat, and how delighted he is with it.

'And how about the love life?' I ask.

'Nothing happening there,' he replies. 'I'm totally focused on work at the moment, anyway. What about you?'

'Nope. As I said before, I'm tired of meeting promising-looking men who subsequently turn out to be hopeless. All of them seem to want someone who can be a mother figure, a housekeeper, or a nymphomaniac at the flick of a switch. None of them, not one, seemed remotely interested in what I might want.'

'Maybe we should have some sort of pact, like this couple did in a film I watched once,' Toby says, suddenly. 'They set a date in the future and, if neither of them had found "the one" by the time the date came, they agreed they would marry each other.'

'And how did that work out?'

'It was a romcom, how do you think it worked out? They realised they were madly in love with each other and it all ended happily.'

'Mm. I don't think that sounds very realistic, do you? Anyway, I wouldn't want to get married out of desperation: that's tragic. I'd rather stay single.'

'Don't you get lonely sometimes, though? I know I do, even though I'm flat out busy. Sometimes I just want someone to share my day with, or talk stuff over with.'

'But that's what friends are for!' I counter. 'You're more than welcome to ring me up anytime and talk to me about stuff. You know me well enough by now that I'll tell you frankly what I think about most things.'

'You are certainly the most, how shall I put this, "direct" person I've ever met,' he laughs.

'Would you rather I was all mysterious and coy, and you never knew what I was thinking?' I ask him.

'No, not at all!'

'Good, because what I'm thinking right now is that you should buy me another one of these delicious negronis.'

17

MAY

'Can I ask you a favour?' Toby says to me, during one of our increasingly regular phone calls. We haven't seen each other since the Corfu trip, but we've taken to speaking on the phone at least once a week since our conversation in the bar.

'Sure, what's up?' I ask.

'I've been commissioned to write a book about Art Nude photography,' he tells me. 'Hints and tips, with pictures to illustrate. I've got a model coming in on Saturday and I need a chaperone.'

'Why, are you worried you won't be able to control yourself?' I ask. I have to stifle a giggle at the thought.

'No, it's just good practice. There are lots of horror stories out there about models feeling that the photographer was pressurising them to go further than they were comfortable with, and something like that could do a lot of damage to my reputation.'

'I don't see you as the pressurising type,' I tell him.

'I'd like to think not. I've shot plenty of Art Nude over the years,' he replies, 'but you can never be too careful. Also, we'll be doing some shooting outdoors, and I need a lookout who can help the model to cover up quickly if anyone comes into sight.'

I think about his request. I don't actually have any firm plans for Saturday, so I could help him out. Also, I owe him; the Corfu article was another great success. On top of that I'm a little curious. I have no interest in naked women, but I'd like to see him at work.

'Sure, I'll be your chaperone. What time do you need me?'

'It's an early start to catch the light, I'm afraid. Would you be able to meet me at the studio at five o'clock?'

'In the morning?'

'Sorry.'

'That's OK. I'm having dinner with Ed and Charley on Friday, but they're hardly night owls these days, so I'll be home in time to have an early night. I'll see you on Saturday morning at five.'

Although I'm often up early to catch a plane, it's not a part of my job that I particularly enjoy, so I set my alarm on Friday night with some reluctance, and it feels like I've barely dropped off to sleep before I'm woken up by its insistent beeping. It's far too early to contemplate breakfast, so I have a quick shower, get dressed, and limit my make-up to the bare essentials. It's still dark when I leave home, and the sun is just beginning to cast a faint glow across the sky by the time I arrive at Toby's studio. He introduces me to the model, a petite young woman called Erin, who is dressed somewhat incongruously in a towelling dressing gown and trainers, with her hair neatly pinned up and immaculate make-up. I clamber into the back of Toby's car, allowing Erin to sit in the front, and we set off.

After around twenty minutes, Toby pulls off the road onto the verge. He unpacks his backpack and various reflective panels from the boot of the car, and we follow him into a field. Although the day ahead promises to be warm, there's a distinct chill in the air at this time in the morning and the ground is wet with dew. I'm grateful for my coat and I wonder how poor Erin is going to cope being out here with nothing on. We go through a gate into another field and Toby leads us over to a fallen tree. Most of the branches have been cut away from it, but two remain, holding the top of the tree around ten feet off the ground. It's obviously been like that for a while, as the wood is bleached from the sun. It's beautiful, in a brutal way.

Toby and Erin busy themselves discussing poses. She acts out a few, wrapping herself around one of the branches and laying in various ways on the trunk. Toby gets his camera out and looks through it, directing her. The sun rises in the sky and soon we're bathed in the early morning light. The tree casts long shadows, and they spend some time altering her positions so that she's lit as he wants her.

'Madison, can you come over here for a minute?' he asks at one point, and I walk over to join them.

'Take this, would you, and hold it as I direct you. Is that OK?'

I take the reflector and stand where he instructs me. He directs me to angle it, and I can see its effect, softly adding extra light to the scene. After some more fiddling with the settings on his camera, he declares himself ready.

'Here's where the hard work begins for you, Madison,' he tells me. 'Erin will be concentrating on her poses and I'll be focused on her, so you have to be our eyes and ears. You need to keep hold of Erin's dressing gown, ready to give it to her as soon as I finish shooting, or if someone comes. You need to let us know the moment you spot anyone. We shouldn't be disturbed at this time of the day, but we don't want to take any chances. You're also in charge of the reflector. OK?'

This is a whole new side to Toby. There's no hint of the reticence that I'm used to. He's exuding confidence and is being positively authoritative. I almost have to blink to reassure myself he's the same person.

Erin takes off her trainers and I put them safely on the grass behind me. Then she undoes the dressing gown, slips it down her shoulders and hands it to me. The next ten minutes are among the most surreal of my life. I'm standing in a field, at this unearthly hour of the morning, trying to follow Toby's instructions about where to position the reflector while also scanning the horizon for any sign of human movement. Meanwhile, Erin is recreating the poses she's just gone through, but this time without a stitch of clothing on. Toby directs her as he shoots and she adjusts her poses accordingly. I'm stunned by Erin's body confidence. To be fair, she has a lot to be confident about; she has creamy, perfect skin without a hint of cellulite, her breasts are small but nicely shaped over her flat belly, and her total absence of pubic hair makes her look like she's just stepped out of a pre-Raphaelite painting. I notice that Toby is careful how he poses her, so that her labia are never visible.

I'm surprised by the total lack of any sexual undercurrent and wonder briefly whether this is down to Toby's sexuality, but he's so professional that I decide it wouldn't make any difference.

As soon as he declares himself satisfied and lowers the camera, I hand her dressing gown back to her and she wraps it tightly around herself. She hasn't uttered a word of complaint, but I'm sure she's freezing. Toby takes a thermos out of his backpack and pours her a cup of hot tea, which she wraps her hands around gratefully as she sips.

'Once you've warmed up, I'd like to do just a few with your hair down before we head back to the studio. Is that OK?' Toby asks her.

'No problem,' Erin replies. She finishes her tea and takes the clips out of her hair, which cascades down over her shoulders in dark waves. She steps out of the dressing gown again and we repeat the performance.

* * *

'You're so brave,' I tell her, once we're back in the car on the way to the studio. 'Don't you feel self-conscious?'

'I did, the first couple of times,' she replies, 'but after a while you just stop thinking about it. I'm careful who I work with, and I'm always very clear about my limits from the start. I don't do open leg, or any of that sort of stuff.'

'Have there ever been any times when someone came along, and you didn't cover up in time?'

'Oh yes!' she laughs. 'I was doing a shoot with this guy in London once. It was early in the morning and we were shooting at this building with lots of gothic pillars outside. I had my dressing gown just behind the pillar, but nobody noticed this old man wandering down the pavement until it was too late.'

'What happened?'

'Nothing! I mean, he obviously saw me, but he just doffed his cap and walked on. He was such a gent, I wanted to run after him and give him a kiss,' she says, smiling broadly.

'I got caught by a policeman once,' Toby tells us. 'I was shooting a model on the steps of a library one morning, and I got a tap on the shoulder.'

'Oh wow, did you get arrested?' I ask.

'No. He was very good about it actually. All he said was, "I'd think about wrapping things up soon if I were you. The market traders will be here to set up before long, and we don't want to give them any unwelcome surprises, do we?"'

'But isn't it illegal to be parading around in public with no clothes on?'

'Actually, no,' Toby replies. 'It's only illegal if, and I quote, "you intentionally expose your genitals with the intention that someone will see them and be caused alarm or distress" or "you commit, in public, an act of a lewd, obscene or disgusting nature which outrages public decency". Simply being naked doesn't fall into either of those categories, which is why events such as the annual London naked bike ride don't result in mass arrests. Having said that, it's better all-round if you're discreet.'

Once we get back to the studio, Erin disappears into the dressing room to fix her hair and make-up and Toby sets up a long trestle table, arranging a light behind it.

'I'm going to do some low-key shots,' he explains, as he fixes a long box over the light. 'This will give a nice soft light from behind her and we'll get some lovely shapes, almost like silhouettes. Art Nude is all about light and shapes. We can't control the light outdoors, so we have to adapt the camera. But in here we have complete control over the light, so we can do what we like.'

There's nothing for me to do now, so I sit in a chair and watch as Toby and Erin work. She lies on her side on the trestle table, moving as he directs, and he moves around her, capturing different details.

'Erin, would you mind if Madison took a few photos?' Toby asks, suddenly.

'I don't need to do that, I'm fine here!' I reply, before Erin has a chance to say anything. 'You carry on.'

'Come on. It'll be good practice, and it might help you.'

'Help me with what?' I retort. 'There don't tend to be a lot of studio lighting set-ups or naked women in my photos!'

'Madison is a travel writer,' Toby explains to Erin, 'and she's come under a bit of fire for her pictures.'

'Come on, Madison. If Toby's prepared to teach you, you'd be mad to turn him down!' she exclaims.

'Oh, for goodness' sake! If it'll shut you two up, hand me the camera.'

Toby rummages in his bag, gets out another camera and fiddles with the settings for a bit. When he hands it to me the first thing that I'm aware of is the weight of it. He shows me how to adjust the zoom and focus.

'Just think about the light and the shapes,' he encourages me. 'Take your time, look at everything. If you think you can improve it then explain to Erin what she needs to do. If you want the light moved, let me know and I'll move it for you.'

I look through the eyepiece and try to follow his instructions. I take a few shots and hand the camera back to him. Erin sits up.

'Let's see,' she says, and she and Toby scroll through together.

'These are good!' she exclaims, and I can't help but smile at her attempt to be encouraging.

'They definitely show promise,' Toby agrees. 'Listen, I don't need you as a lookout for this phase, so why don't you hang on to this camera and take a few pictures after I've done each set. I'm sure Erin won't mind, will you?'

'No skin off my nose,' she replies. 'You've paid me for the day. How you use it is up to you.'

The rest of the day is actually fun. Erin is bubbly and encouraging, and Toby patiently shows me different angles I could shoot from and the effects that I can create from each. As I scroll through the pictures I've taken while Toby is setting up the final set, I can see quite a few that I'm pleased with.

When I look up, I notice that Toby has brought the trestle table back out, along with a bottle of baby oil and one of those sprayers that you use for house plants. I watch, transfixed, as Erin rubs the baby oil into her skin, and then lies on her back on the table. She flinches from the cold a few times as Toby sprays her with the water, and then giggles.

'What on earth are you doing to the poor girl now?' I ask.

'The oil makes the water form into droplets,' he explains. 'After a few minutes we'll get the most incredible effect.' Sure enough, after a minute or two, she looks like she's covered in condensation, and he begins to shoot again.

* * *

'Thank you. I actually quite enjoyed that,' I say to him, after everything has been put away and Erin has left for the station. 'Although I'd got so used to seeing Erin naked that it was a bit odd when she came out of the dressing room in jeans and a jumper. I half expected her to wander off to the station as she was!'

'She's really good. I like working with her,' he tells me. 'You got some good shots. I'll put them on a memory stick for you to keep. I've got some other models coming in over the next few weeks, different body shapes and so on. If you're around, you're welcome to come and chaperone me again, and take some more pictures.'

'I think I'd like that,' I tell him. 'Now, I'm starving. How about I buy you the fish and chips this time?'

'I think I should probably buy them,' he replies. 'A thank you for helping me out today.'

'No, let me. It's my turn and I have a favour to ask you, anyway.'

'Sounds intriguing,' he tells me, as we walk out of the front door.

18

MAY

'I know it's short notice, but can I bring Toby with me to the christening as a plus one?' I ask Charley later that week.

'Of course!' she replies. 'We'd love to meet him.'

I've been struggling to find a suitable christening present for Amelia and, in the end, I landed on the idea of a nice set of photos that I could give them. I'd found some sites online where you can upload pictures and make an album, so my plan was to ask Toby for some tips to make sure the photos weren't too awful. He surprised me by offering to come and take them himself and, despite my protests that I didn't want to take advantage of him, he eventually persuaded me to let him. We did at least agree that I would cover the cost of the album. He also suggested we frame a few for them to have at home, which I thought was a lovely idea.

I have mixed feelings about the upcoming christening. Charley has sent me the order of service and there are some vows I have to make about renouncing evil and turning to Christ, as well as promising to ensure Amelia is brought up to become a Christian. I'm happy enough to say the words, but I have to confess that I'm not particularly religious. I'm not an atheist; I just don't think God and I have a lot to say to each other. At school we had to go to chapel every morning, which wasn't too bad as the services were pretty short and I quite enjoyed singing the hymns. On Sundays, however, we had longer services, often with visiting speakers who would drone on for hours about their pet cause or charity. They were unbearably dull, and the hard wooden pews would make my bum go to sleep. Since then, I've rather enjoyed having Sunday mornings to myself without God muscling in. If I'm not travelling, I sometimes go out for breakfast, buying the Sunday broadsheet I write for on the way and enjoying a few sections over a poached egg on toast and some strong coffee.

I arrive at the studio a little early on the day of the service, and Toby isn't quite ready when I ring the bell, so he invites me up to the flat to wait. This is the first time I've been in here since the day he moved in and the transformation is amazing. The sitting room ceiling has been replastered and he's redecorated in warm, light colours. The biscuit-coloured carpet also adds to the feeling of airiness in here, and there are pops of colour from the artwork on the walls and the large squishy sofas. The obligatory flatscreen TV is mounted on the wall, with speakers and all sorts of other man paraphernalia beneath.

The bedroom door is ajar, and I stick my head around it. Toby is rummaging in his wardrobe, with a towel around his waist. 'Am I OK to have a look around?'

'Help yourself!' he replies.

I walk into the kitchen, which now features sleek, modern units. It's a little more sterile and masculine than I would choose, but it's still a very pleasant room. I run my fingers over the granite work-tops, which feel cool and smooth to the touch. Toby evidently doesn't do 'cheap and cheerful'. Out of curiosity I open one of the drawers. There isn't much in it apart from a few utensils. I push it shut and it closes softly, as if it's cushioned from behind. There's a small round table in there with two chairs, and I find myself imagining Toby and a boyfriend having breakfast together at it. The bathroom now contains an expensive-looking white bath suite, with bright lighting and a powerful-sounding extractor fan. I doubt very much that you'd get steamed up with that thing whirring away.

'What do you think?' Toby asks from just behind me, making me jump.

'Bloody hell, Toby, you gave me a fright!' I say, turning to face him. He's wearing a dark blue suit, white shirt and a red and blue striped tie, and his aftershave is woody and spicy.

'It's amazing,' I continue. 'You must have spent a fortune!'

'It wasn't cheap, but having waited so long for my own space, I wanted it to be *right*, do you know what I mean?'

I think of the effort I put into my flat when I first moved in there, and nod. 'Show me the rest then,' I tell him.

The second bedroom has been repurposed as a study, with a desk, filing cabinet, and swivel chair. There's a bookcase with hundreds of well-thumbed books on various aspects of photography, and the walls are adorned with framed photographs. A powerful-looking computer sits on the desk. In the master bedroom, the single mattress on the floor has gone, replaced by a wooden-framed king-size bed with crisp white bedlinen and matching bedside tables with lights. The revamped en-suite bathroom has a lingering aroma of Toby's aftershave.

'I'm particularly pleased with this,' Toby says, indicating the mirror in the en suite. 'It's heated, so it doesn't steam up. I got the idea after the first place we stayed when we went to Courchevel. I came out of the shower, couldn't see a damned thing in the mirror and thought, there must be a better way. A bit of internet research led me to this.'

'I think it's probably a man thing,' I laugh. 'I just rub my mirror with the towel.'

* * *

As we drive to the church, I fill him in on the other people who are likely to be there. The other godparents are Ed's sister, Lily, and Charley's brother, Simon. Both sets of parents are also coming, as are quite a few of their friends. The church is the same one that Charley and Ed got married in, which is a nice piece of continuity. The only downside is the vicar, who was a rather decrepit old man with yellow teeth and terrible breath. I hope he's going to be strong enough to be able to hold Amelia without dropping her.

The church is already full when we get there, but we have reserved seats at the front with the family. I can just make out faint organ music above the hubbub of chatter. Amelia seems to be loving being the centre of attention and grins toothlessly at everyone. I introduce Toby to Ed and Charley, and also to Charley's parents, John and Christine.

'I hope you're coming back to ours afterwards,' John says to Toby. 'We have enough to feed the whole of Kent from what I can see!'

'Nonsense,' Christine retorts. 'I just wanted to make sure that nobody was hungry, and you always end up with more people than you think you're going to have at these things.'

'I'd be delighted,' Toby says to them. 'If you've been slaving away over a hot stove it would be terrible to have anything go to waste.'

John laughs. 'The only thing she's been slaving over is the menu! She was on the phone to the caterers as soon as the date was set.'

A hush falls over the congregation as the vicar comes out of the vestry and walks over to the desk at the front. I do a slight double take as she's not only a woman, but appears to be barely older than me.

'What happened to the old guy?' I whisper to Charley.

'He retired, thank goodness. This one is really lovely. Ed and I like her so much we're talking about coming regularly.'

'Really?'

'Yes, Ed's got this whole "pillar of the community" bee in his bonnet, and also there's a crèche for Amelia when she's older.'

The vicar welcomes everyone warmly and makes a particular fuss of Ed, Charley and Amelia. I'm glad to discover that the hymns are all familiar to me from my school days, and I sing along lustily, drawing amused side glances from Toby. When we get to the actual baptism part, we all gather around the font and say our vows, before the vicar takes Amelia and carefully pours the water from the font over her forehead. Amelia looks surprised but doesn't cry. We're then sent back to our seats and the vicar takes Amelia on a sort of victory lap around the church, introducing her to various people in the congregation before returning her to Charley.

When the service is over, Toby asks the vicar if she would mind re-enacting some of the baptism so he can take pictures, and she gladly agrees. Toby also takes pictures of Amelia with her parents, grandparents and godparents. It feels a little bit like a wedding, and I worry that Amelia will get bored and start crying. Thankfully, he's quick and efficient and the whole thing only takes a few minutes.

Charley's parents' house is quite close to the church, so we leave the car where it is and walk down there after the service. There are signs directing us around the house to a large marquee, which has been set up in the garden. At one end of the marquee there is a bar, and the food has been laid out at the other. John was right, there is enough here to feed an army; the tables look like they might buckle at any minute under the weight of it all. We help ourselves to a glass of champagne from the bar and circulate. Ed and Charley are happily passing Amelia round to anyone who wants a cuddle, and she still appears to be loving the attention. Every so often Toby gives me his glass to hold so he can take a picture.

'Madison, isn't it?' a voice says from behind me, and I turn to find myself face to face with the vicar. 'I'm Sharon. I didn't get a chance to say hello properly before, so I thought I'd come and do it now.'

'Nice to meet you, Sharon,' I reply. 'How long have you been here? The last time I came the vicar was an old guy.'

'That would have been Tom,' she tells me. 'He retired just over a year ago, and I've been here for six months.'

'Where were you before?'

'This is my first incumbency. I was a curate in a church in Northamptonshire before I came here.'

'I hope you'll forgive my ignorance, but what's the difference between a curate and a vicar?' I ask. 'I watched a few episodes of *Grantchester*, and James Norton was a curate in that, wasn't he?'

'A curate is like a trainee vicar,' she explains. 'When you're first ordained, you're ordained as a deacon and you go off to work as a curate under an experienced priest and learn the ropes. For the first year you can't do the ABCs, meaning you can't absolve anyone from their sins, you can't bless anything or anyone, and you can't consecrate the bread and wine for communion. After the first year they ordain you again, as a priest this time, and then you serve another two or three years as a curate before you can apply for your own parish.'

'So you apply? You don't just get told where to go?'

'No. Some churches are like that. In the Salvation Army, for instance, they give you your "marching orders" and you have to go wherever they send you, but in the Church of England you apply and go through a selection and interview process in the same way that you would for any other job. My husband—' she indicates a man out playing with a small boy in the garden '—was particularly keen to move here because it's much easier for him to get to London than it was from Northampton.'

'OK, and when you get your own parish, that's when you become a vicar?'

'Not necessarily.' She smiles. 'It depends on the parish. It gets quite complicated, but basically you could be a vicar, a priest-in-charge or a rector, depending on the set-up.'

My mind is starting to spin. Who knew this was all so complicated? I decide to head back to safer ground.

'Well, I have to say I was relieved it wasn't Tom. I had visions of him dropping Amelia into the font.'

'Yes, I heard he was quite frail towards the end. Babies can be a hazard; some of them wriggle, and you have to watch they don't grab your glasses or the lapel mic. Amelia was good as gold though.'

'Isn't she supposed to cry when you baptise her? I thought that was supposed to be a sign of the devil coming out.'

'I'm afraid that's a bit of an old wives' tale. Quite a few of them do cry though. Even though we make sure the water is nice and hot when we pour it into the font, the stone cools it down pretty quickly, and I think it shocks them a bit. Is this your partner?' she asks as Toby approaches.

'No, he's just a friend.'

'Oh, I'm sorry. It's just that you looked so close.'

At that moment there's a howl from the little boy, who has evidently fallen over and grazed his knee.

'Oh, bloody hell, what's he done to himself now?' Sharon exclaims, and my eyebrows shoot up. 'Sorry, I'd better go and check he's OK.'

'What did I miss?' Toby asks.

'Apart from the sweary vicar and the fact that the Church of England is the most confusing organisation I think I've ever come across? Nothing much. Charley was right though, she's nice. Misguided, but nice.'

'Misguided how?' Toby asks.

'She thought we were a couple,' I laugh.

'Yes, that is misguided.' He smiles. 'I'm way out of your league!'

'You think that, if it helps,' I tell him, putting on my most patronising voice. 'Quick, Charley and Ed are free. It's time I had another cuddle with my god-daughter.'

'For someone who professes not to be maternal, you're not very convincing, you know that?'

'Amelia's special, that's all. She's not just any baby, she's my best friend's baby and my god-daughter.'

By the time we've eaten lunch and drunk a series of toasts to Amelia it's nearly five o'clock. I've got to be on an early morning flight to Oslo, so we make our excuses and leave. As I drive home, Sharon's remarks come back to me and I chuckle to myself at the thought of Toby and I being a couple. I wonder if she's friends with the mad woman we met on the plane the first time we travelled together.

19

AUGUST

'You know the wedding I'm doing in a few weeks?' Toby asks me, as I help him to tidy up the studio after his final set of Art Nude photos. In addition to chaperoning him with the various models he's brought in for the book, I've taken to coming down and helping out when I'm around and not working. Toby says he enjoys the company, and he has shown me how to set up the lights and what the various different umbrellas and soft-boxes do, so I actually feel useful in here now. I've also learned quite a lot about cameras, and how changes in the various settings affect the final picture. It's been surprisingly interesting, although I think I've seen enough female flesh in the Art Nude sessions to last me a lifetime. The models have been very varied, from tiny waif-like things that look like they'll blow away in the breeze, to plus-sized women with curves aplenty. They've all radiated with confidence in front of the camera though, and I'm sure the book will be beautiful.

'The incredibly lavish one? Sophie double-barrelled something and James double-barrelled something else?' I reply.

'That's the one. Sophie Beresford-Smith and James Huntingdon-Barfoot. It's the first weekend of September. Are you around?'

I consult my phone diary. Toby and I have not long returned from a whirlwind trip to Morocco, with two nights staying in a traditional riad in Marrakesh followed by one night to experience the beaches of Agadir. It wasn't without incident, as Toby got distracted during our visit to one of the souks, and for a while I thought I'd lost him forever in the maze. The traditional hammam was amazing though. As well as writing that up, I know I'm going to the West Country to review a number of boutique hotels in the next week or two. I've also got a trip to the Caribbean in September, which I'm in two minds about. Although I love the Caribbean, it will still be the hurricane season, so the weather might not be great.

'I am,' I tell him. 'It's the weekend before I fly to Barbados.'

'Do you fancy coming along as my assistant? I thought you might enjoy it.'

'Won't I just get in your way?'

'No. I'll do all the main stuff, but I can find things for you to do. If it were a celebrity wedding, such as the one I did last week, then there would be no chance because you'd have to be vetted and everything. There's no issue with this one though, and it promises to be quite a spectacle.'

I think about it. I do love weddings and, from what he's told me about this one already, it promises to be seriously over the top. The bride is the only daughter of a billionaire, so no expense has been spared.

'Count me in.' I grin.

'Excellent. It will be a fairly early start, as we have to get to the bride's house to capture her getting ready, and we're there until the first dance, so it will be a long day. Can you get here for seven o'clock?'

I make a note in my diary, and we head across the road for our traditional fish and chips. We've graduated from sitting on the floor in the studio, and now we eat it at the table in the kitchen of his flat.

* * *

On the day of the wedding, I arrive at Toby's studio bang on seven o'clock. He's already loaded his car, but there's an extra rucksack by the back door, which he offers to me.

'I thought it was time you had your own kit,' he explains, 'so I've got you a camera, a flash, and some lenses. Have a look.'

I open the rucksack and see a camera pretty much identical to the one he's taught me to use, with a standard zoom lens, a telephoto lens and a wide-angle. There's also a flash unit in there.

'It's for you to keep,' he tells me as I adjust the settings and take a couple of test shots to check the results.

'Oh, Toby. I can't possibly accept this!' I exclaim. 'It must have cost a fortune.'

'Nonsense, of course you can accept it. Think of it as payment in kind for all the help you've given me over the last few months. Also, I need the camera you usually use as backup today, in case anything goes wrong with the main one.'

'Well, if you put it like that...'

'I do. There are spare batteries and memory cards in the bag, so you're all set up.'

On the way to the bride's house, Toby explains how the day is going to work.

'First of all, we have to capture the bride getting ready. It'll be a mixture of posed shots and reportage. I'll focus on the bride, the bridesmaids and her parents. What I'd like you to do is look for little details; maybe a pattern on her shoes, or a detail of the dress, OK?'

'Yes, I can do that,' I reply. 'What's reportage?'

'It's literally just telling the story of an event in photos. So, you aim to capture the emotions, the special moments, the things that will bring the memories to life for them.'

Toby turns off the road and we are confronted by a pair of tall wrought iron gates. He presses the button, announces himself, and they silently swing open, as if they're being moved by a giant invisible hand. We follow the driveway through woodland for what seems like miles before the view opens up and we catch our first glimpse of the house.

'Bloody hell, it's like something out of a Jane Austen novel!' I cry. The enormous house is Georgian in style and is surrounded by immaculately kept lawns with ruler-straight stripes. The front of the house overlooks a substantial lake, and I can see a tennis court and a croquet lawn off to one side.

'When do you think it was built?' he asks.

'I don't know, early eighteen hundreds?'

'It's actually only fifteen years old. There's a bit of a story to it, although I don't know if it's true. Apparently, old man Beresford-Smith fell in love with the grounds, but he didn't like the house that originally stood here. He applied for permission to demolish it and was refused because the house was listed. So, as a massive "fuck you" to the council, he used it to store animal feed. Very mysteriously, a few months later, a load of hay he was keeping in there caught fire and the whole place burned to the ground. Shortly after that, he got his planning permission and work on the new house began.'

'That doesn't sound like very aristocratic behaviour!'

'Oh, there's nothing aristocratic about him, don't be fooled by the name. From what I understand, his original name was just

Smith. He made an absolute fortune in the dot-com boom back in the nineties and changed his name by deed poll to celebrate his first hundred million. Apparently, he and his wife had elocution lessons at the same time, although I think she's probably taken it a bit too far. Last time I came, the housekeeper told me that Sophie and Mrs Beresford-Smith were waiting for me in "the withdrawing room". How pretentious is that?'

Just before we reach the front of the house, Toby turns right onto another track, which is signposted 'Tradespeople and Deliveries'. It leads us to a large forecourt at the back of the house, where he neatly parks the car. We retrieve our rucksacks from the boot and he rings the bell by the door. It's answered by a middle-aged woman in a pinafore, who I'm guessing must be the housekeeper.

'Mrs Beresford-Smith has instructed me to give you free rein to go wherever you please, but she asks that you do not enter either the master bedroom or Mr Beresford-Smith's study. Miss Beresford-Smith and her entourage are using the east wing for their preparations. I imagine you'd like to start there?'

She leads us through to the main hallway, a breath-taking double height room with a magnificent, curved staircase leading up to the first floor. We follow her along seemingly endless corridors, until the sound of female voices and laughter indicates that we're nearly there. The housekeeper knocks on a door, waits to be invited in, and then announces us. I'm stunned to see that she curtseys before she speaks.

'Mr Toby Roberts and his assistant for you, Miss Beresford-Smith.'

'Thank you, Margot,' a young woman wrapped in a white towelling dressing gown replies.

Although I have strong suspicions by this point that Mr and Mrs Beresford-Smith are probably awful people, Sophie proves impossible not to like. I was expecting a spoiled diva, but she's kind, down to earth, and takes a genuine interest in everyone around her. I discover that we were actually at school together, although she was a couple of years below me and in a different house, so our paths never crossed. The Beresford-Smiths obviously have good genes because she is incredibly beautiful. Her face is almost doll-like, with wide blue eyes, a straight, well-proportioned nose and a rosebud mouth framed by shiny blonde hair. Her skin is flawless, and I suspect some very expensive dentistry has gone into her perfect teeth. I'm surprised I never noticed her when the whole school came together for chapel.

'I was a bit different at school,' she says, when I remark on it. 'I was going through a gothic, rebellious phase so I dyed my hair black and wore a lot of kohl eyeliner. Mum and Dad absolutely hated it, which only made me do it more. There was one time when I got a temporary tattoo on my arm. I thought Dad was going to have a coronary. Do you remember that, Maudie?' she asks one of the bridesmaids.

'How could I forget?' Maudie replies. 'It was both terrifying and hysterically funny all at once. I've never seen your dad so angry, and you kept him going for ages before you admitted it was temporary.'

'Honestly, she was evil,' Maudie says to me. 'She made up all this stuff about how she'd gone to some dodgy-looking tattoo place, and how she wasn't sure how clean the needle was. I'm amazed he didn't disown her there and then. He did see the funny side eventually, but it took him a while. To be fair, they were a lot more tolerant about the rest of your gothic phase after that, weren't they, Soph?'

The storytelling is interrupted by another knock on the door, and the housekeeper announces the hairstylist and make-up artist. Toby and I unpack and get to work as Sophie and the bridesmaids take turns being primped and polished. I get some nice detail shots of the dress, which is still on its hanger, and one that I'm really pleased with of Sophie's shoes just peeking out of the box. When the time comes for her to get dressed, Toby is banished, but Sophie insists that I stay. It turns out that her 'something blue' is a garter that she pulls midway up her thigh, and I take a couple of (hopefully) tasteful pictures of it in situ.

'Are you going to get James to remove it with his teeth and throw it into the crowd?' another one of the bridesmaids asks. I think her name is Kate.

'I don't know,' Sophie replies. 'On the one hand, it might be fun, but it might also set James' rugby mates off and that would be bad. I might wait until we're alone, that might be safest.'

'Spoilsport!' Kate replies. 'Maybe I'll get one of James' rugby mates to help me with my underwear instead.'

Sophie rolls her eyes exaggeratedly. 'Kate, I love you to bits, but try to control your raging libido, just for my wedding day, would you?' She turns to me with a smile. 'She's hopeless. At my twenty-first birthday party she disappeared with one of the boys for half an hour. She swore blind that nothing had happened, but the grass stains all down the back of her dress told a very different story. At our engagement party she hooked up with Robert, one of James' rugby pals. I'm sure you can spot the theme.'

'I assume Robert is going to be at the wedding?' Kate asks, not making any effort to hide her eagerness.

'He is,' Sophie replies.

'Sorry darling. In that case I can't promise anything,' Kate says, with a giggle.

Sophie sighs theatrically, but smiles indulgently at her.

Once the bride and bridesmaids are all decent, Toby is read-mitted for a few final shots before they head downstairs to the cars. He pauses them at the staircase and takes a couple of them standing one behind the other, before we're joined by Sophie's parents. I almost do a double take when I meet them, because Sophie doesn't look like either of them at first glance. Mr Beresford-Smith is short and squat, with a squashed offset nose that looks like he's been in a few fights, and a thin, mean-looking slit of a mouth. His wife, on the other hand, is waspishly thin, with a pointy nose and dark, glittering eyes. There's something almost rat-like about her. I conclude that Sophie is either adopted, or their recessive genes really came to the fore when they made her.

Toby takes a couple of photos of Sophie with her parents, and then her mum heads off to the church. Three vintage Rolls-Royces stand outside the front door and, with a certain amount of pushing and shoving, everyone finds their place.

'Right,' Toby says to me. 'They're going to let us go first, so we get to the church before them. Have you got everything?'

'Yup, all set, boss,' I reply, as we hurry through the house to retrieve Toby's car. 'Bring on act two.'

20

SEPTEMBER

'You can relax during the service,' Toby tells me, as we park at the church. 'I've already agreed the shots I'm going to take with the vicar. It's always a balancing act; the vicar wants as little disruption to the service as possible, but the couple want the photos. I know some 'togs who just shoot all the way through the service on the basis that the vicar isn't really in a position to stop them, but I think that's disrespectful. I always make a point of phoning and speaking to them in advance and agreeing which points I'll capture.'

He puts on some sort of harness and attaches two cameras to it, one with a standard zoom lens and the other with a telephoto.

'You look like photography's answer to a gun-toting sheriff in the Wild West!' I laugh.

At that point, the bridal cars arrive and we rush over. Toby choreographs various shots, one of Sophie and her father in the car, another of him helping her out, and so on. I focus on the bridesmaids. The vicar fits my stereotype much better than Sharon did; he's an older man with a shock of white hair, half-moon glasses perched on the end of his nose, and little tufts of stubble here and there that he's missed while shaving.

The procession begins to form up and Toby vanishes into the church to capture Sophie walking down the aisle. I slide into a chair at the back. The church is packed to the rafters; the men are all wearing morning coats, and the ladies appear to be in a competition for who can have the largest hat. They're all craning round, trying to get a glimpse of Sophie. There are flowers absolutely everywhere and the air is thick with the scent of expensive perfumes and colognes. It takes me straight back to the way the hallway in my house at school used to smell at the start and end of term, when the parents descended en masse. I can see James, the husband-to-be, standing with his best man at the front. He's a good match for Sophie physically, being tall, broad and good-looking. They will have beautiful children, that's for sure.

The organist strikes up the 'Wedding March', the congregation get to their feet, and we're off. The vicar enters first, followed by Sophie and her father, with the bridesmaids behind. Sophie is beaming, and even her father seems to be enjoying the moment. I smile at Maudie and Kate, and Maudie gives me a friendly wink as she passes. I can't see James' face any more as all the hats are blocking my view, but I hope he's as delighted as she is. Eventually, they obviously reach the front, because the music stops and the vicar's voice comes over the PA system, welcoming everyone and asking them to sit down. As they do so, James comes back into view, and I'm pleased to see that he's looking at Sophie with an expression of complete adoration on his face. This all bodes very well indeed.

I'm aware of Toby appearing by my side. 'How did you do that?' I whisper to him.

'How did I do what?'

'Get back here from the front of the church without ploughing through the wedding procession!'

'Oh, there's a side door that the vicar had opened for me. I went out of that, round the outside and here I am.'

'Do you know anything about James?'

'Not a huge amount. His family are rich, of course, but they're old money. Extensive estates down in the West Country somewhere. I think they're moving down there after the wedding.'

The vicar announces the first hymn, which is a well-known traditional number. I notice that hardly anyone in the congregation is singing. Some of them are mouthing the words, but others are just standing with their mouths shut, staring at the orders of service. Thankfully, I can hear the choir giving it all they've got at the front, including an ambitious descant in the final verse. At the end, the congregation sits down again, and the vows begin. Both Sophie and James say their vows loudly and confidently, and I can hear them clearly. They've obviously been coached, because most of the brides and grooms at other weddings I've been to have been practically inaudible. A big cheer goes up from the congregation when the vicar declares that Sophie and James are husband and wife, and Toby uses his long lens to capture their first kiss from the back of the church.

I let the rest of the service wash over me. It's familiar, and even the vicar's address isn't too bad. He's obviously done his research because he seems to know a lot about how they met, what their interests are, and what attracted them to one another. When it comes to the signing of the register, the bridal party disappears into the vestry and Toby follows them in. The choir sing a couple of pieces, but nobody appears to be listening, if the hubbub of conversation is anything to go by. After ten minutes or so, Toby reappears and takes up position about halfway down the aisle. He's followed by the vicar, who tells the congregation to get their cameras ready because Mr and Mrs Huntingdon-Barfoot are about to make their appearance. The organist strikes up again, and Sophie and James emerge from the vestry, followed by their parents, and then the bridesmaids. Cameras and phones flash madly as they make their way back down the aisle towards the waiting cars. Toby gets them to pause and look back by the door, and then they disappear outside. The rest of the congregation follows in a slightly haphazard manner, and soon the church is empty. I wander around, getting some pictures of the floral decorations, the hassocks that Sophie and James knelt on to be blessed, and any other details that I think might be of interest. After a little while the vicar comes back into the church and approaches me.

'Please do tell Mr Roberts that it was an absolute pleasure to work with him,' he tells me. 'Such a courteous young man, and he stuck to everything we'd agreed. I'm afraid I don't have a very good opinion of your lot; I've had photographers using flash all the way through, which is incredibly distracting, and one fellow even commandeered my pulpit. That was a bridge too far.'

I open my mouth to tell him that I'm not a real wedding photographer, but then think better of it. 'Thank you,' I say. 'I'll let him know.'

Everyone is still milling around outside as I walk out of the church into the sunshine. Some of the women are struggling with their stiletto heels on the grass, which makes me smile. Toby is nowhere to be seen, so I take a few candid shots of some of the guests to pass the time.

'I bloody hate this bit,' a female voice close to me says, and I busy myself fiddling with the camera so I can eavesdrop.

'Yah,' another voice chimes in. 'So boring. Why can't they do the photos at the venue, so we can have a drink at least? I just hope the photographer guy hurries up. I can't decide what I want more, a glass of fizz or a wee!'

They dissolve into fits of giggles and I move on. Eventually, I spot Toby with Sophie, James and their families. He's trying to organise them into a group shot where everyone can be seen, but I can see it's a bit like herding cats. I go over to help him.

'Last one before the confetti shot,' he calls and puts the camera up to his face. As soon as they hear the click, the group starts to disperse and Toby shepherds Sophie and James down towards the lychgate. One of the bridesmaids hands round a basket of confetti and I notice that it's real dried rose petals, rather than the cheaper paper or rice. Toby positions himself, counts to three and a cloud of petals fills the air, along with a cheer from the throwers. After a couple more pictures of them getting into the car, Toby comes to find me.

'We've got to get moving,' he tells me. 'They're going to take a slightly circuitous route to the reception venue, but we need to make sure we're there before them. Are you OK?'

'I'm fine,' I tell him, as we jump into the car and set off. 'I'm actually really enjoying myself, more than some of the guests are, anyway.' I fill him in on the conversation I overheard.

'The reception is at a large country house hotel,' Toby informs me. 'When we get there, I'm going to take Sophie and James off for a few portraits in the grounds. Are you happy to carry on recording the guests? Also, see if you can get access to the dining room. Get details of the table decorations and any favours that have been laid out. Everything in there has been thought about and planned, so it's worth recording. Does that make sense?'

'Yes, boss!' I laugh.

'What's so funny?'

'You. I've noticed this before when you're working. It's like there are two Tobys. There's social Toby, who's quiet and reflective, and then there's work Toby, who is a whip-cracking slave driver!'

'Sorry,' he says. 'I do get very focused when I'm working. I'm sure you'll tell me if I overstep the mark.'

'Don't worry. Like I said, I'm enjoying myself. You keep telling me what you want, and I'll try to do it. OK?'

The reception venue, when we get there, is exactly the sort of grand hotel that I would have expected. Some of the guests have already arrived, and I can see them on the terrace as smartly dressed waiters circulate with champagne and canapés.

'I wonder what all this is costing,' I muse, as Toby and I unpack our gear from the boot.

'Mm. It's got to be the wrong side of half a million, I would have thought. Apparently, they've taken over the whole hotel. The bride and groom are staying here tonight, along with the brides-maids and quite a few of the guests, and there's a big breakfast planned for the morning, before Sophie and James go off on their honeymoon. They're flying first class to some mega-exclusive place in the Seychelles, I believe. At one point they were talking about asking me to stay over and record the breakfast and their departure, but thankfully they changed their minds. I find one day of wedding stressful enough.'

'Do you really find it stressful? Why?'

'Weddings are probably the least favourite part of my job. You've only got one chance to get it right, and if a camera decides to misbehave, or something else goes wrong, you're potentially seriously in the shit. I carry sufficient liability insurance to pay to restage the whole thing if that happens, but that's not the point, is it? They want the memories of the actual day. So yes, it's pressure, but it's also one of the most profitable things I do, so it balances out in the end.'

Before Toby can disappear with the bride and groom, the

guests are all asked to assemble on the lawn. A man fiddles with a large crate and takes out two birds, handing one each to Sophie and James.

'No way!' I whisper to Toby. 'They're doing a dove release. That's so tacky!'

'Shit, I forgot about this bit,' he replies. 'I got the impression Sophie wasn't that fussed about it, but Mrs Beresford-Smith absolutely insisted. Put your camera onto continuous mode. The crowd is going to count down from three, so start shooting just before they release, and keep going until all the doves have gone. There are fifty more in the crate, which will be opened at the same time, so there are going to be birds everywhere.'

'Where do they go, once they're released?' I ask him. 'Do they just fly off and make a new life in the wild?'

'Not likely. They're homing birds, so they'll just fly back to their dovecote until they're needed the next time.'

I set up my camera as Toby has instructed. The crowd counts down from three, and I start shooting. Suddenly, the sky is filled with white doves, all clearly delighted to be free from the crate. As they fly over the assembled guests, there's a shriek from one of the women.

'One of them bloody shat on me!!' she cries, furiously reaching into her handbag to find something to wipe the mess off her jacket with. Without thinking, I take a few shots of her as she dabs away at the stain.

'Don't worry about it, Caroline. It's supposed to be a sign of good luck,' one of the other guests tells her.

'Well, forgive me if I don't feel very lucky!' Caroline retorts, dabbing frantically. 'This is Givenchy, you know.'

As promised, Toby disappears with the bride and groom after the bird release, and I continue taking candid shots of the guests. A member of staff lets me into the dining room, and I take photos of all the details as Toby has instructed. The decorations are tasteful in a way that only comes about when a lot of money has been spent. The table linen is thick and crisp and the glasses shimmer in the light from the windows. The tiered wedding cake stands on a table at one end of the room, and I carefully record some of the details from the icing, which is covered with exquisite tiny sugar roses. Eventually, the guests start to file in and Toby and I withdraw to allow them to enjoy their meal in peace.

'Just the cutting of the cake and the first dance to go, and then we can get out of here,' he tells me, as he hands me a thermos flask and a Tupperware tub back at the car.

'What's this?' I ask.

'Rations, to keep us going. If we're lucky we'll get back in before the chippy closes, but this will keep you going in the meantime. Tea and sandwiches. Not very interesting I'm afraid.'

I realise that I haven't actually eaten anything today and I'm ravenous, so I tear into the sandwiches enthusiastically, washing them down with some tea from the flask.

'Right, final push,' he says when we've finished. 'Ready?'

'I think so. All I can think about is fish and chips now, if I'm honest.'

21

SEPTEMBER

The speeches seem to go on forever, and it's after nine o'clock when we finally start the drive home. As we head back towards Kent, I do some calculations in my head.

'What time does the fish and chip shop close?' I ask Toby.

'Ten o'clock, I think.'

I get my iPhone out and put Toby's address into the navigation app.

'According to this, we won't get back to yours until ten thirty,' I tell him. I'm feeling a bit grumpy now. The sandwich and tea have long worn off, and my stomach is rumbling fiercely. An idea comes to me.

'I tell you what. There's a chippy near my flat that stays open late. It's not quite as good as yours, but it's OK. Why don't we detour via Tunbridge Wells, have something to eat, and then I'll come on with you to collect my car afterwards. What do you think? We're practically going past my door on the way back to Sevenoaks, so it's hardly out of the way.'

Toby considers my plan. 'OK,' he says, after a few moments. 'Let's do that. I've never been to your flat.'

'Very few people have. This is a huge privilege for you, Toby. I hope you realise that?'

'Surely your boyfriends stayed over and saw it?'

'No. One or two came for coffee or lunch, but that's it. I have a golden rule that nobody stays the night.'

'In that case, I am honoured.' He smiles.

He's silent for a while, but I can sense his curiosity.

'It's not a big deal,' I tell him. 'I'm not hiding some huge trauma or anything. It's just that my flat is my space, I have everything exactly as I like it, and I decided early on that I would keep it as a haven just for me. If I let someone stay over then, before I know it, there will be toothbrushes and mess in the bathroom, pants on the floor, and some guy's hairy arse farting into my sofa when he's not raiding my fridge. So, nobody stays the night, and only the special few are allowed across the threshold at all.'

'For someone who professes to like men, you have a very low opinion of them, you know that?'

'That's not fair!'

'It is. You say you like men, but your generalisations about us are pretty critical. "Some guy's hairy arse farting into my sofa", that doesn't sound very pro-men to me.'

I consider his words before replying.

'I do like men. I like their company and, not to put too fine a point on it, I mostly enjoy sex. Or, at least, I used to. It's just that men can be extraordinarily inconsiderate and selfish in my experience. And it's not just the normal things like leaving the loo seat up, although that drives me insane. It's leaving stuff lying around, or not clearing up after themselves. I'll give you an example. The last guy I went out with was called Ross. I met him through Tinder and, on the surface, he seemed perfect. He was good-looking, funny, attentive, and pretty good in the bedroom too. His flat was always immaculately clean, and I thought I'd hit the jackpot.

We went away for a few days to the Lake District together, staying in a little stone cottage. All very romantic, you'd think. Turns out that he was a total slob when he was out of his own space. He left half-drunk cups of coffee around, expecting that I'd clear them up and wipe up the ring marks on the table as well. He left his towel on the bathroom floor every time he showered, and he was pretty careless using the loo, so I'd find splashes of his pee when I went to use it. We broke up as soon as we got back. That's fairly typical of my experience.'

'Did you say anything to him? Give him the opportunity to mend his ways?'

'I'm looking for a man, not a dog to train!'

'I see. So, in order to gain access to your flat, a man has to pass a series of Madison tests that he's unaware of. Did I pass these tests?'

'Yes, but it's different with you because you're a friend rather than a boyfriend. I make no apology for being very protective of my space. As an introvert, it's important to have a refuge where I can go to recharge my batteries.'

'Of all the terms I would use to describe you,' Toby laughs loudly, 'introvert is definitely not among them!'

'How would you describe an introvert then?' I ask him.

'Well, someone more like me I guess,' he says, after his trade-mark pause. 'Quiet, inward-looking, a little shy in company. You're ballsy and confident; you like to be in charge. I would say those were extrovert qualities.'

'Ah, but you've fallen into the classic trap of thinking that extroverts are loud and introverts are shy. In fact, it's nothing to do with that. Do you remember my friend who told me about systematic desensitisation and flooding?'

'How can I forget?' He smiles. 'It was, umm, a pivotal moment in our friendship.'

'She also explained this to me, because I always thought I was an extrovert for the same reasons you just outlined. But what she told me was that the difference between an extrovert and an introvert is nothing to do with how you interact with people, it's about where your strength comes from.'

'Go on.'

'So, to put it bluntly, an extrovert feeds off other people.'

'Like a vampire?'

'No, idiot. They get their energy from being in the company of other people. They don't like being alone; they need social interaction to charge them up, if that makes sense. So, they will seek out situations where they can be in company.'

'OK, and an introvert?'

'Many introverts come across as confident and outgoing, and we can be good in a crowd. The difference is that, unlike the extrovert, being in a crowd doesn't charge us up. Social interaction drains us, and we often have to have some downtime on our own to recharge afterwards. So, much as I like seeing people and socialising, I always sigh with relief when I get home and shut the front door behind me.'

Toby is silent for a long time, digesting this.

'I think,' he pronounces eventually, 'that you're the most fascinatingly confusing person I've ever met.'

'Thank you!' I smile at him in the darkness.

* * *

When we get to Tunbridge Wells, I direct him to a parking space near my flat, we grab the backpacks out of the boot and head for the fish and chip shop. It's just before ten o'clock and it's quiet, so we have to wait while they cook our cod. As soon as we get back, I hastily grab plates, glasses and cutlery and place them on the table. I add tomato ketchup and two glasses of water, and rip open the paper, inhaling the strong scent of vinegar. I'm ravenous and I dig in eagerly. Toby, typically, takes his time unwrapping the fish, arranging it on the plate with the chips, and adding just the right amount of ketchup.

'I know it's not as good as the place over the road from you, but I'm so hungry I don't care,' I tell him after the first few big mouthfuls.

'I can see.' He smiles. 'Would it be easier if you lay on the floor with your mouth open, and I just tipped it all in?'

'Don't tempt me! I think watching the wedding guests eating all that sumptuous food probably didn't help, particularly when that sandwich was the only thing I'd had to eat all day.'

Toby reaches down into his rucksack and pulls out his laptop, firing it up while he eats.

'Can I borrow your camera for a moment?' he asks. 'I want to download your pictures from today, if you don't mind.'

I stuff a couple of ketchup-covered chips into my mouth before retrieving my new camera from the bag and handing it over. Toby flips open the cover, ejects the memory card and sticks it into his laptop. We resume eating in silence as the pictures download.

'I like your flat,' Toby observes later, as I'm clearing away the empty plates and stacking them in the dishwasher. 'It's very cosy. I can see why you love it so much.'

'By cosy, I assume you mean small? I'd give you the tour, but this is pretty much it.'

My flat is probably less than half the size of Toby's. It's in a modern, purpose-built block, and the front door opens directly into the main living space, which is one large open plan room. The kitchen is positioned at one end of it, with my dining table next to it. At the other end is my L-shaped sofa and the TV, along with my bookshelves, which are crammed with travel books and pictures of friends and family. There's a small corridor leading to my bedroom and bathroom, and that's it. It's not big or lavish, but it's mine and I love it. The only thing it lacks are a couple of houseplants, but I learned early on that frequent travel and houseplants don't mix.

'It's nice though. Very you.'

'What do you mean?'

'I don't really know. It's a very feminine space, but not floral or chintzy. Does that make sense? It's sophisticated – Chanel rather than Laura Ashley.'

I decide that's a compliment and smile at him, just as the progress bar on his laptop screen disappears, indicating that all the images from my card have downloaded.

'Right, let's have a quick look, shall we?'

I feel suddenly nervous, like he's marking my homework, and I'm astonished to discover I'm holding my breath, awaiting his verdict. He flicks through them silently, pausing every so often to examine one in detail.

'These are excellent,' he declares when he's seen them all. 'They're exactly what I was looking for. You've got an eye for the details, and you've thought about composition and depth of field. I love the picture of the bride's shoes in the box particularly, but there are a lot here that I can use. Thank you!'

'You're welcome.' I smile, blushing slightly from the compliments. 'You've been a good teacher.'

Toby pulls the card out of the laptop and pops it back into my camera, then slips his laptop back into the rucksack. He rummages around in one of the other pockets for a bit, and then retrieves an envelope, which he hands to me. I open it and find it stuffed with twenty-pound notes.

'What's this?' I ask him.

'Your fee. It's five hundred pounds, I hope that's OK?'

'Oh, Toby, you don't need to pay me. I enjoyed it!'

'I do need to pay you. You've earned it fair and square, and I've done extremely well out of this wedding.'

'Yes, but I did it as your friend. You've already given me a camera today; I don't think I can accept this as well.' I push the envelope back towards him.

'Paul's my friend too, but he'd expect a cut if he came on a job with me. It's only fair, Madison. I charged the Beresford-Smiths a small fortune to shoot Sophie's wedding, and your images form part of the package they've paid for. I wouldn't be happy to use them if I didn't pay you for them. Forget about me, imagine this is a payment from the Beresford-Smiths.' He nudges the envelope back in my direction.

'Are you sure?'

'I am.'

Toby asks to use the bathroom before we leave, and I'm pleased to see he's left the seat down when I go in after him. In fact, now I come to think about it, I don't think he's ever left the seat up. I suppose I'm only noticing it properly now because of the conversation we had earlier.

* * *

It's past midnight by the time I return home after collecting my car. Even though it's been a really long day, I'm still wide awake, so I pour myself a glass of wine and settle on the sofa to drink it. I expect the wedding is winding up now, with just a few diehards milking every drop out of the free bar. The envelope with the five hundred pounds in it is still on my dining table, and I mentally run through some ideas for things I could spend it on.

As I reflect on the day, a thought strikes me. Whenever I invite someone to my flat for the first time, I'm usually slightly on edge all the time they're here, and secretly relieved when they leave. Apart from the anxiety I felt while Toby was reviewing my pictures, I felt completely comfortable with him. It reminds me a bit of how I used to feel when Charley popped round, in the days when she lived in the flat opposite with her then-boyfriend, Josh. I know she'll be asleep, but I fish out my phone to send her a WhatsApp message.

Invited Toby to have fish and chips at my place on the way back from the wedding. It was nice, and he even left the loo seat down! Think I've lucked out on the GBF stakes…

I can feel my eyelids starting to droop, so I drain my glass and head off to bed.

22

DECEMBER

'What are you doing on Saturday?' Toby asks me when I drop him at his studio. We've just finished our sixth and final trip of the year, a marathon eight days in Cape Town. It was my first time in the city, and we've worked hard to take in all the places recommended in the famil packs, including Table Mountain, the Victoria and Alfred Waterfront, Camps Bay, as well as the various bars and restaurants on Long Street. We've toured the winelands, done a day safari to the Aquila Reserve (where my telephoto lens came into its own) and visited the Cape of Good Hope. On top of all of that we've stayed in four different hotels. It's been exhausting and exhilarating at the same time, but now I'm just feeling tired and grimy from the eleven-hour overnight flight home.

'I don't think I'm doing anything, why?'

'I've got a free day. I thought we could celebrate our first year of collaboration by doing something that's neither travel nor photography related.'

'What do you have in mind?'

'I don't know yet. Why don't I surprise you?'

'I'm not a great fan of surprises.'

'Trust me, it's not going to be anything bad.'

'If it's skydiving you may not survive the day.'

'OK, no skydiving, I promise. Anything else?'

I think for a while. 'I don't want to be cold, wet or dirty. So, no assault courses or anything silly like that.'

'No assault courses, got it. Shame, because an assault course is exactly what I thought you'd love most,' he says, with a wink. 'Anything else?'

'Not that I can think of,' I reply.

'Good. I'll collect you from your flat at nine in the morning. I'll text you the day before to give you an idea of the dress code. OK?'

When I get home, I take a long, hot shower and wash my hair to get rid of the weird aroma that seems to cling to me after long-haul flights. It's a mixture of the overall smell of the plane and a slight whiff of the breakfast they served us before we landed. I don't sleep well on planes, so my bed looks particularly inviting, but I resolve to keep going rather than risk messing up my body clock. I can have an early night tonight if necessary.

Once I've restocked the fridge and put a load of washing on, I ring Charley.

'Oh, hi, Mads,' she answers, sounding slightly breathless. 'Can you hang on a minute?'

'I can call back if I'm interrupting,' I tell her.

'No, it's fine. I've just got to corral Amelia. Hang on.'

I hear the sound of doors being closed, followed by a few whimpers from Amelia, who is obviously cross at having her freedom curtailed.

'Sorry about that. Since she started crawling, she's become a complete liability. She's into everything! We've had to buy covers for all the plug sockets, and we've got baby gates across all the doorways. It's like living in Fort Knox, but she still finds ways to put herself in danger. She's trying to walk, so she'll grab at anything to pull herself up. God knows what it'll be like when she actually starts walking. I think I might have to buy a lead. Anyway, how was your trip?'

I fill her in on the details, although she has to stop me regularly to prevent Amelia from hurting herself. I can sense her exasperation mounting, and I'm just about to suggest I call back when things come to a head.

'Oh, for fuck's sake!' she exclaims. 'Sit there and I'll put the bloody *Teletubbies* on for you.'

'I try to limit her screen time,' she explains to me a few moments later as the theme tune plays in the background, 'but sometimes putting her in front of the TV is the only way I can get anything done. Thank goodness I'm back at work three days a week now. I need adult contact to keep me sane. Does that make me a bad mother? I look at the other mothers at nursery, and they all seem much more together than me, somehow.'

'Of course you're not a bad mother!' I tell her. 'Amelia's thriving, isn't she? I bet those other mothers either have nannies, or they're so full of Xanax they don't even know what day of the week it is. If you went to the nursery at drop-off time on a Saturday or Sunday you'd probably find them all there, wandering round in a daze and bumping into the door, like flies trying to find their way out of a locked window.'

Charley laughs softly. 'Thanks, Mads. I can always rely on you to lift my spirits. So, how's the GBF?'

'He's fine,' I tell her. 'He's planning a surprise for me on Saturday, to celebrate our first year of working together.'

'But you hate surprises! What on earth is he thinking?'

'I know, but I was tired, and he promised it would be something nice. Maybe I should ring and cancel, though. I don't know. I'll think about it. How's Ed?'

'Busy. He's representing the soon to be ex-wife of a Russian oligarch. Trying to identify the assets is proving to be a nightmare, as you'd expect. He's not allowed to tell me much about it, but occasionally he drops a detail here and there. It's a totally different world when you're arguing about who gets which yacht, and whether she should continue to have use of a private jet!'

'I hope he's not abandoning his parental duties.'

'He's trying not to, but he is a bit. He tried working from home a couple of times, but it's such a madhouse here when Amelia's awake that he soon had to give that up. So, he's going into the office, and sometimes he doesn't get home until after I've gone to bed. We had a couple of arguments about it, because I suspected him of using work as an excuse to get out of doing his fair share with his daughter, but deep down I knew I was being unreasonable. He is potty about her and makes a real effort when he's here, so it's not all bad. He's found some baby floating thing that they do at the local swimming pool on Saturday mornings, and he takes her every week so I can have a lie-in. I think there might be a hidden agenda there though.'

'Why?'

'Well, he's started going on about how much easier things are now that she sleeps through the night and, the other day, he actually suggested we could try for another baby.'

'Another one? What did you say?'

'I told him I'd chop his cock off if it came anywhere near me wearing fewer than three super-strength condoms. I think he got the message!' she laughs.

After a few more minutes of conversation, we book a date in the diary for me to pop in and drop off their Christmas presents, and I ring off.

* * *

I'm sitting on the sofa typing up the Cape Town trip on Friday when the text arrives from Toby.

Hi. I will collect you at 9 a.m. Dress casually and warmly. You won't be cold/wet/dirty, but we will be outdoors for part of the time. Bring walking boots. Tx

My heart sinks. What have I let myself in for?

My mood has barely improved when he arrives to collect me and, after I've given him a few monosyllabic answers, we complete the first part of the journey in silence. At least it isn't raining; the sky is cloudless and it's a perfect, crisp winter day. After a while, I start to suspect where he's taking me, and my spirits lift a little.

'Are we going to Hever Castle?'

'We might be. Have you been before?'

'No, never, but I've always wanted to go.'

'The gardens aren't great at this time of year, but we can look inside the house and walk around the lake. I've booked us into a pub for lunch.'

At the sound of a pub lunch my bad mood lifts completely. Toby parks the car and we put on our coats and walking boots. I can see that the gardens would be much better in summer, but they're still magnificent, and the castle is fascinating. I stand in Anne Boleyn's childhood bedroom and try to imagine her in it as a girl, full of hopes and dreams, completely unaware of the tragic direction her life will end up taking.

'It's extraordinary to think that it's still privately owned, isn't it?' Toby remarks, as we set off on a walk around the lake. 'I wonder whether the owners ever close it and just come and live in it for a bit. That would be fun, don't you think?'

'I don't know,' I reply. 'What if it's haunted? What if you're lying in bed and Anne Boleyn appears, waving her severed head at you?'

'How do you think that works, if you're a ghost?' he counters. 'Do you have to stick your head on to be able to see and talk, or can you do those things with it detached?'

Our conversation about the practicalities of being a ghost carries us all the way around the lake, and most of the way to the pub. The pub itself is in a tiny hamlet, but the number of cars in the car park indicates that it's popular. A blast of warm air greets us as Toby opens the door and ushers me into the bar, which has plenty of tables and a roaring fire at one end. Everything on the menu sounds delicious, and I sip my cold white wine thoughtfully as I try to decide what to have.

'I chose this because I remembered what you said about poncy food on our first trip,' Toby explains. 'I could have gone for fish and chips, as that's our signature dish, but I thought I'd broaden the horizons a bit. There is fish and chips on the menu if you want to go traditional though.'

'No, I think I fancy a burger,' I tell him. 'I reckon a burger tells you all you need to know about a place. If it's good, then you can bet that everything else on the menu is good. If it's not, then chances are the rest isn't great either.'

Toby goes up to the bar to place our order and returns with a second glass of wine for me. I'm surprised to notice that I've pretty much drained the first one already. I make a note to drink more slowly, otherwise I'll be asleep for the whole afternoon.

'I need to ask your advice about something,' Toby says. I look at him and notice that he has his serious face on.

'Go on,' I reply. My mind is already feeling slightly fuzzy from the wine and the warmth in the room.

'Well, the thing is, I've met someone special.'

Suddenly, I'm fully alert, and I'm surprised by the pang of jealousy that shoots through me. I've always known he and I would never be more than friends, but the idea that he's met someone else, who is going to muscle in on our friendship and take him away from me, hurts in a way that I'm unprepared for. I take a moment to compose myself, and remind myself to approach this carefully, because Toby has always been very guarded about stuff like this.

'That's great!' I say, plastering a smile on my face and trying to sound sincere. 'Congratulations!'

'It's a little early for that, I'm afraid.'

'Why?'

'It's complicated. I'm in the friend zone at the moment, and I don't know if they feel the same way about me as I do about them. Part of me thinks it's safer to leave things as they are and not risk ruining a friendship, but then I wonder whether I'm missing a chance at happiness. What would you do?'

My first thought is to tell him to say nothing, but I realise that's just me selfishly trying to stop him from pursuing a relationship with this person. Toby feels like a part of my life now and, although I know he'd make an effort to keep our friendship going, I also know that we'd inevitably drift apart if things got serious between him and whoever the other guy is. I tell myself to pull myself together. I've been hoping he'd find a boyfriend almost from the moment I've known him. Maybe it'll be fine.

'What's your gut feeling about how they would react?' I ask him.

'I can't call it. On one level we're really close, but I don't know if it's enough to get me out of the friend zone.'

'Have they given you any signals?'

'No.'

'Tricky. Do they have any friends you could sound out?'

'None that I know well enough to have that conversation with.'

'If they aren't giving you any signals, I think I'd play it safe if I were you. Give it time and see what happens. If they're interested in you, they'll find a way of letting you know.'

'Yes, you're probably right. Ah, here's our lunch.'

I'm fairly certain I see a look of disappointment flash across his face. As soon as it appears, though, it's gone, and I don't think any more about it. The burger is excellent, and the wine combines with my full stomach and the fresh air earlier to make me feel pleasantly dozy. He doesn't broach the subject again, but I do find it playing on my mind after he's dropped me back home. I'm not sure my motives were as pure as they could have been when I told Toby to bide his time, but I can't help feeling a bit possessive of him. This person, whoever he is, had better be worthy of him.

23

CHRISTMAS EVE – THE MORNING AFTER THE GALA DINNER

'What the bloody hell are you doing here, Toby?'

He looks at me blankly from the bed.

'You invited me,' he says.

'Bollocks. I would never have done that. You know how I feel about people staying over.'

'I do, which is why it was such a surprise.'

The soothing effect of the shower is wearing off and I can feel the throbbing headache returning. I need paracetamol before I can deal with this. I grab the packet from the drawer in my bedside cabinet and swallow two, washing them down with water from the glass on top. Another anomaly: how did I remember to bring fresh water to bed, but not take off my bra? It's all too confusing, and I slump back onto the bed and close my eyes. My stomach, having emptied itself so comprehensively when I woke up, cramps in protest at the addition of the pills and water, and I silently beg it to keep them down; I need to be well enough to drive to my parents' house in Oxfordshire later, and the very thought of being anywhere near a car at the moment makes me feel nauseous.

'How bad is it?' Toby asks.

'It's bad. How much did I have to drink?'

'You did put it away,' he chuckles. 'After that chap went for you—'

'Peter,' I interrupt. 'He's always had a problem with me. I have no idea why.'

'Well, you shouldn't be in any doubt now. He was pretty explicit.'

'I remember him being pretty upset about us winning the award.' An image of a puce-faced Peter, with little bits of spittle flying out of his mouth, swims into my mind. I remember being shocked by the ferocity of his tirade, but I'm struggling to remember what he said.

'That's putting it mildly.'

I try to cast my mind back to the previous evening, to see if I can remember the conversation. After a while a few phrases start to trickle to the surface.

'Did he call me spoilt?' I ask.

'To be precise, and leaving out the worst of the expletives, he called you a spoilt little bitch who'd had life handed to you on a plate. He accused you of treating your job as nothing more than a hobby, something to amuse you until your trust fund kicked in. How you had no idea what hard graft was, and that you should have been fired for your incompetent first review of the Bellavista instead of being given awards. There was quite a lot more, but that's the basic gist of it. It was pretty strong stuff.'

'Please tell me I didn't reciprocate. I can tell you that there's definitely no trust fund, so I need this job. Giving one of the editors of *Voyages Luxes* a piece of my mind is not going to go down well, however much I might have wanted to put the little prick right.'

'No, you were brilliant! When he finished, all you said was "I'm very sorry you feel that way." It earned you a round of applause from the rest of the table, who were all listening in. To be fair to them, he was so loud it was impossible not to. I think that was the final straw for him, because he stormed off and we didn't see him again. Then you bought the champagne and, well, here we are.'

'Did I really invite you to stay?'

'You did and, even if you hadn't, I would have stayed anyway, regardless of your golden rule. You were pretty far gone, and I was worried you might throw up in your sleep and suffocate yourself. I tried to stay awake for as long as I could, to keep an eye on you, but obviously I didn't quite manage it. Sorry.'

'Bloody hell, I feel awful. Why did you let me drink so much?'

'Hang on, don't start trying to blame this on me! I did suggest you slowed down at one point, but you gave me such a filthy look that I didn't dare intervene again.'

'I'm supposed to be driving to Oxfordshire later. How am I going to do that without throwing up?'

'You also promised to drop me home, remember? I'd like you a little bit more with it than you are now before I get in a car with you.'

I glance around the room. Something is missing, and it takes me a while to work out what it is.

'Where's my dress?'

'I hung it up in the wardrobe for you.'

Suddenly, all the pieces of the jigsaw that I haven't been able to put together yet, the T-shirt, bra, thong, make-up and water, slot into place.

'Did you... Did you *undress* me?'

'If I hadn't helped you out of your dress, you probably would have gone to bed wearing it and ruined it. I knew I'd find the T-shirt under your pillow.'

'Was I that bad?'

'I'm afraid so. You were all floppy and you just kept muttering on about how much you wanted to sleep, except you were slurring your words, so it sounded more like "schleep". It was quite funny, actually.'

'It doesn't feel very funny this morning, but at least it explains why I was still wearing that bloody uncomfortable thong when I woke up. Why did you leave my bra on? You know I don't wear a bra to bed.'

Toby blushes. 'Two reasons really. Although I've seen you naked lots of times, it still seemed too intimate a thing to do. Also, I'm not entirely sure how the clasp works.'

Despite the headache, I can't help laughing.

'I suppose I should thank you for looking after me,' I admit.

'You're welcome. Now, what are we going to do to help you to feel better? There's only one guaranteed hangover cure I know.'

'If you mention hair of the dog I will throw up, probably on you.'

'No. You need fat, and you need carbs. Basically, only a full English breakfast is going to save you from this, the bigger the better.'

My stomach lurches horribly at the thought.

'I don't think so,' I tell him.

'Trust me. You'll feel like a new woman afterwards. Why don't you throw on some clothes while I look up the nearest greasy spoon, and I'll take you out for breakfast.'

Toby busies himself with his phone while I dry my hair. Once that's done, I stand up, slip out of the towel and start getting dressed. I've been naked in front of Toby so many times now that I don't really think about it, and he's showing no interest, as usual.

Once I've got knickers and a fresh bra on, I rummage in the wardrobe and end up with a pair of black leggings and a grey soft cotton hooded top. I put a pair of thick soled trainers on my feet, hoping that the cushioning will protect my delicate head from too much movement as I walk.

'Found one.' Toby gets out of bed and starts putting on his dress shirt and trousers, which were folded neatly next to the bed on his side.

'Don't you want a shower?' I ask him.

'I'll have one when I get home. I wouldn't want to run the risk of leaving a pube or something in yours. I'd be ostracised for ever!'

'A pube in the shower would be forgivable as a first offence,' I call to him as I return my towel to the rail in the bathroom. 'A pube on the soap, however, would be an entirely different matter.'

'I don't even want to think about it,' he calls back.

'You're OK. I don't have soap in the shower anyway. It just goes all manky.'

* * *

As we step out of the apartment block into the cold, crisp December morning, I inhale deeply, hoping that the fresh air will help to clear my head. We make our way along the pavements, with Toby checking his phone periodically to make sure we're going the right way. After ten minutes or so, we reach the café. I steel myself for the smell of frying and my stomach lurches again as Toby pushes open the door and leads me inside.

It's busy in here, and we're directed to the last remaining free table. The first thing I notice is that there's no stench of stale oil, like there was at Nora's. Instead, the much more welcome aroma of freshly ground coffee fills the air, and I breathe it in appreciatively. We remove our coats and hang them on the backs of our chairs, and I notice one or two of the other customers glancing curiously at Toby, still wearing his dinner jacket in the morning. They probably think he's doing the male equivalent of the walk of shame after a night of wild sex with me. Do men have a walk of shame, or is it more of a walk of pride? I'm struggling to care.

'What can I get you?' the server asks, with a strong Australian accent. He's a hipster young man with a long beard, wearing a crisp white T-shirt, black jeans and an apron emblazoned with the name of the café.

'Can we have two full English breakfasts please with extra egg, hash brown and bacon, and a flat white and a latte to drink?' Toby asks.

'Great choice. Coming right up!' the server replies and disappears towards the kitchen.

'I didn't even get a chance to look at the menu!' I complain. 'I might have wanted something else.'

'Trust me, you don't.'

The server returns with our coffees and I sip mine slowly, taking care not to overwhelm my grumbling stomach.

'It's a bit of a step up from Nora's, isn't it?' Toby remarks.

'Yes, I can't believe I've never been here before,' I reply.

'It had excellent reviews when I looked it up,' he tells me, 'especially the full English, so I have high hopes.'

Sure enough, the breakfast looks delicious when it arrives. Tentatively, I cut a piece off one of the hash browns, dip it in the egg yolk, and pop it in my mouth.

'Mmm, this is good,' I murmur, as I take small mouthfuls of bacon, sausage mushrooms, and baked beans. I add a splodge of brown sauce to the plate and sigh contentedly as the food begins to work its magic. I can feel my headache receding, and my stomach begins to rumble with pleasure.

'Feeling better?' Toby smiles.

'Much better. This was an excellent idea.'

'I told you. Best hangover cure there is, apart from shutting your finger in a door.'

'I've never heard of that one!'

'Neither had I, until it happened to me. It was the only time I was invited to a party by someone from school. It was his eighteenth, and his mates had concocted some sort of punch in a huge bowl. I have no idea what was in it, but it was potent. When I woke in the morning, the pain was so intense that I was convinced I was going to die, and I was throwing up every five minutes. I couldn't face the bus ride home, but one of the other guys there took pity on me and offered to drive me. We had to stop several times on the way for me to be sick, but he was very good-natured about it. He kept saying, "We've all been there, mate," and laughing. When he dropped me off, I wasn't looking what I was doing and shut my finger in the door. My finger hurt like hell for a while, but the headache and nausea completely disappeared. Weird, huh?'

'Yeah, I think I'll take a rain check on that one. This is better.'

'I think you're right. It took me ages to live it down at school, as I'm sure you can imagine.'

The rest of the meal passes pretty much in silence, as we focus on our food. Much to my surprise, especially given the extras that Toby ordered, I clear my plate. Toby pays the bill and I link my arm through his as we saunter back towards my flat.

'So, what else do I need to know about last night?' I ask him.

'Well—' he looks at me with a sparkle in his eye '—you told me that you loved me.'

'Did I?'

'Yes. You said, "I bloody love you, Toby Roberts." It made my evening, even though you were very drunk. In vino veritas, I reckon.'

'Of course I love you!' I exclaim. 'You and Charley are my best friends, and I love you both.'

Toby stops walking and detaches his arm from mine. I turn to look at him and, to my astonishment, he looks stunned, like I've slapped him.

'What? What's the matter?' I ask him.

'Nothing. Never mind,' he replies, curtly, and starts walking again. I notice he's thrust his hands into his pockets, so that I can't link arms with him again.

'Come on, Toby. Something's bothering you. Tell me what it is,' I urge. I grab his arm to force him to stop. When he turns to face me, I can see that his eyes are watery, as if he's on the verge of tears.

'What is it? What have I said?'

'I'm sorry Madison,' he replies, his voice shaking with emotion, 'I can't do this any more.'

'Do what?'

'Do you remember, when we went to Hever, I told you I'd met someone, but that I was in the friend zone?'

Relief washes through me. This is about the guy he met. He's probably given him the brush-off and he's hurting. I can deal with this.

'Yes. What happened?'

'Did you really not know who I was talking about?'

This question catches me by surprise. Why would I know who he was talking about? The only one of his friends I've met properly is Paul, and I'm pretty sure Toby hasn't fallen in love with him. They've known each other for ages, so surely something would have happened by now if it was going to happen. Also, I'm pretty sure Paul is straight.

'Is it someone I know?' I ask, tentatively.

'Oh, for fuck's sake, Madison! Do you honestly not have a clue?'

I stare at him. I literally have no idea what he's on about.

'It's you, Madison. I've fallen in love with you.'

24

CHRISTMAS EVE

My first instinct is to laugh. He's got to be joking, right? But one look at his anguished face tells me that he's deadly serious. I'm completely confused; nothing makes sense here.

'But, Toby, you're gay!'

'What? What on earth made you think that?'

'You. You know, the way you are!' I feel like I'm lost in fog, with no landmarks to help me get my bearings. 'For example, the very emphatic way you said, right back when I first met you, that I had *nothing* to fear from you.'

'I was being a gentleman!' Toby exclaims, almost shouting.

'But you've never shown any interest in me! Even when I've been naked around you, you've just buried yourself in your laptop, or whatever.'

'Would you have preferred it if I'd stared at you, maybe wolf-whistled a few times? For God's sake! Tell me, what else about me makes you so certain I'm homosexual?'

I stand there like a goldfish. My mouth opens and closes but nothing comes out. I can't believe I've got this so completely wrong. I was so certain he was gay.

'Well, this has been a fucking car crash,' he says, when it's clear I have no answer for him.

'I'm really sorry, Toby. If I'd have known...'

'Yes, well, evidently you didn't. I feel like a total idiot.'

'You're not an idiot, Toby. It's just that this has come so totally out of the blue, I don't know what to make of it.'

'I think the fact that you're not dancing for joy tells me everything I need to know, don't you?'

He looks angry and hurt, and I still don't know what to say to him. I want to make this better, but it's as if some invisible barrier has come down between us.

'Look,' he says, after an uncomfortable pause, 'I think I need some time, a bit of space. I'm sure you understand.'

'Of course I do,' I say quickly, 'I'll drop you off at your studio and we'll talk after Christmas, when I've had a chance to digest all of this.'

'Actually, I think I'll get a taxi. I don't think I can be around you right now. I'll call you when I'm ready.'

He turns and strides away. I want to call out to him, but the words won't come. I watch his retreating back, willing him to turn, but he doesn't even glance back. My mind is stuck on just one question: What the fuck just happened?

* * *

I don't know how long I stand there, immobile, looking in the direction that Toby took. I'm not even sure what I'm expecting to happen. Is he going to come back, smiling, and tell me that this was all a joke, a prank he dreamed up?

'Are you all right, dear?'

I turn to see an elderly lady looking at me with concern on her face.

'I'm sorry?' I ask her.

'I wondered if you were all right. I don't mean to pry, but I was waiting for my bus over there, and I saw you and your young man walk past, and then you seemed to have a bit of an argument and he stormed off, and you've just been standing there for nearly five minutes without moving.'

Shit. I need to pull myself together. I'm starting to worry innocent passers-by.

'I'm fine,' I tell her. 'I've just had a bit of a shock, but I'm fine now. Thank you.' I give her what I hope is a warm smile and set off towards home. When I get back to the flat, everything looks the same. How can it look the same when, within the space of a couple of hours, everything has changed, and everything I thought I knew has been turned on its head? My headache, soothed by the breakfast, has decided to reappear. I walk into my bedroom; there's a dent in the duvet where Toby sat down to do up his shoes. I hastily smooth it over, before ripping off all the bedclothes and shoving them in the washing machine. I don't want any trace of him in here. How dare he drop a bombshell like that and just disappear? How am I supposed to make sense of this? This is the reason why I've never allowed anyone to stay over; the atmosphere in my flat, my sanctuary, feels polluted and foul. My head throbs as I yank the hoover out of its cupboard and hurl it angrily over all the floors. As I feverishly wipe down every surface, I realise I'm muttering obscenities like a madwoman.

By midday there's nothing left to clean. I've been over the entire flat and it's spotless. I've put new sheets on the bed, and I just need to wait for the tumble dryer to finish before I leave for Oxfordshire. I've packed my bag and loaded it, along with the presents for my parents, into the car. I opened all the windows earlier to refresh the place with clean air, so it's now freezing in here and I'm sitting huddled in my coat. After what feels like an age, the tumble dryer bleeps to let me know that it has finished. I remove the sheets, fold them and stack them in the airing cupboard, before doing my customary pre-departure tour, making sure that all the windows are closed and locked, and everything is turned off. My rage has subsided now and the fresh air, aided by another dose of paracetamol, has taken the edge off my headache.

The Christmas Eve traffic is typically awful and the drive to Oxfordshire takes nearly four hours. I use the time to continue to try to make sense of what happened this morning. How could I have been so wrong about Toby? I was so absolutely convinced he was gay. And how on earth do we come back from this? I try to work out how I feel about him. I meant what I said when I told him I loved him, but I'd never even contemplated that we could be anything more than friends. I try to picture us as a couple, but my mind just isn't able to make that shift. Maybe he's right. Maybe we both need space to come to terms with his revelations, and then we can talk about it after Christmas like the grown-ups that we both are, and figure out what to do.

* * *

It's dark when I arrive at my parents' house, but I'm illuminated by the blaze from the security lights as I pull up behind my mom's BMW. The dog has obviously noticed that the lights have been triggered and I hear him barking inside. I retrieve my case and the presents from the boot and lug them across the gravel driveway to the front door, where I let myself in with my key.

'Hi, Mom!' I call, as the dog bounds up to me, wagging his tail furiously. I set my case down and fuss over him while he wriggles in absolute delight.

My mother emerges from the kitchen and wraps her arms

around me. She's wearing a dress and high heels, with an apron over the top, and she smells of her trademark Jo Malone scent.

'Hi, honey. You're very late, I was beginning to worry.'

'I'm sorry. I was a bit late leaving and then the traffic was awful.'

'Well, you're here now, and that's all that matters. Your father isn't home yet. He rang earlier to say something had cropped up that he needed to deal with, but he hopes that he'll be home in time for dinner. He's looking forward to seeing you. Why don't you take your stuff up to your room, freshen up, and then I think we can treat ourselves to a glass of wine, don't you?'

At the mention of wine, my stomach heaves slightly. I've still got the slight trace of a headache and don't really fancy anything to drink, but Mom will think it odd if I don't have a glass with her, and I don't want to admit to being hung over. Both of my parents have strong views about 'people who drink too much'.

'I see you've entered into the festive spirit already,' I tease her. 'I hope you haven't been raiding Dad's cellar. You know he'll notice.'

'Heavens no! I think your father has set aside a couple of bottles for Christmas Day, but I wouldn't dare set foot down there. Apart from anything else, I wouldn't have the first clue what I was looking at. No, I've got a bottle of Sancerre from Waitrose as it's a special occasion.'

Dad's wine cellar is a bit of a standing joke between Mom and me. He's practically teetotal, but you'd never know from the size of it. Plenty of bottles seem to go down there, but very few ever come back up again. He told me once that he likes to buy fine wines young and then sell them on when they've matured and the price has risen, but I think he just likes looking at his collection and cataloguing it.

After bringing my bag up to my old room, I splash some water on my face and dry it, before changing out of my leggings and hoodie into a dress. My father stops short of dressing for dinner, but we are all expected to look smart. I put on some simple make-up, brush my hair and tie it back, give myself a quick spritz of scent, and wriggle my feet into a pair of black ballet pumps.

'Ah, there you are,' my mom says, as I walk into the kitchen. 'Your father just called from the car. He should be here in around an hour. I've opened the bottle and poured us each a glass.' I'm relieved to see that her idea of a glass of wine is still little more than a thimbleful, as that's probably as much as I can cope with, even as hair of the dog.

'Thanks, Mom.'

'I'm pretty much ready for tomorrow, I think. I hope you don't mind but I've invited the Wheelers to join us for lunch. Their children live overseas, so it's just the two of them, and I thought that sounded a bit sad. We're going British on the main course, with turkey and roast potatoes, but I'm rebelling on the pudding because I can't understand how anyone could like Christmas pudding, so I've made a pumpkin pie instead.'

My mom is an excellent cook, and the kitchen is very much her domain. I'm not sure if my dad even goes in there. They both have very traditional views where gender roles are concerned; he earns the money and she runs the house. It seems to work for them, but I would find it suffocating. Sometimes, in the summer, Dad invites a load of his business friends over and makes a big show of cooking large quantities of meat on his enormous, gas-fired barbecue, but all the hard work has already been done in the background by Mom, who has prepared all the salads, the marinades and so on.

'Tell me about you,' Mom is saying. 'How's work, and your homosexual friend? Tell me about Charley's baby, she sounds completely adorable.'

'Work is good. Toby and I won an award for the most innovative content at the gala dinner last night,' I tell her. My gut wrenches slightly as I say Toby's name, and I momentarily wonder what he's doing now.

'And the baby?'

'You would absolutely love her, but she's driving poor Charley round the bend. She's still into everything, but she is the cutest thing. Charley and Ed completely adore her, and she'll definitely have Ed wrapped around her little finger when she's older.' I get out my phone to show Mom some pictures, and she coos with delight.

'I would so love to have given you a brother or sister,' she sighs. 'I always dreamed of a big family.'

'I know, Mom,' I tell her, pulling her into an awkward hug. 'But it wasn't to be, and you're stuck with little old me.'

Thankfully, before she can go any further down into the rabbit hole of her inability to have any more children, the security lights come on again, indicating that my dad has arrived home. The dog rushes off to grab a toy to present and he, Mom and I assemble in the hallway. Once more I'm reminded of a Jane Austen novel and, for a moment, I wonder whether I should stand behind my mother to indicate my lower rank as his unmarried daughter.

As my father comes through the door, the dog can contain himself no longer and launches himself at him. Dad makes a huge fuss of him, rubbing and patting his flanks and scratching his ears, before he turns his attention to us.

'Hi, honey,' he says to my mom, giving her a kiss on the cheek. 'Sorry I got held up. There was some paperwork missing on a deal we're closing in Malaysia, and I had to track it down. It's all under control now, so I'm ready for Christmas. I will have to do some work on the twenty-sixth, but I can do that from here.'

His eyes alight on me. 'Madison!' he exclaims. 'How is my favourite daughter?' This is a long-standing joke, dating back to a difficult time in our relationship when I was a teenager and he and I didn't seem to agree on anything. 'No matter what you think or say, you'll always be my favourite daughter,' he used to say. In the years since, I've learned that it's easier for everyone if I don't contradict him and our relationship has improved, even if we're not exactly close. He's a slightly forbidding personality, and he's never made any secret of the fact that he disapproves of my job.

I step forward to give him an awkward hug. 'Hi, Daddy. Merry Christmas.'

Mom fusses over him, pouring him a glass of lemon barley water before he goes upstairs to change. Later, as we sit down to our dinner, he does at least make an effort to ask about my work, but it's not long before he's back on his hobby horse.

'What I don't understand, Madison, is where this job is *going*. As a freelance writer you have zero job security, zero opportunity for promotion, no pension or medical benefits. You're over thirty years old, for God's sake! If you're not going to marry, then you need a career that's going someplace, not this piecemeal hand-to-mouth existence you've had going on for the last however many years. You've had your fun, but now it's time to wake up and smell the coffee.'

'Madison won an award yesterday, didn't you, honey? Tell your father,' my mom prompts, trying to help me out without appearing to take my side. 'What was it? Most innovative content?'

'That's great,' my father counters, 'but awards don't pay the mortgage, do they, Madison?'

'No, sir,' I concede.

It's going to be a long Christmas.

25

DECEMBER

After two full days with my parents, I'm relieved to get back home on the day after Boxing Day. I find the atmosphere in their house somewhat oppressive. My mother always appears happy on the surface, but there's a slightly manic, brittle edge to her, as if she's only just keeping it together and it could all disintegrate at any moment. My father is a brooding presence when he's at home, devouring either the *Financial Times* or some weighty tome about a famous historical general or political leader while Mom waits on him hand and foot. I think the only truly happy and joyous occupant of that house is the dog. I suspect he's a surrogate child, a vessel for them to pour their love into, that loves them uncondi-tionally in return and doesn't answer back. Certainly much easier to deal with than their actual daughter, with her disappointing dead-end job and lack of husband.

I sigh with pleasure as I close the door of my flat behind me. A few days away has cleared the air and it feels like my sanctuary once more, particularly after my stay with my parents. I haven't heard anything from Toby, but he's very much on my mind. I wake up each morning thinking about him, and I'm devoting a lot of time to trying to work out where we go from here. I can't imagine life without him; I feel a physical ache when I try to contemplate that. I know he was spending Christmas with his parents, and I've decided to give him space until the New Year. If I haven't heard from him by then, I'll ring him.

For some reason, my father's words on Christmas Eve have hit home this time. I'm pretty certain that, whatever happens with Toby and me in the future, our days of travelling together are probably at an end. The problem is that I've got used to travelling with him. I never used to mind travelling on my own, but recently I've found myself missing his company on solo trips, if only to share a joke or an experience. I realised yesterday, when I was thinking all of this through for the umpteenth time, that the time has probably come for me to follow my father's advice, give my battered passport a rest, and look for a new career.

I have deliberately not checked my emails while I've been away, not that I would have expected anyone to be emailing over Christmas. It's usually pretty quiet from Christmas Eve until the beginning of January. Nevertheless, I fire up my laptop just to make sure nothing has come through that I need to deal with before the New Year.

There is the usual collection of spam, including one from a Nigerian prince who claims to have a deal that could be 'highly advantagius' to me, but my eye is drawn to one from Mark at *Voyages Luxes*. I know he usually takes the whole Christmas period off, so getting an email from him today is not a good sign. I check the timestamp and find that he sent it first thing this morning. I open it and read:

Dear Madison,
Congratulations to you and Toby on your award. I have something I

need to discuss with you face to face. Would you be able to meet me
at our offices at 11 a.m. on Tuesday 2 January please?
Regards
Mark

The tone is more formal than he usually uses in our emails,
and my mind is uncomfortably drawn back to the summons I
received pretty much exactly a year ago. This one feels more
urgent, though; he's asked me to go in on the first proper working
day after the Christmas break. I reply to the email, saying that I
will be there, and try to put it out of my mind.

* * *

By mid-afternoon, I'm in a frenzy. As well as wondering when, if
ever, I'm going to hear from Toby and how on earth to salvage our
relationship, I'm now also worrying about what I've done that has
earned me a second summons to the *Voyages Luxes* offices. I'm
pacing around my flat like a caged animal. I've tried reading a
book to distract me, and watching TV, but neither have worked.
My mind just keeps on trudging round the same old loop.

In the end I can take it no more. I pick up my phone and call
Toby's number. It rings, but he doesn't answer and it goes to
voicemail.

'Oh, umm... Hi, Toby, it's Madison here. I just wanted to check
in to see how you are. I know you said you wanted space and
everything, but I'm worried about you. Maybe you could give me
a call when you're free?'

As soon as I hang up, I kick myself. What have I achieved
from that? I feel no better, and he's going to be pissed off that I'm
not respecting his boundaries and giving him the time he asked
for to clear his head. For a brief moment I consider calling Mark

to see if I can find out what he wants to see me about, but I manage to talk myself out of that one. He won't thank me for invading his Christmas, even if he's taken time out to email me, and it might actually do more harm than good.

I text Charley to see if now is a good time to call her. After the slightly tense start to the call before Christmas I don't want to catch her at a bad time again, particularly as I'd quite like to ask her opinion about the situation with Toby. Her reply is pretty much immediate.

Yes, absolutely. Ed and Amelia are out, so please call. Save me from laundry!

She answers straight away. 'Hi, Mads, how are you? How was your Christmas?'

'You first,' I tell her.

'Oh, you know, all the usual. We went over to Mum and Dad's for Christmas Day. Simon, Emma and the girls were there too. It was nice. Did I tell you Amelia's walking now? If I thought the crawling was bad, walking is a whole new world of pain, literally. When she first started, she would manage a few steps at a time before she toppled over, and we'd have to try to predict where she was going to fall to prevent her bumping her head. The worst one was when she banged it on the corner of the TV cabinet. I thought she was never going to stop crying, and then she got a massive bruise. I was just waiting for someone from Social Services to arrive, decide I was an abusive parent, and take her away. She is completely adorable, though. Don't tell Ed, but I'm softening to the idea of another baby. Thank you for her Peppa pig jumper, by the way. She loves it and looks absolutely sweet in it. I'll send you a picture next time she's wearing it.'

'Aww, bless her. Send her love from her Auntie Mads, will you? Are you seeing Ed's family at all?'

'Yes, we're going down there for New Year's Eve. They throw a party every year and they always invite us. I've warned them I'm likely to be asleep in a corner by half past ten this time, party animal that I am. Anyway, enough about me, what about you?'

'Life's a bit shit at the moment, if I'm honest,' I tell her. 'Toby and I had a massive bust-up on Christmas Eve, and I've been summoned to the *Voyages Luxes* offices again.'

'Oh no! What happened with Toby?'

'He stayed over, and then he told me he was in love with me. I...'

'Whoa, back up a bit. Start from the beginning and give me all the details. He stayed over? Nobody stays over!'

I go back and fill her in on everything, from winning the award, the fight with Peter Smallbone, waking up to find Toby in my bed, the breakfast, to us standing on the pavement with him telling me he was in love with me.

'But you said he was gay!' she exclaims, after I've taken her through the last bit.

'I know.'

'So he's bi?'

'No, from the way he reacted, it seems he's straight.'

'Why did he say he was gay, then?'

I sigh. 'He didn't. I just assumed he was. You know how you get a feeling about people...'

'Are you telling me you never actually had a conversation about it with him?'

'He's very private about stuff like that. I figured he would tell me when he was ready.'

'Oh, Mads. I love you, but you are a little quick to make your mind up about things sometimes.'

'Yeah, well this one just turned round and bit me on the arse. I did drop some pretty heavy hints and he never contradicted me, though. Don't you think that's odd?'

'For example?'

'I said that I wasn't his type and stuff like that. Why didn't he tell me I was barking up the wrong tree?'

'Maybe he just thought that you were saying you weren't the right type of woman for him, rather than the wrong gender. Maybe he thought you didn't think he was your type, but you were trying to be tactful about it.'

'But he completely ignored me when I was naked around him. Surely that's a big bloody red light right there? I'm not saying that I'm irresistible or anything, but any red-blooded male is going to take some interest in a naked woman prancing around, isn't he? But no, nothing. Is it any wonder I was knocked for six when he declared that he was in love with me?'

'What are you going to do? I take it you don't feel the same way about him.'

'I've just never thought about him in that way,' I confess. 'I thought we would always be friends, but this has kind of chucked a hand grenade into all of that. I just wish I knew what he was thinking. I called him, but he didn't answer.'

'I hate to say it, darling, but I think you're going to have to play the long game here. Give him the space he's asked for.'

'Yeah, but it's so hard. You know me, I like to get things out in the open and resolve them. I feel like he's dumped this on me and run away, leaving me holding this "thing" that I can't do anything with. It pisses me off a little. I didn't ask him to fall in love with me!'

'No, you didn't, but shit happens. He's probably feeling really embarrassed and wishing he'd never said anything at all. Avoiding you is the safest way to protect his feelings while he tries to come to terms with the fact that you gave him the brush-off.'

'I didn't give him the brush-off, though! I was just so surprised that I didn't know what to say or do. He didn't really give me a chance to take it in, he just dashed off.'

'OK, so if he rang you up and said it all again, what would you say?'

I sigh. 'I still don't know. I miss him, and I want what we had back. But I know that, whatever happens now, we can't have that.'

'Do you fancy him?'

'Of course I do! You've seen him, right? I mean, it's a shame he's shorter than me, but...'

'What is this obsession you have with men who are shorter than you? Why is it such a problem?'

'Small man syndrome. Men who are shorter than me tend to be very competitive about everything, as if they're trying to make up for it. Ugh.'

'And has Toby ever done that?'

'No.'

'So, what's actually wrong with him?'

'Nothing! He's perfect in a lot of ways. I just... Oh, I don't know.'

'It sounds to me like you also need a bit of space then. You need to work out how you feel about him before you have any further conversation with him.'

'I know you're right,' I tell her. 'It just goes against my nature to let this thing fester between us.'

'You've got no choice, I'm afraid. Now, what's all this about *Voyages Luxes*?'

'I don't know, but I'm worried. Peter Smallbone was so angry at the dinner, and he's always hated me, so it wouldn't surprise me if he's come up with some new reason for them to let me go. It shouldn't bother me, because I've pretty much decided to give it up anyway, but I just want to go on my terms, rather than being thrown out.'

'This is new. What's brought this on?'

'Oh, lots of things. Part of it's related to Toby, because I've really enjoyed working with him, and doing it on my own just doesn't seem like fun any more. My dad had another go at me as well, the same old "you need to stop faffing around and get a proper job" routine. I always knew I wouldn't do this forever, and I suppose now feels like the right time for a change.'

'But what will you do?'

'I don't know yet. I've got some savings that will tide me over for a while, so I don't need to rush into anything. I'd like to stay in the travel industry if I can, otherwise all the experience I've had so far kind of goes to waste.'

'Well, good luck. Ring me afterwards and let me know what happens, OK? I should be around, as I don't go back to work until the fifth. Oh, and ring me if you hear from Toby, or you come to any definite conclusions.'

'Thanks. Sorry, this wasn't much of a fun call, was it?'

'I must admit it's very unlike you to get yourself in quite such a mess. But you're a fighter. You'll sort it all out, because that's what you always do.'

'I really hope you're right,' I tell her, as we end the call.

26

JANUARY

My nerves are jangling as I approach the *Voyages Luxes* offices. Over the last few days, I've concocted ever more fanciful scenarios, from simple mistakes in my expenses, to a dream I had last night where Toby and I were accused of taking bribes to write positively about a hotel that hadn't even been built yet. At least Toby was in the dream, so it wasn't all bad.

I still haven't heard anything from him. It's been nine days now, not that I'm counting. The longest we've gone without speaking over the last six months has been a week, and that was because I was in the middle of nowhere in Botswana with no internet connection. Despite promising myself that I'd leave him alone, I've tried to ring him twice more and got his voicemail both times. I miss him so much. I just want to hear his voice, to laugh with him again. It sounds ridiculous, particularly from someone who values their independence as much as I do, but I feel kind of incomplete without him, like there's a part of me missing because he's not around.

I'm the only visitor today and, after announcing myself to the receptionist, I take a seat in the waiting area. Being here reminds me of meeting Toby for the first time. It's amazing to think that it was only a year ago. It feels like I've known him for much longer. My anxiety about what this meeting might entail combines with my ache of longing to hear from Toby to form a heavy pool of misery in the pit of my stomach. It's all I can do to stop myself from just getting up and running away.

I spot Mark in one of the meeting rooms as I look around. Peter Smallbone and a woman I don't know are also in there with him. Oh great, Peter's going to get to witness my humiliation this time. I feel the bile rising inside me and focus all my energy on not being sick. I shouldn't be this nervous; I've already decided I don't want to do this any more, but I want to walk out of here with my head held high and my pride intact. Looking at the occupants of the room, it seems like that's not going to be how this ends.

After what feels like an age, they all get up and leave the meeting room. Peter and the woman walk back through the barriers into the main office area, and Mark starts walking towards me. It seems Peter is being denied his moment of ultimate victory after all, and he doesn't look very happy about it. I stand up straight, determined to face my firing squad with courage. For the last few minutes, I've been silently repeating the phrase 'I won't let them break me, I'm worth more than this' to myself, and it seems to have helped a little.

'Madison, thank you for coming in.' Mark extends his hand to me, and I notice that he looks tired. I shake his hand and follow him silently to the meeting room. He closes the door but leaves the blinds open. I wonder if this is so Peter can watch from a hidden location, and then tell myself I'm being paranoid.

'Please, take a seat.' His voice is very downbeat and serious, and my palms start sweating. Maybe, if what I've done isn't too bad, we'll be able to agree on a narrative where I decide not to pitch for any more work from *Voyages Luxes*, rather than him letting me go. That might work. I sit ramrod straight in the chair and prepare myself to hear what he has to say. Another woman I don't know slips into the room.

'OK,' he sighs, as he slumps into a chair opposite me. 'Madison, this is Jane, from our HR department. She is here to make sure that due process is followed. I have a statement here, which I have to read to you in full. You can comment at the end. Do you understand?'

My heart is thudding and I'm now genuinely worried that I'm going to throw up. I look around to see if there's a bin or something, in case of emergency, and spot one in the corner of the room. This all sounds much more severe than even my bribery dream.

'I understand,' I tell them, and my voice croaks with tension.

He puts on his glasses, looks down at the page in front of him and begins to read: 'It has been brought to our attention that an incident took place at the gala dinner on the twenty-third of December last year, involving you and Peter Smallbone. We understand that Peter was verbally abusive to you, and also acted in a physically threatening manner towards you. *Voyages Luxes* takes all incidents of this nature extremely seriously. We expect our staff, and anyone else representing our company, to adhere to our code of conduct at all times when carrying out company business. This includes social occasions hosted by the company, such as the gala dinner. We have therefore conducted a full investigation and spoken to everyone who was on the same table as you, as well as those on neighbouring tables. Without exception, those who were aware of the incident have described his behaviour as unprovoked and shocking, and some even went so far as to make special mention of your calm professionalism in such an extreme situation. We have spoken with Peter and explained the severity of his breach of our code of conduct. He is leaving *Voyages Luxes* with immediate effect. On behalf of *Voyages Luxes*, I would like to offer you a formal apology. I'm bound to advise you that it is within your statutory rights, even as a self-employed agent, to make a claim to an employment tribunal, should you feel that our actions in this instance have been insufficient. Do you have any comment you would like to make at this stage?'

'Fuck.' The word is out of my mouth before I can stop it. I see Jane's eyebrows shoot up.

'Sorry,' I continue. 'This is such a complete shock.'

'That's OK, Madison,' Jane says. 'You don't need to commit now, and obviously you can change your mind at any time, but it would be incredibly helpful if you were able to give us some idea about whether you intend to take this further.'

'God, no!' I exclaim. 'Poor Peter. I know we never got on, but is he OK? You didn't have to fire him because of me. I bet he hates me even more now.'

'We didn't fire him "because of you",' Jane explains, gently. 'On the twenty-seventh of December we received a complaint, via email, from another occupant of your table, who was concerned by the way he spoke to you and his threatening behaviour. Mark and I have been working flat out to establish what happened since then, and the evidence we uncovered left us with no option but to dismiss him on the grounds of gross misconduct.'

No wonder Mark looks tired. I bet he's been having a hell of a time.

'I'm sorry,' I say to him. 'I didn't mean to ruin your Christmas.'

'For God's sake, Madison!' Mark exclaims, causing Jane's eyebrows to shoot up again. I don't think she does strong language. 'If anyone ruined my Christmas, it was Peter, not you.'

'There's just one thing I don't understand,' I say. 'If you only got the complaint on the twenty-seventh, why did you invite me in straight away, before you had a chance to investigate?'

'Although we knew we had to look into it properly, the complaint was detailed enough that we suspected it would come to this. We agreed that it was better to have something in the diary, rather than prolong this any more than was necessary. If it had all turned out to be nothing, we would have cancelled it.'

'I think my role here is finished,' Jane says. 'Before I go and help Deborah finish processing Peter's paperwork, do you have any further questions for me?'

'No, thank you,' I tell her.

As soon as she leaves the room, Mark lets out a huge sigh.

'Sorry about all that. Because of the severity of the situation, we have to make sure we dot every i and cross every t. Are you OK?'

'I'm fine,' I tell him. 'Shocked, but fine. I honestly thought I'd done something wrong, and you'd called me in to let me go.'

'Not this time.' He smiles. 'In a funny way, you've done us a favour. I probably shouldn't tell you this, but Peter isn't a natural editor. Over the years he's been here he's tried really hard and worked incredibly long hours, but I could see he finds it a struggle. It was something we were going to raise in his next annual appraisal, but obviously this episode brought things to a head. Anyway, I hope we can put this sorry mess behind us. I've got some great ideas for you and Toby this year.'

'Mark, there's something I need to tell you before you go any further. I've been reflecting over Christmas, and I've decided that I won't be tendering for any more work.'

'What? I thought that you'd accepted our apology. Look, if there's something more that we need to do...'

'It's not about that. I've really enjoyed the last ten years, but you know as well as I do that you can't do this job forever. There comes a point where you want to spend more time in just one place and start to have a more normal life. I've reached that point.'

He studies me for a long time before he speaks.

'I can't say I'm not disappointed, because you're one of the best writers I've worked with. I'm not just saying that to make you feel good, you genuinely are. You have an ability to bring a place to life and make the reader feel that they've been there. It's a rare talent, and I doubt I'll find anyone as good to replace you. But I do understand. You're describing exactly how I felt when I gave it up. The stuff you have done this last year with Toby has been truly exceptional. I'm not exaggerating when I say it's game changing.'

'Thank you. I have enjoyed working with him—' I'm surprised how hard this is to say '—and we were both very grateful for the award. However, even if I hadn't decided to give this up, Toby and I wouldn't have continued working together.' I search for a plausible excuse. 'It was becoming too much pressure.'

'I understand. You two have been revolutionary though, and our circulation figures have risen sharply over the last year. I think you can both take some credit for that.'

I smile at him. 'It's been a lot of fun, and I just want to say thank you to you and *Voyages Luxes* for all the opportunities you've given me over the years. I really appreciate it, and I wish you every success in the future.'

I stand up to go. Now that the initial shock from the start of the meeting has subsided, and I've had the opportunity to say my piece, I feel strangely calm and detached. I'm just about to step out into the main reception area when I see Peter come back through the security barriers into the reception area. He's carrying a box, and is accompanied by the woman I assume is Deborah. I watch as they walk to the reception desk, where he hands in his pass. He looks completely defeated and, despite his efforts to destroy my career, I feel terribly sorry for him.

'Where do you think he'll go?' I ask Mark.

'No idea,' he replies. 'We've promised him a fair reference that focuses on his years of service rather than the manner of his departure, and this might just be the shock he needs to make him reflect on what he really wants out of life. Hopefully, he'll find something that suits him better.'

As Peter turns around, he sees me through the glass. I'm expecting his face to contort with anger, as it did at the gala dinner, but it doesn't. For a moment it looks like he's mouthing the word 'sorry' at me as he walks towards the front door, but I'm sure my mind must be playing tricks on me.

'Before you go, I've just had a thought,' Mark pipes up, suddenly. 'Have you got five more minutes?'

'Sure,' I reply, and sit back down at the table.

'Peter's departure leaves us with a vacancy in the editorial department. How would you feel about applying for it?'

'Are you offering me a job?'

'Not exactly. We have to advertise the vacancy, but off the record I'm sure we'd be very receptive to an application from you. You have tons of experience, you know the market, and you know good writing when you see it. These are all qualities we look for. Plus, your spelling and grammar are first rate. I can't remember the last time we had to correct your work. Think about it? I imagine the vacancy will be posted on our company website in the next few days.'

'Thank you, Mark,' I tell him as I stand to leave again. 'I will think about it, I promise.'

* * *

It's all I can do not to cartwheel down the pavement as I leave the offices. Not only did I get to leave on my own terms, but the perfect job is within my grasp. I'm just about to do a little skip of joy when I spot Peter sitting outside the same café I sat outside almost a year ago. He's got a cup of coffee, and his box of possessions is balanced precariously on the rickety table. He looks so pathetic that I find myself drawn to him, even though he's never had a nice word to say to me in the entire time I've known him.

'I'm really sorry, Peter,' I say to him.

He looks up at me, and I'm surprised to see no malice in his face at all.

'Don't be,' he replies. 'I brought it on myself, I know that. In a funny way it's probably a good thing. I've wanted to be a travel writer since I was very young. All the other kids in my class wanted to be footballers or pop stars, but I wanted nothing more than to see the world and write about it. It turns out, of course, that it's not as easy as that. You can't just will yourself into a job like that, you need talent, and it didn't take me very long to realise that I didn't have any. But I was lucky, and I managed to get the editing job instead. It was as close to my dream as I knew I was ever going to get, so I slogged away dutifully at it. Unfortunately, it turned out that I wasn't much good at that either, and I found it a real struggle.

'When I first met you, I was so envious of you. There you were, young, beautiful, posh, and so, *so* fucking talented. Excuse my language, but you are. You made it look easy, and I hated you for it, because you were producing stuff that was better than anything I'd dreamed of writing, and you didn't even appear to break a sweat. It all just seemed so unfair, and I started to get a bit obsessed about bringing you down. When I saw what people were saying online about the Bellavista, I thought this was my opportunity to prove that you weren't as infallible as you appeared to be. You were supposed to be Icarus, and I reckoned I was the sun that was going to melt your wings. I was so pleased when I showed my findings to Mark and he called you in. I knew he was going to let you go and I thought I'd won. Only you took it, made something even better from it, and then won a bloody award! I think that tipped me over the edge. I knew that I'd gone too far as soon as I woke the next day, so I wasn't surprised when I got called in this morning. I'm sorry, Madison. I really am.'

'What will you do now?' I ask him.

'Nothing to do with writing or editing!' he laughs. 'I don't know yet. They were kind enough to give me a severance package, which they didn't have to do. It was "in recognition of my many years of service", apparently. I'm sure I'll find something.'

'I hope you do. Good luck, Peter.'

'Thanks. Good luck yourself.'

27

JANUARY

'So they offered you a job? That's amazing!' Charley says, down the phone. I've called her with the update, as promised.

'No, they haven't offered me the job, but they've "encouraged me to apply", which isn't far off. I had a chat with Peter as well. He was surprisingly nice about it all. I think he realises he's been a complete dick to me. Shame it took him so long.'

'Does he know you're going for his old job?'

'No, I thought that might be rubbing unnecessary salt in the wound.'

'Good point. I really hope you get it, though. It sounds perfect for you, and it will be nice to have you around more, instead of travelling all the time. Have you heard anything from Toby?'

'Not a thing, and he still isn't answering my calls. I don't know what to do. I can't even go to the studio and confront him, like I did with Ed at his office that time, because there's no guarantee he'll be there. I could be sitting outside for weeks if he's away on a shoot. I can't tell you how much I'm missing him.'

'Try.'

'What?'

'Try to tell me how much you're missing him. I have a theory.'

'It feels...' I start, and then dry up.

'Yes?' she prompts. 'Oh, I don't know. It feels like a part of me is missing, does that make sense? If I've had a dream with him in it, which I do a lot, I feel all warm and fuzzy when I wake up, and then reality comes crashing in and it's like a punch in the gut. Thank goodness I don't have any deadlines looming, because I'm completely unable to focus on anything except him. I keep wondering what he's doing, what he's thinking, who he's with. Sometimes I just sit, staring at the phone, willing it to ring and be him.'

'Mm. That's what I thought,' she says. 'Has it occurred to you that you might be in love with him?'

'What?? God, no!'

'OK, answer this. What do you think it would be like to kiss him?'

'Oh, I'm sure he's a good kisser!' I say, confidently. 'He'd be gentle, but not sloppy. He wouldn't be one of those guys who rams their tongue in your mouth as if they're trying to force-feed it to you, but it wouldn't be flopping around like a piece of raw liver either.'

'I worry about your imagery sometimes. And what do you think he'd be like in bed?'

'He'd be a considerate lover,' I tell her. 'He'd be attentive, wanting to make sure that everything was right.'

'So, to recap what we know so far. You miss him so much you practically feel like you've lost a body part. You fancy him. You've obviously thought about what he'd be like as a lover and your descriptions are very positive. This doesn't sound like "just good friends" to me. Face it, you are in love with him. I've never heard you speak about a man like this before. Surely you can recognise the symptoms. You must have been in love before, how does the way you feel now compare to that?'

I cast my mind back through my previous relationships and try to remember how I felt about them.

'Are you still there?' Charley asks.

'Yes, sorry, just thinking. Do you know what, I don't think I have?'

'Have what?'

'I don't think I've ever been in love. I've been in "like", and I've been in "lust", but I've never felt the way I do now about any man, ever.'

'That's love.'

'Fuck.'

'Yep. Question is, what are you going to do about it if he won't take your calls?'

'I need a way to get him to answer,' I say to her. 'In fact, I need more than that, because what I really need is to talk to him face to face. I know! You could ring him for me, and tell him he has to meet me.'

'Oh no. Leave me out of this.'

'But I went and got Ed for you!'

'Yes, and you'll never know how grateful I am, but the difference is that you did that behind my back. I never asked you to get involved and, if I had, I'm pretty sure you would have been just as robust with me as I'm trying to be with you. Come on, Mads. Where's all that resourcefulness you normally have?'

I have the beginning of an idea. 'You're right,' I tell her. 'I think I know what to do.'

'Attagirl!' she replies. 'Good luck and keep me posted. Keep me posted on the job too!'

'I will,' I promise, and ring off.

* * *

A few minutes later I'm in Carphone Warehouse, buying the cheapest pay-as-you-go phone they have available. I did think about just getting another SIM card, but the phone is only ten pounds and the idea of owning a 'burner' phone tickles me. It's not a make I've heard of, the screen is tiny, and it has actual buttons for dialling numbers rather than a touchscreen. It's perfect. As soon as I get it home, I insert the SIM and plug it in to charge. I start to put flesh on the rest of my plan while I wait.

By the time the charge indicator has got to 50 per cent, my patience has run out. I unplug the phone and punch in Toby's number. I realise my hands are shaking with excitement and my heart is in my mouth.

'Toby Roberts. How can I help you?'

It's him. The rush of relief at hearing his voice nearly derails me, but I force myself to stick to the plan. He'll probably hang up if he finds out it's me, and I can't risk that.

'Hello,' I say. I lower my voice so it hopefully doesn't sound like me, and I'm trying to speak in what I think is an Eastern European accent.

'I vish to book photo shoot. Sexy photos, you know? As gift for boyfriend.'

'A boudoir shoot? Yes, I can certainly help you with that. What did you have in mind?'

'Must be vairy discreet. Boyfriend is, how you say, high profile. Must be vairy private. You haff back door? Nobody must see.' I'm really not sure about this accent, but he doesn't appear to have twigged, and that's the main point.

'All of our shoots are discreet; I can assure you. We do have a back door, so that's no problem. It will just be you, me, and a chaperone that I trust.'

'No!' I practically bark. 'No chaperone. Vairy private. Just you and me.'

'I'm sorry, but I have to insist. It's for your protection as well as mine.' Damn. I need him on his own. I can't do this with an audience.

'Vairy well. I vill bring this chaperone.' I won't, but he doesn't need to know that.

I can practically hear him thinking down the phone line. Eventually, he replies.

'OK, that's fine. When would you like to come?'

'Must be soon. Boyfriend is out of country on business. Ven he comes back, he does not like me to go away from him.' What is this gibberish that I'm spouting?

'I do have a slot free on Friday afternoon next week, from two until five. It's a cancellation. After that the earliest slot I could give you would be...' I hear him flicking through the pages in his diary, 'April the fifteenth.'

'Next Friday is good. I cannot wait until April.'

'Let's get you booked in then. Can I take your name?'

'Name is Kristina.'

'And your surname?'

'Vot for you need my surname?' I ask, trying to sound angry. This accent is terrible, and I'm struggling not to laugh.

'I don't technically need it. It's just a detail I normally take, along with your address and email.'

'Surname is Olgatov. But no address. No email. Must be vairy discreet, I told you.'

'I normally email the studio address and a copy of the paperwork that needs to be signed.'

'Vot paperwork?' Shit, I didn't consider that I might need to sign stuff.

'Because of the intimate nature of the shoot, I need proof that you're over eighteen years of age, and written consent from you that you're participating of your own free will.'

'But I can sign this on Friday, no? Ven I come? I can bring passport with me.'

Again, he pauses.

'I suppose so,' he says. 'OK, the cost of the session is four hundred pounds, and I normally take a deposit of one hundred pounds from your debit or credit card to secure the booking.'

How much?? Bloody hell, no wonder Mark complains about how expensive he is.

'No credit cards. I pay cash,' I tell him.

'I understand that, but I do need a deposit to secure the booking, I'm afraid.'

Damn. Another factor that I didn't take into account. How am I going to pay the deposit without him finding out who I am? I decide to get money from the cashpoint, but I need to figure out a way to deliver it without revealing my identity. I look at my watch to see how long I have before the shops shut.

'Text your address to this number. I vill get driver to post deposit in cash through your front door tonight.' I tell him. 'Envelope will say "From Kristina", so you know is from me. Ven you have money, you text again to confirm.'

'OK. This is all highly unusual, but I can see you're keen to protect your privacy, Ms Olgatov. I look forward to meeting you next Friday. I normally include a list of items to bring with you on the confirmation email, shall I text those as well?'

'Yes. Text is good. Goodbye.' I ring off and punch the air with sheer relief. I've done it! I'm going to see Toby again. Now all I have to do is work out how to stop him from slamming the door in my face, but I've got a week and a bit to figure that part out. I plug the burner phone in to finish charging and, within a few minutes, it pings to let me know that I've received new text messages. The first text contains the studio address, which of course I already know. The second one contains advice about hair, make-up, nails and waxing, and a list of items I might want to bring with me, including lingerie (obviously), high-heeled shoes and boots, a white shirt, plus fetish wear if I want to.

'I don't want to, thank you,' I say to the phone.

I had a boyfriend once who was very into fetish gear, and I was curious enough to give it a try. I hated it. Apart from anything else, the squeaking sound the rubber made had the same effect on me as someone dragging their nails down a blackboard, which was a massive turn-off. It was also very difficult to get into and out of, and I sweated profusely in it. Unsurprisingly, the relationship didn't last. I do have some sexy lingerie – the type that's scratchy and uncomfortable but not designed to be worn for very long – but I think I might treat myself to some new stuff for this. I'm not actually sure whether I'll go through with the photo shoot, but I ought to be prepared, just in case it's the only way I can buy enough time to force him to hear me out.

It's just after two thirty, which means I have plenty of time to get to Bluewater, do some shopping and, most importantly, get a hundred pounds out of the cashpoint to post through Toby's door on the way back. I grab a suitably sized envelope, write 'From Kristina' on it (taking care to disguise my handwriting), stuff it into my bag and head down to the car.

* * *

I love Bluewater. To be fair, I love most shopping centres, but Bluewater is the closest one to me and therefore has a special place in my heart. The post-Christmas sales are still on, but it's not too busy now that most people are back at work. I decide to go for two different styles of lingerie. In Ann Summers I buy a very tarty-looking push-up basque set in black, with crimson detailing. In Rigby & Peller I spend a fortune on a beautiful matching bra and knickers set; I like it so much I decide this is the first underwear I want Toby to see me in for the shoot, if it happens. Next, I pop into M&S, where I buy a man's white shirt. I don't currently own any high heels; I'm tall enough as it is, so I would tower over people if I wore heels. Despite that, I decide to push the boat out and end up spending far more than is decent on a pair of red stilettos in Russell & Bromley.

By the time I come out, it's dark and I'm ready to put the next part of my plan into action. I stuff the hundred pounds I've just withdrawn into the envelope and set off for Sevenoaks. When I get there, I pull my hoodie up and keep my head down as I approach the studio, so that he can't see it's me if he's watching. I hurry away as soon as I've posted the money through the door. By the time I arrive home, another text has arrived on the burner phone.

Dear Ms Olgatov, I can confirm that I have received your deposit, and I look forward to seeing you on Friday 12 January at 2 p.m. Regards, Toby Roberts.

We're on.

28

JANUARY

The vacancy appears on the *Voyages Luxes* website the next day. I force myself to concentrate and spend the morning redrafting my CV. I also check it several times for spelling and grammatical mistakes, before sending it to the email address given. It's a strange feeling, having all my eggs in one basket like this. I've already told both of the airline magazines that I'm not accepting commissions at the moment, as they've been in touch with offers of work in January and February. I haven't said anything to the Sunday supplement yet, as that doesn't require any actual travel, and I may even be able to continue doing it alongside the editing job, if I get it.

If this were any other job, I'd spend the time between applying and hopefully being invited to interview doing research about the company, looking up their mission statements and corporate values. As I've already worked with *Voyages Luxes* for so many years, I pretty much know their mission statement and their values off by heart. I'm therefore at a bit of a loose end and full of nervous energy. My flat is spotless, I've taken my car to the car wash and hoovered it out, and it's too soon to be going to Bluewater to buy work clothes; I don't want to jinx it.

I'm also trying not to count the days until Friday 12th, when I will see Toby again, but it's hopeless. I'm so aware of the passage of time that I might as well have a chart on the fridge to mark off the hours. I still haven't decided whether to go ahead with the photo shoot or not; I think I'll wear the Rigby & Peller underwear and decide when I get there. I do at least have a rudimentary plan to stop him from being able to slam the door on me.

The email arrives on Monday.

Dear Ms Morgan,

Thank you for your application for the position of Assistant Editor at Voyages Luxes. I am delighted to be able to invite you for interview on Friday 12th January at 2.30 p.m. The interview will last approximately two hours, and will consist of the following elements:

- You will be asked to edit a submitted article, removing spelling and grammatical mistakes, and also making changes where necessary to improve readability.
- You will then be interviewed by the Commissioning Editor, Mark Stevens, and me. The interview will consist of questions that will help us to ascertain your suitability for the role. These are designed to enable you to showcase yourself; we are not trying to trap you!
- You will have the opportunity to ask any questions that you wish to.
- During the interview we will share with you information including office hours, annual leave, pension schemes, medical cover and salary.

I look forward to meeting you,

Deborah Reynolds
Human Resources Manager

My elation at having been offered an interview is short-lived. It's right in the middle of the session I'm supposed to be having with Toby! What on earth am I going to do? If I try to rearrange the interview, I risk looking unprofessional and denting my chances of getting this job. If I cancel Toby, I might not get another opportunity to see him until April, and I can't wait that long.

In the end, I know there's only one option. Nervously, I reach for the phone, dial the offices of *Voyages Luxes* and ask to be put through to Deborah.

'Deborah Reynolds speaking.'

'Hello, this is Madison Morgan. I've just received your email inviting me for interview.'

'Your CV was impressive. I'm looking forward to meeting you.'

'And I you. There's just one thing. I have an appointment that I can't reschedule between two and five on Friday 12th. Is there any possibility at all that I could come in at a different time?'

I feel like a fraud. If she knew I was putting this job at risk because I'd booked a boudoir photo shoot with a man I think I might be in love with, she'd tell me to get lost. For some reason, I'm convinced that she's going to see through me and I feel the same sense of dread that I did as a child, when I lied to my mother about something, knowing full well that she already knew what had really happened.

I wait for Deborah to produce the evidence of my guilt with the same triumphant voice that my mother used to use.

'That's no problem at all, I quite understand. This sort of thing happens all the time, don't worry. Let me check the calendars,' she tells me, and I start breathing again. I hadn't even noticed that I was holding my breath.

'We have another candidate coming in on Thursday afternoon, but we could see you on Friday morning, if you're able to get here for eight thirty. Is that any good?'

'That's perfect,' I tell her, hoping I don't sound as relieved as I feel. 'Thank you so much.'

'Excellent. I'll look forward to meeting you at eight thirty on Friday morning.'

As soon as the call is over, I heave a huge sigh of relief and berate myself for being so paranoid. Of course they must have to move interviews around; she probably didn't think my request unusual at all. After texting first to make sure it's a good time, I ring Charley to fill her in. She's delighted when I tell her.

'It was a close-run thing, though,' I tell her, when her shrieks of joy have died down. 'The first slot was the same time as my photo shoot with Toby.'

'Are you two speaking again then? That's even better news. What did he say? Are you an item now?'

'Umm, no. Not exactly.' I fill her in on the details of me pretending to be Kristina Olgatov, the burner phone, and even give a demonstration of my appalling Eastern European accent. She guffaws with laughter.

'That is the funniest thing I've heard in ages,' she tells me. 'I've literally got tears running down my cheeks from laughing so much. I told you you were resourceful, didn't I?'

'You did, and I am quite pleased with myself. It just took me a while to figure out how to get hold of him without him realising it was me. It's all going to unravel the moment he claps eyes on me, but I think I have a plan for that.'

'Which is?'

'I've paid a deposit and he's accepted it. That's a contract. He has to let me in. If I have to take all my clothes off and force him to take pictures of me, I'll do it to make sure I have the full three hours to try to get through to him.'

'Well, technically Kristina paid the deposit. He could simply return it on the basis that you aren't who you said you were on the phone.'

'I've just got to hope he doesn't do that, haven't I? Anyway, I've bought new lingerie and everything.'

'Would you actually do the photo shoot then? I'd be too embarrassed.'

'If I have to, yes.'

After I hang up, I realise Charley has a point. There's nothing to stop Toby simply returning the hundred pound deposit and telling me to get lost. I need him not to know it's me until I'm actually inside the studio. I need a disguise. Some big sunglasses and a wig ought to do it.

It doesn't take much internet research for me to work out that a wig is not going to work. My hair is long, and I'll confess to being a bit vain about it. In order to get it to sit under a wig, I'd have to braid it and wrap it around my head; it would need professional attention to hang properly after that kind of abuse. A search on facial disguises proves to be equally useless, unless I want to pitch up in a Marx Brothers moustache with comedy eyebrows and glasses. This is hopeless.

Eventually I decide that some big sunglasses and a hoodie will probably work, as long as I keep my head down until I'm actually inside the studio. I still have a couple of days to fill, so I pencil in another shopping trip; I need an interview outfit, and I need a hoodie that Toby hasn't seen, as well as the sunglasses.

* * *

My debit card takes a pounding the next day, and I find myself begging any deity that will listen to help me get this job. I'm going to have to raid my savings to pay myself back for the fortune I've spent in the two shopping trips I've embarked on in the last few days. My haul today includes a charcoal grey suit with subtle pinstripes for the interview. It was much more than I planned to spend, but the jacket fits beautifully, nipping in to emphasise my waist, and the matching pencil skirt flattens my stomach and flatters my thighs before ending just above the knee. It's corporate, but also feminine, and I fell in love with it as soon as I tried it on. I bought myself some black patent leather court shoes with low heels to go with it, some new tights, and another set of 'lucky' Rigby & Peller underwear. I know the underwear will make no difference whatsoever to the interviewers' opinion of me, but I will know I'm wearing it and it will boost my confidence. Of course, that's complete nonsense, but it's as good an excuse as any to justify another set of hideously expensive lingerie.

For the meeting with Toby, I buy myself a pair of mirrored pilot's sunglasses that are so big they obscure most of my face, and a new hoodie in Superdry that will cover my hair. I also brave the electronics department in John Lewis, coming away with a memory card that I know will fit Toby's camera.

* * *

I'm up early on Friday morning. I had set my alarm for half past six, but I'm wide awake an hour before that. I've planned the day with military precision. I'm going to arrive at the *Voyages Luxes* offices at eight twenty, which is early enough to indicate that I'm serious, without being so early that I come across as desperate. The interview should be finished by ten thirty, although I've allowed half an hour of contingency time, just in case. That still gives me plenty of time to come back home, shower again, and change into Kristina's outfit of tracksuit bottoms and the hoodie, complete with the second set of underwear underneath. I've decided to arrive fifteen minutes late for my appointment with Toby. Not only does this seem the sort of thing that 'Kristina' would do, it also ensures I won't accidentally overlap with whatever he's doing before me and have to wait.

As I shower, I focus on the interview and the questions they might ask me. I need not to think about Toby for this part of the day. Once the interview is over I can focus fully on him but, for now, I need to nail this and secure my future. I'm a little bit early and have to walk around the block a couple of times before presenting myself at reception at eight twenty precisely. I only have to wait a few moments before Deborah appears to meet me.

'Madison.' She holds out her hand. 'I'm Deborah Reynolds, nice to meet you. The editorial exercise is all set up. Would you like a cup of tea or coffee before we begin?'

'No, I'm fine, thank you.'

She leads me into one of the meeting rooms, where a computer is waiting for me.

'The article for you to edit is on the screen in front of you. When you make changes, you'll see that there is a red line to the left. Don't worry about that, it's purely so that we can see what you have altered so we can get a flavour of your editing style. You have an hour to complete the exercise, so take your time.'

She loads up the article, notes the time, and leaves. I turn my attention to the screen and my heart sinks. I've read this article before. It's one of Peter Smallbone's, and it's so turgid I have little chance of turning it into anything useful unless I throw it away and rewrite it from scratch. I sit and stare at it for a few moments before I realise what they've done. Despite all the warm words in the email, this is a trap. If I rewrite it, I prove that I'm not an editor but a writer. If I merely edit it, it will never bring the place alive in the way that I would want an article to do. I allow a few profanities to seep out under my breath.

At the end of the hour I'm not happy, but I've done as much as I can for Peter's article without losing what he wrote originally. It's not fit to be published, and I'm hoping that I'm right that the brief was to make the most of what I was presented with, rather than turn it into an article that I'd be happy to put my name to.

The interview itself appears to go well. Mark and Deborah read what I've done, ask a few questions that I don't find hard to answer, and then fill me in on the practicalities of the job. The salary isn't huge, but I'll be able to live on it fairly comfortably. More importantly, I'll get perks that I'd never have dreamed of as a freelance journalist; I'll have four weeks of paid holiday per year rising to five, private medical insurance, and they will contribute to my pension. There's even a bonus scheme. I'm starting to see why my father had such a problem with me being self-employed.

'You're the last of the candidates we selected for interview,' Deborah tells me as she shows me out. 'You should hear from us soon. Thank you for coming in.'

As I drive home, I replay the interview in my head. I'm relieved to find that I can't think of any questions that I wish I had answered differently, so I allow myself to focus fully on the shoot this afternoon. I have to prepare for the performance of my life.

29

JANUARY

The nerves are back with a vengeance as I ring the back doorbell of Toby's studio at two fifteen. I've pulled the hoodie as far forward as it will go and I'm wearing the sunglasses. It's not the greatest of disguises, but I just need it to get me past the threshold. My heart leaps with joy as he opens the door and I see him for the first time. He looks well, but his face falls when he sees me and, for a moment, I wonder if I've completely misjudged this and made a colossal mistake.

'Madison, you can't be here. I'm waiting for a client,' he says, woodenly. So much for the disguise then. This going off the rails before I've even had a chance to get out of the starting blocks. With no other options to choose from, I decide to remain in character. Hopefully it will keep him off guard for long enough to get me inside.

'Who is this Madison? I am Kristina. I haff appointment,' I tell him, using my ridiculous accent. He looks completely dumbfounded, and I use the opportunity to sweep regally past him into the studio. He's laid out the consent form on a table, and I slap down the three hundred pounds next to it, while hastily signing

Kristina's name on the forms. Toby follows me, obviously completely confused.

'Madison, I don't understand. What's going on?'

'Name is Kristina!' I tell him again. 'You are going to take photos of me, yes? Vairy private photos.' I rummage in my bag and fish out the memory card.

'Put this in camera. You give it to me when we finish. This way I am sure I haff only copies.'

I don't know how, but he manages to look sceptical, baffled and annoyed all at the same time. I'm certain he's going to ask me to leave, so I play my (very weak) trump card in desperation.

'Vot is problem? I haff paid money. Haff signed form. Is contract, no? You take pictures now.'

I can almost hear his brain churning. He really doesn't want me here, that's plain to see. But there's no way I'm leaving until I've had a chance to talk to him properly. Looking at his current expression, it looks like I'll have no option but to go through with the photo shoot to get him calm enough to hear me out, but I always knew that was a risk. I just have to hope like hell he's going to overlook the fact that there isn't a chaperone in sight. I'm relying on a gamble that he doesn't want to play out this next scene in front of an audience any more than I do.

'OK, "Kristina",' he says eventually, making little quote marks in the air as he says the name. 'Let's do this.'

I walk into the dressing room and strip down to the Rigby & Peller bra and knickers. I put on the red stilettos and the man's white shirt, rolling up the sleeves as they're way too long. I'm going for the 'morning after' look, but I'm not sure how successful it is. It's a long time since I've had a morning after, so I'm a little rusty.

Toby is waiting for me as I come out of the dressing room. The porno bed is in place, with black cotton sheets and lights set up around it. I can see he's used the time that I was changing to switch, as best he can, into professional mode, but it's all I can do not to launch myself at him.

'Patience,' I tell myself, firmly.

'What was that?' he asks.

'Nothing,' I reply, as Kristina. 'I am ready. We start now.'

To begin with, I feel incredibly embarrassed as Toby directs me. I've never done anything like this before and I feel a bit silly as he puts me in poses that are evidently supposed to maximise my cleavage and instructs me to lower my head so that I'm looking up at him because, apparently, that's sexier. As time goes on, though, I start to relax. Even though we haven't had the conversation I'm here for, and I still have no idea how I'm going to start it, I'm just so happy to see him that I stop worrying about the fact that, to all intents and purposes, I'm writhing around on the porno bed like a wannabe glamour model.

Every so often he makes adjustments to the look. At one point, I remove both the shirt and the stilettos, and he changes the bed sheets from black to white. We also do some shots without the bed, thankfully.

'We've been going for an hour,' he announces. 'Would you like a break?'

It feels like we've only been doing this for five minutes, but I realise I am thirsty, so I agree. He hands me a dressing gown to cover myself up with, fetches me a bottle of water from the fridge in the kitchen area, and I sit on the bed to drink it. I check my phone, but there's nothing from *Voyages Luxes* yet, so I slip it into the pocket of the dressing gown. An awkward silence descends.

'Why are you here, Madison?' he asks, eventually. His voice is so sad that I want to wrap my arms around him.

'For vairy private photo shoot!' I reply, in Kristina's voice.

'No, why are you really here?'

Even though I've been writhing around in next to nothing for the last hour, desperately trying to work out how to start the conversation we're obviously about to have, it's only now that I truly feel exposed and vulnerable. This is a new sensation for me and I don't like it. What if I bare my soul, but he's decided he's not actually in love with me after all and turns me down? Why on earth didn't I work out what I was going to say when I was planning this? He's looking at me expectantly, so I steel myself, open my mouth and start to wing it.

'You know when you told me you'd met someone special, and I didn't realise you were talking about me, so you had to spell it out?'

'Yes. How can I forget? I think Christmas Eve rates quite highly among the worst days of my life and, believe me, there are quite a few to choose from.' He laughs, bitterly.

'Well, what I didn't realise at the time, but I know now, was that I'd met someone special too.'

I've obviously said the wrong thing, because he looks absolutely stricken. This isn't going to plan at all.

'And these photos... are for him?' Toby asks, his voice barely above a whisper. 'Didn't you think about how I'd feel at all?' He drops his eyes to the camera and I see him eject the memory card. Without looking at me, he holds it out.

'Take it,' he says, hoarsely. 'Take the money as well. I can't do this, and I can't believe you would be so insensitive as to ask me to do it. You can get changed back into your clothes, but then I'd like you to leave.'

Oh no you don't. I haven't gone through this entire rigmarole for it to end like this. If he thinks I'm just going to slink away, he's got another thought coming.

'Look at me,' I command him, and I'm aware that my desperation is making me sound much harsher than I want to, but it has the desired effect. Slowly, he lifts his eyes and meets my gaze. His expression is one of pure misery, and he's still holding out his hand with the memory card in it. I reach out, take his hand gently in mine and close his fingers around the card.

'They're for you,' I explain. 'Look, Toby. What I'm trying to tell you, and making a complete hash of, if the look on your face is anything to go by, is that I've realised that I'm in love with you too. I'm yours, if you still want me.'

He says nothing for what feels like an age, and my heart is pounding so hard I'm worried that I might be on the brink of a seizure, but I finally see the faintest hint of a smile start to play on his lips.

'Are you saying...' he begins, tentatively.

'Yes!'

'But on Christmas Eve...'

'I know. I'm really sorry about that. It's just that you caught me completely by surprise and, at the time, I didn't know how I felt about you. Believe it or not, I've never been in love before.'

'Never?' he asks. 'But what about the other guys you went out with?'

'I can honestly tell you, Toby, that I've never felt the way I feel right now about anyone else. When you walked off and left me standing there on Christmas Eve, I was in shock, like a part of me had been torn off. Since then I've missed you so much it has felt like an actual, physical pain. But I still didn't understand what it was. It was only when Charley pointed it out to me that I finally got it. I wanted to tell you, but you wouldn't answer my calls.'

'I'm sorry. I saw them, and the voicemails, but I couldn't bring myself to listen to them, much less actually talk to you. I felt so stupid and embarrassed. I was sure you were going to tell me that we could pretend it never happened and carry on as we were before, and I couldn't stand the thought of hearing the pity in your voice.'

'I understand, but not knowing when, or even if, you'd speak to me again was tearing me apart. So I came up with the idea of the burner phone as a number you wouldn't recognise, and Kristina.'

'I knew something was off with her! I've worked with a lot of Eastern Europeans and none of them sounded even vaguely like her. I assume it was an Eastern European accent you were attempting?' He's smiling widely now. God, he has a beautiful smile. I could stare at it all day.

'It worked, didn't it?'

'So, what happens now?'

'I think I'd like you to kiss me.'

To my surprise he looks terrified, like a rabbit caught in the headlights, but he does come and sit next to me on the bed. 'Umm, I should warn you that I'm not very experienced in these things. I haven't exactly had a girlfriend before.'

'And by "exactly", you mean?'

'I mean I haven't.'

'I'm sure you'll figure it out.' I smile, lean forward and kiss him lightly on the lips. We stay like that for a while, just kissing gently, and I feel him start to relax. Our arms wrap round each other as if on autopilot as our kisses start to deepen. I was right. He may be inexperienced, but he's a fantastic kisser and I can feel my body coming alive and responding to him. At some point we shift position, so that we're lying on the bed, and I become aware of his arousal.

'Toby,' I break off from kissing him.

'Yes?'

'What is this?' I ask, putting my hand on his trousers. His face blushes so red that I can't help laughing.

'If we're going to do this,' I tell him, without moving my hand, 'and I want to just as much as it appears you do, I don't want our first time to be on the porno bed. I'm sure we'll christen all the areas of your studio in time, but can we go up to your flat now?'

He hesitates, and I wonder if I've gone too far too fast.

'What's the matter?' I ask him.

'I don't have any condoms,' he replies. 'They haven't been something I've ever needed before.'

I grin at him. 'Well, it's lucky I'm on the pill then, isn't it?'

He takes my hand and we practically run up the stairs to his flat.

* * *

'What are you thinking?' I ask him, as we're lying naked in his bed some time later. Things had been a little awkward at first; Toby was keen, but his inexperience made him a little clumsy. In the end I had taken charge and showed him what to do and what I liked. After that it all improved dramatically. I'm confident that he'll make an extremely good lover with a little bit of guidance.

'You know I said that Christmas Eve was one of the worst days of my life?'

'Yes.'

'I think today ranks as one of the best.'

'Only one of the best??'

'Well, I was pretty happy when my parents bought me my first bike...'

'This could be a very short-lived relationship, you know!'

'I'm kidding,' he laughs. 'It's definitely the best.'

We're interrupted by the sound of my phone ringing inside the pocket of the dressing gown, which got thrown on the floor at some point. I disentangle myself from Toby and retrieve it. The caller ID tells me it's *Voyages Luxes*.

'Madison Morgan.' I try to sound cool and professional, rather than post-coital and loved up.

'Hello, Madison, it's Deborah Reynolds from *Voyages Luxes*. Is now a good time?'

'Absolutely!' *I'm standing stark naked in my new boyfriend's bedroom, but you don't need to know that, Deborah.*

'I just wanted to say thank you for coming in this morning. As you know, we shortlisted two candidates for interview. You were both very strong, but obviously we only have one position available.'

Oh shit, she's ringing to tell me that I haven't got the job after all. I brace myself for the bad news.

'Mark and I spent some time discussing it after you left, and I'm delighted to be able to offer you the position.'

I'm so delighted I nearly drop the phone. 'Really? That's fantastic news, thank you so much!'

'I probably shouldn't tell you this, but you were in a totally different league to the other applicant. Your work on the test article was first rate. The fact that you know the company so well from your time as a freelance writer also gave us confidence that you would fit in well here. I'll send you confirmation in writing, of course, and we'll be in touch soon to discuss your starting date. Congratulations, and welcome to *Voyages Luxes*.'

'Thank you so much for calling.' I ring off and turn to Toby.

'I got the job!' I tell him, breaking into a victory dance.

'What job?'

I realise that I haven't told him anything about the fallout from the gala dinner, so I climb back into bed and wrap myself around him. Even though he's shorter than me, we just seem to fit together naturally.

'And the best part,' I tell him, after I've filled him in with all the details, 'is that I don't have to travel any more, unless I'm actually on holiday.'

'I'm so pleased for you,' he says. 'I'm pretty pleased for me too, actually. I don't think I could bear being apart from you for long.' As I snuggle in closer to him, I become aware of something pressing into my thigh.

'Again? Already?' I ask him, with a smile on my face.

'I've got a lot of catching up to do. Plus, you were just gyrating round my bedroom in the nude!' he laughs.

* * *

'There's one thing that I still don't get,' I say to him, much later. We're sitting at the table in his kitchen, with the obligatory fish and chips in front of us.

'What is it?'

'OK, so I think we have established beyond doubt that you're not gay.'

'I'd certainly hope so!'

'When we were in that hotel, with the shower that left nothing to the imagination, I'll confess that I sneaked the odd peek at you. Did you notice?'

'There were a couple of times when I suspected, but you looked away very quickly so I could never be completely sure.'

'You, on the other hand, didn't show any interest at all. You just buried yourself in your work. So, either my naked body is repulsive to you, which doesn't seem to be the case if this afternoon is anything to go by, or it would have been fair for me to assume that you weren't interested in naked women generally.'

He smiles, in a slightly embarrassed way.

'What?'

'I might have a small confession about that,' he tells me.

'Go on.'

'My laptop has a very shiny screen. When you were in the shower, I discovered that, if I had something fairly dark on the screen, I could use it almost like a mirror. I had a very good view of you, actually.'

'Unbelievable! So you were watching me the whole time?'

He nods.

'I don't know whether to be flattered or slap you!'

'Oh, come on. You'd have done the same if you'd have thought of it. You're just annoyed that you didn't.'

'Maybe. But from now on, if I'm naked around you, I expect your full attention, OK?'

He smiles. 'I think I can manage that.'

EPILOGUE
SIX MONTHS LATER

Toby is waiting for me as I leave the *Voyages Luxes* offices at lunchtime. We're completing the purchase of our new house tomorrow, so I've taken the afternoon, and all of next week, off. We've spent the last few weeks going through our joint possessions to decide what we'll take with us. My L-shaped sofa lost out to his big squishy ones and, unsurprisingly, we're bringing his enormous TV rather than my small one. We're taking both beds, but mine is going to be the main one, as we decided (after an awful lot of testing) that it was slightly more comfortable than his.

We're going to base ourselves at Toby's flat until the end of next week, so we can decorate the house and get the carpets laid before our furniture goes in. The removers are coming first thing in the morning to take everything that's still in my flat into storage, and then they'll come and empty Toby's flat next Friday morning and take everything to the house. I sold my flat within two weeks of putting it on the market, and Toby has a new tenant lined up for his.

We agreed that we would get somewhere that was new for both of us, rather than one of us moving in with the other, so that it was 'ours' from the beginning. Toby initially preferred the idea of renting rather than buying, due to his aversion to debt, but I wasn't wild about that idea as my dad has always told me that paying rent was 'money down the drain'. With the help of a lot of spreadsheets, we were able to work out that the proceeds from the sale of my flat, plus his (once more) buoyant savings, would give us a big enough deposit that the rent income from the two flats above the studio would pretty much cover the mortgage payments, and he relented.

The house is a three-bedroomed semi in Tonbridge, with a small garden behind. The vendors have been very accommodating and we've been able to arrange for various people to go in and measure up for the carpets, new kitchen and bathroom. Toby has planned the renovations in meticulous detail; everyone should pitch up on Monday morning, and the kitchen and bathroom work should be complete by the end of play on Wednesday. The carpets are going down on Thursday, ready for us to move in on Friday. Toby and I will be frantically decorating while the work goes on, so hopefully everything will be complete, apart from painting the kitchen and bathroom, by the time the furniture arrives. It's daunting, but exciting too.

It's a beautiful summer's day, and Toby takes my hand as we walk away from the office. We're going to have lunch together in Tunbridge Wells before 'a mooch around the shops', as he described it. I'm not quite sure what he has in mind, as he's not really a shopping person; we agreed early on that clothes shopping was something I was better off doing alone.

I started working at *Voyages Luxes* a couple of weeks after they offered me the job. I didn't have anywhere I needed to hand notice in to, and they were keen to get Peter's replacement up and running as quickly as possible, so it made sense for both of us. I was amused to find, after I'd picked up my pass and walked through the security barrier on the first day, that the offices were just as chaotic as I'd always imagined them to be. It took me a little while to get used to regular working hours in an office and, even now, I can't quite believe that I'm going to have a week and a half off and they're still going to pay me. I am really enjoying the work and Mark seems happy with me, so I've definitely landed on my feet.

'I've booked us into a little Italian restaurant I found online,' Toby tells me. 'It's got good reviews, so I'm hopeful.'

'Sounds lovely. And what are we looking for this afternoon?'

'That depends.'

'On what?'

'Wait and see!'

The restaurant is tiny, the sort of place you wouldn't notice unless you were looking for it, but it has a garden behind it, and Toby and I are seated outside. I tilt my face to the sun, enjoying the warmth on my skin. The waiter brings menus and tells us he'll come back shortly for our drinks order.

'Before we order, there's something I need to ask you,' Toby says, his face suddenly very serious.

'What? What's the matter?'

'Nothing's the matter. I'm really looking forward to this next stage of our lives, are you?'

'Oh yes, I'm really excited!' I tell him. 'The next week is going to be hard work, but it'll be fun seeing our new home taking shape. Was that what you wanted to know?'

'No.' He reaches out and grasps my hand.

'Would you mind taking off your sunglasses for a moment? I want to see your eyes.'

I edge them up onto the top of my head. Toby looks so severe that I feel a bit unnerved.

Without warning, he slides out of his seat and goes down on

one knee. It takes me a moment to realise what is happening. I totally wasn't expecting this.

'Madison, will you marry me?'

'Are you serious?'

'I've never been more serious. I love you, and I would be the happiest man alive if you agreed to become my wife.'

I know it's cruel, but I just can't seem to help myself. Suppressing the joy bubbling up inside me, I twist my face into what I hope is a thoughtful expression.

'I don't know, Toby. Marriage is a pretty patriarchal concept. Do we buy into that?'

He looks absolutely mortified. I can't keep it up.

'Of course I'll marry you! Yes!' I tell him. I bend down and kiss him passionately.

Some of the other diners have obviously realised what's going on and start applauding. Toby gets to his feet and beams. He pulls me to my feet and envelops me in a passionate clinch. I can hear the other diners still applauding and cheering, but they feel far away, as if they're in another room. All I'm aware of is Toby and me.

A polite cough from behind me brings me back to reality and, somewhat reluctantly, I break off the kiss. It's the waiter, obviously wanting to take our order.

'I think a glass of prosecco, don't you? We can celebrate properly with champagne later,' Toby suggests, as we sit back down.

He places the order and I grin stupidly at him. Suddenly, a thought occurs to me that wipes the smile off my face.

'Wait. Sorry, Toby, but we need to do this properly. I know it's ridiculous, but my father will expect you to ask his permission before you can propose to me. It won't change my answer, but you'll have to ask me again after you've asked him.'

'Relax.' He smiles. 'I spoke to him yesterday and he gave his blessing very happily. I think your mother is already planning the guest list.'

It's fair to say that my father didn't like the sound of Toby at all when I first told him that we were dating. 'Freelance photographer', unsurprisingly, didn't count as a real job to him, and he warned me about getting involved with 'some loser who will probably just be a drain on you'. It was only after he'd Googled 'Toby Roberts', and I'd explained that Toby earned comfortably more than I did, that he changed his opinion. The fact that Toby has always been polite and deferential to him helped, and now he thinks Toby is very good for me.

'How long have you been planning this?' I ask him.

'A while, but I was having trouble coming up with the perfect proposal. If I'd dragged you up a mountain or anything like that you would have been suspicious, and I wanted it to be a surprise. In the end, I decided to keep it simple. Was it a surprise?'

'Total surprise! I'm so happy, though.' Another thought occurs to me. 'Hang on a minute. Aren't you supposed to give me a ring?'

'I struggled with that so much,' he tells me. 'I looked at loads, but I couldn't find one that I was absolutely sure you'd love. And then I thought, we're going into this incredible partnership, and it seems wrong to start out by me imposing my choice of ring on you without you getting a say. Also—' he grins '—if you'd have said no, I would have had to go through all the rigmarole of taking it back for a refund.'

'Who said the art of romance was dead?' I smile at him. 'So, what's the plan?'

'We eat our lunch, drink our prosecco, enjoy each other's company, and then I thought we could go and choose a ring together this afternoon. What do you think?'

'That sounds absolutely perfect.'

ACKNOWLEDGMENTS

Firstly, a massive thank you to my ever patient editor, Tara, and the entire Boldwood team. Working with you continues to be a revelation.

Writing a book with so much travel in it during lockdown has been a huge challenge. I'm massively grateful to Paul, Nikky, Guy and Ros for all their helpful input on skiing holidays, as well as my mother and sister for checking my Istanbul homework. I'd like to thank the Coach House photographic studio for my introduction to Art Nude photography, and Irida, who was the inspiration for Erin.

I need to say a huge thank you once again to Frances, for her patient and good-humoured spell checking of the first edition.

I also need to thank Fiona and the wonderful members of the ChickLitChatHQ Facebook group, who came to my rescue when I was struggling to come up with a title for the book.

Finally, I need to thank Mandy once again, this time for checking my Church sections, and correcting the order of the bridal procession at Sophie's wedding.

MORE FROM PHOEBE MACLEOD

We hope you enjoyed reading *Not the Man I Thought He Was*. If you did, please leave a review.

If you'd like to gift a copy, this book is also available as an ebook, digital audio download and audiobook CD.

Sign up to Phoebe MacLeod's mailing list for news, competitions and updates on future books.

https://bit.ly/PhoebeMacLeodNews

Someone Else's Honeymoon, another brilliant read from Phoebe MacLeod, is available now.

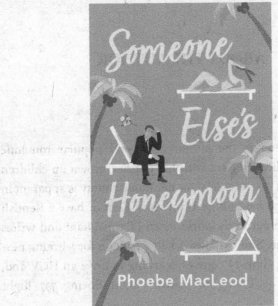

ABOUT THE AUTHOR

Phoebe MacLeod is the author of several popular romantic comedies. She lives in Kent with her partner, grown up children and disobedient dog. Her love for her home county is apparent in her books, which have either been set in Kent or have a Kentish connection. She currently works as an IT consultant and writes in her spare time. She has always had a passion for learning new skills, including cookery courses, learning to drive an HGV and, most recently, qualifying to instruct on a Boeing 737 flight simulator.

Follow Phoebe on social media:

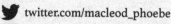 twitter.com/macleod_phoebe

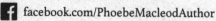 facebook.com/PhoebeMacleodAuthor

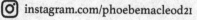 instagram.com/phoebemacleod21

Boldw**oo**d

Boldwood Books is an award-winning fiction publishing company seeking out the best stories from around the world.

Find out more at www.boldwoodbooks.com

Join our reader community for brilliant books, competitions and offers!

Follow us
@BoldwoodBooks
@BookandTonic

Sign up to our weekly deals newsletter

https://bit.ly/BoldwoodBNewsletter